Lies and Revelations

Lies and Revelations

A Novella

and

Two Short Stories

Linda Blackwell Billingsley

ISBN: 9798354047734

For Mary Welp

My Good Friend

Books, wine, food, life…
May the conversation never end!

Table of Contents

Acknowledgments

I am grateful to have friends who lend their time and talents to my endeavors.

Thank you to Katharine Phelps, Mary Welp, and Cate Fosl who read an early version of *The Center of the Quilt* many years ago when I thought it was finished. I later discovered the story was not quite finished with me. Cate and Mary both read all three stories in *Lies and Revelations* (Sometimes more than once!) and provided helpful criticism. Mary, as always, read with her editor's eye, but all mistakes and infelicities that remain are, of course, mine.

Dale Billingsley, my husband, read something very close to the final draft. His comments were insightful and helpful as I moved toward a final draft. As always, his love and support encourage and sustain me.

The Center of the Quilt

I

It was mid-morning on a bright day in early April. Ready for work, coffee cup in hand, I walked toward my office, savoring the profound quiet of the house after the chaotic meals, late nights, and ever-changing plans of our daughter and son's spring break.

"I must be getting old," I was thinking, when the doorbell rang.

I looked out the front window and saw a tall, young man with jet black hair and olive skin. He was wearing a backpack and shivering in a jacket too light for the chilly morning. He looked about twenty, and I assumed that he must be one of the twins' friends.

I opened the door and said, "I'm sorry if you're looking for Will and Dana. They went back to school yesterday."

He shifted nervously as his dark eyes met mine.

"No. I'm looking for Noel Bjorn."

"My husband? He's at work."

"My name is Tomás Noel Rodriquez. Most people call me Tommy."

"How do you know my husband? Why are you named after him?" I asked, expecting a story about an old friend or colleague.

The young man shivered and shifted uneasily before saying, "He's my father."

Stunned, I pulled out my phone and called Noel.

"Hi, honey. What's up?" he asked in his usual gentle voice.

"There's someone here to see you. His name is Tommy—no, Tomás Noel Rodriquez--and he says he's your son."

"Oh, my God," gasped Noel, and I knew it was true.

"Oh, God, Marcia. Oh, my God. I'll be right home."

The shock and anguish in his voice told me his worlds had unexpectedly collided, but the bottom had dropped out of mine.

"Please come in," I said calmly, opening the door wider. "It's chilly today," I continued inanely as a polite autopilot I did not even know I possessed took over. "It will warm up. Later you won't even need a jacket. Why don't you come in the kitchen and have something to drink?"

"Thank you. I'd like that," he said, his voice sounding, in spite of the faintest Spanish lilt, remarkably like Noel's.

He followed me into the kitchen, and I gestured for him to sit down at the table.

"Coffee? Tea? Cocoa? A Coke?"

"Cocoa would be very nice," he said, "If it isn't too much trouble."

As I warmed the milk and stirred the chocolate in, I studied his profile and could see Noel in his jaw line and the set of his dark eyes.

"Where have you come from?" I asked, trying to sound conversational. Seeing how young he was, knowing he was Noel's son, and sensing his vulnerability prevented me from seizing the occasion to interrogate him. Or perhaps I simply wanted to delay moving from knowing one awful fact to confronting a host of others.

I set the cup of cocoa down in front of him, and he smiled. He had a beautiful, wide smile that made me smile back.

"Thank you," he said, sipping the cocoa. "I'm from Los Angeles. Actually Van Nuys—in the San Fernando Valley."

"I know where that is," I assured him, noticing that he also had Noel's long, slender fingers. "Do you go to school?"

"Yes, I'm at a community college, but next fall I'll be going to UCLA if I get a scholarship. I'm waiting to hear. That is," he paused and seemed to have difficulty speaking. He cleared his throat and murmured, "My plans might change."

"I need to go get my coffee cup," I said as an excuse to leave the kitchen. In the front hall, I stood clutching my favorite mug and taking deep breaths, trying to stop my heart from pounding.

The front door opened and Noel came in, saying, "Marcia...."

2

Before I could respond, Tommy had Noel in an embrace, had started to cry, and was saying, "Papá! Papá!"

"Tommy, what is it? What are you doing here? How did you get here?" Noel held him by the shoulders so he could look into his face. "Does your mother know where you are? What's wrong?"

"Papá, she's so sick," the boy said, wiping his eyes with his sleeve.

"Come in here and sit down."

Noel led him toward the kitchen. He shot me a desperate look but did not invite me to follow so I grabbed a coat off the rack and went out to sit in the porch swing. My mind was blank with shock.

"He has another family," I tried whispering to myself, but my mind recoiled, unable to reconcile this fact with the man I had known and loved for over twenty years.

In a few moments, Noel came out with Tommy.

"I'm taking Tommy to a motel and then I'm going back to work for a couple hours. I absolutely have to be in this meeting, but then I'll be home."

I looked up at them standing side by side. Tommy, like the twins, had inherited Noel's height and long legs, but his build was stockier, his shoulders broader.

"Mrs. Bjorn," said Tommy, his eyes red from crying, "I'm sorry for upsetting you. I didn't mean to do that."

Not trusting myself to speak, I nodded.

"I'll be back as soon as I can. Marcia, please wait for me," pleaded Noel.

I nodded and watched them leave. Then the tears came. As a journalist, I was supposed to investigate and write about this sort of situation. It was not supposed to happen to me.

II

The early spring chill finally drove me inside where I paused to listen to the small sounds of the house and then went to get another cup of coffee. I had an article to write as the lead up to a gardening festival, sponsored by a local ecology group. Although the deadline was two weeks away, I wanted to write it while the interviews and research were fresh in my mind. I forced myself to walk toward my office.

"I want to talk to Suzanne," I thought and reached for my phone but then realized that I had only the barest essentials of the story and, more importantly, if I heard my best friend's voice, I might go to pieces. Instead of calling Suzanne or going to my office, I carried my coffee up two flights of stairs

Fifteen years earlier, after moving into the house, Noel and I had worked for over a year to finish the attic and create an office for him. I had never questioned either the existence of his sideline—a prosperous tech consulting company--or his need for a quiet, organized place to work. The children had grown up knowing both our offices as places that were off limits unless they were expressly invited in.

Noel and I shared an in-bred sense of privacy and respect that meant we did not snoop. We were not the kind of parents who read their children's journals or search their rooms. We never opened mail addressed to other people. As a consequence, I stood in Noel's office for a long moment before my sense of betrayal silenced any qualms I had about violating his privacy.

I opened the top drawer of the file cabinet. It contained literature about various software products and companies. In the second drawer, I found the beginning of an alphabetical sequence of files. I recognized a few personal names among the company files. I opened the third drawer and flicked through files until I found the first name I did not recognize: "Rodriguez, C." There were three fat files. My hands trembled as I pulled the first file out and laid it on the desk.

At the front was a check book for an account I had never seen before at a bank where, to my knowledge, we had never banked. The checks had Noel's name printed on them and his business address. I opened the register where Noel had methodically recorded a monthly deposit and various payments to "Consuela Rodriguez," the woman with whom Noel had been involved during college. There were more recent checks to "Tomás N. Rodriguez."

I immediately realized that if Noel had fathered a child with Consuela, that child should now be several years older than Tommy appeared to be. I knew that Noel had wanted to marry Consuela, but her father had threatened to disown her if she married an Anglo. As far as I knew, Noel's relationship with this woman had ended several years before we met, and he had had no further contact with her.

"As far as I knew…." I mentally rolled my eyes. It was clear that I did not know much.

I looked at the most recent checks. Besides the monthly check for $700, there was a large check the past June (graduation present?), a large check in August (tuition?), a smaller check in early September (books?), two checks written to "Tomàs N. Rodriquez" in December (Christmas and what?), and two checks in January (tuition and books for the spring?).

I set the checkbook aside and began to look through the letters and pictures. The most recent letters were from both mother and son. I found a picture of Noel with Tommy, in cap and gown, holding a diploma. The date, neatly written on the back of the picture, was from the past June. I remembered that immediately after the twins' graduation in June, a "business trip" to California had suddenly come up. The note on the back of the photo said, "Thank you so much for coming to Tommy's graduation. He was so proud to have his Papá there."

As I flipped back through the files, I was moving back in time. There were school pictures of Tommy each year and some snapshots with notes on the back: "Tommy loves his new bike. Thank you!" and "Tommy's learning to swim very well!" on the back of a picture taken at what looked like a public pool. Young Tommy stood, tanned dark, smiling widely, with his arm around a smaller boy who was laughing up at him.

I had never before seen Consuela's round, even handwriting or Tommy's almost illegible print-scrawl so I was certain that none of these letters had been delivered to the house. I guessed that Noel might have received them at work, but then I found an envelope with an address for a post office box at a zip code a good distance from our home. In each discovery, I could see my brilliant, logical husband at work.

I closed the files, put them back in the cabinet, and sat staring at the brightly colored Guatemalan cross that hung on the wall in front Noel's desk. For the first time since I had opened the door that morning, I tried to pray. As often happens when I am seriously troubled, not my own but the psalmist's words came to me: "Out of the depths I cry to you, O Lord! Lord, hear my voice!"

Raised by a Catholic mother and an agnostic father, I made my first communion and went through confirmation, but our church commitment did not extend beyond attendance at Mass. In elementary school, I played basketball and volleyball on school/parish teams, but I always felt like an outsider because I attended public school. In college, I stopped going to church.

In my twenties, I started doing yoga. I found that I enjoyed the quiet spirituality of the practice and realized that at some level I still believed in a divine, creative force in the universe. Noel was an agnostic and had not been raised in a religious tradition so we were married by a justice of the peace in a ceremony that mentioned God in passing but did not press the point.

When the twins were two, I was flying back from a free-lance assignment in New Mexico when the plane lost an engine and had to make an emergency landing. I was terrified, less for myself than for Noel and the babies. In the midst of my blind terror, my hands in the sweaty grip of my fellow passengers, the woman next to me began to pray, "Our Father, who art in Heaven...." As I found the familiar words that I had not said in years, I suddenly knew that I was in the hands of the living God. I did not know that we would land safely, but, with laser-like clarity, I knew that we would ultimately be safe.

When Noel picked me up from the airport, I was giddy with joy and love.

"I know God!" I told him insistently, "And we need to make sure that Dana and Will know God too! This is such an incredible blessing!"

I am sure that Noel attributed my euphoria to my brush with death, but a few days after I got home, I went to see a priest at the local church and told him my story. Father Gerald had seen his fair share of death-bed conversions, but he listened to me with great kindness. He loaned me several spiritual classics, suggested that we visit again, and enrolled me in the parish. He asked about baptism for the twins, and I promised to talk with Noel. Rather than being threatened or annoyed by my spiritual journey, Noel treated my rediscovered faith with respect. We signed up for baptism classes, and two months later, the twins were baptized. I had given Noel the Guatemalan cross to commemorate the occasion.

The person who seemed to understand most clearly what had happened to me was my best friend. Suzanne Levy and I had met as first-year roommates in college. The first night that we spent in the dormitory, she told me that she would not date anyone who was not Jewish because "My faith is the center of my life."

I had found her attitude narrow-minded but, in some strange way, enviable. She had certainty about her God, while I was drifting in the sea of rebellion against eighteen years of Sunday and Holy Day obligations. Years later, when I called to tell her about my re-found faith, she rejoiced, and in addition to the fiction we often shared, we began reading feminist theology and religious history that explored both Judaism and Christianity.

Noel remained agnostic. He loved raising the children Catholic and seemed to feel toward me the sort of envy I used to feel toward Suzanne. He went to church with us, and when I asked him why, he said, "I like the order and quiet, and I love your faith. I love the joy it brings you." He shook his head and sighed. "I think that I'm waiting for a lightning bolt to strike me."

Dana and Will went to public school. They attended religious education classes and played on the parish sports teams while Noel and I volunteered for various parish activities.

While lightning did not strike Noel, it did strike me. The increasing conservatism of the Catholic church arrived at our liberal parish in the form of a young priest who swooped in denouncing, "liberal, humanistic tendencies," the use of inclusive language, women serving on the altar, and lay speakers at Mass. His homilies were pretentious, ignorant, politically conservative, and filled with efforts to demonize "secular humanism" and abortion rights. Noel soon stopped coming to church with us.

As we learned of the extensive clerical abuse of children and hierarchical conspiracy to protect the abusers, I was horrified by the church's denial and feeble excuses at every level. Then came the Sunday when this poorly educated, unmarried man chose to preach on "Wives be obedient to your husbands...."

There is no way to construe Paul's words as good news for women or as anything other than evidence of the Catholic church's adoption of patriarchal Rome's attitude toward women. As the priest blathered on about the words "metaphorical meaning," never acknowledging the literal way these words have been used to control real women, a clear, white-hot anger filled me.

I stood up and told Dana and Will that we were leaving.

"Why, Mom?" they whispered.

"Because we've heard enough of this drivel," I said in a normal tone, hustling them out with no effort to go quietly.

Noel greeted us at the front door.

"You're back early. Is anything wrong?"

"Not with us," I said. "We need to have a family meeting."

We all sat down in the living room and I said, "I can't sit through or make the kids sit through these homilies any more. Today he was banging on about 'Wives be obedient to your husbands.'"

"Sounds like a plan," said Noel, chuckling.

"I'm not joking. I don't think the kids should be exposed to ideas that we don't believe. I don't think it's healthy to go to church and then have to come home and correct what was said. And, God forbid, they might believe some of this drivel."

"I hesitated to say anything, but I agree with you," said Noel, meeting my eyes.

"You mean, we don't have to go to church?" asked Will, looking at Dana, his wide, dark eyes dancing.

"Would it bother you if we stopped going to St. Mary's?" I asked. "If we aren't in the parish, you can't play sports, and I know you both enjoy that."

Dana and Will looked at each other, and Dana finally said, "The kids aren't very nice to us."

"What do you mean?"

"They're always saying stuff about public school—how they don't teach you as much and the kids are all wild and there are lots of drugs. Stuff like that. Even though they don't know anything about it," added Dana angrily.

"And Coach Bob is always making jokes about how they wouldn't allow my hair to be this long in a Catholic school," said Will.

"But you never said anything!" I exclaimed, looking at Noel in shock.

"We like playing basketball," said Dana. "And I like volleyball, too. I have friends at school so I don't care if the girls don't want to be my friends."

"There are other sports programs," I said firmly.

"Can we finish the season?" asked Will. "My team's really good!"

"Sure," I said, "But we're going to look for another church."

"Do we have to?" asked Dana and added earnestly, "Can't we just say prayers and read the Bible at home? Kind of like what we do at Aunt Suzanne's?"

I met Noel's eyes and could barely refrain from laughing.

"I think your mother and I need to talk about what we're going to do, but we both think church is important," said Noel firmly.

"So we don't get a say?" demanded Dana.

"You're having your say now," replied Noel evenly. "Your mother asked you about leaving St. Mary's."

"Can't we just say we don't want to go to church anymore?" demanded Will indignantly.

"Sure, you can," I replied and added, just as Will and Dana leaned toward each other to exchange a high five, "When you're eighteen!"

"Mom!" they wailed.

"I don't want you growing up like heathens," I said.

"Dad's a heathen," they protested.

"He's an exceptional heathen," I said, patting Noel's hand.

"Your mother and I want you to grow up having a chance to explore the spiritual side of things," Noel said firmly. "I didn't have that, but I think it's important. I want it for you."

After the twins left the room, Noel said, "Maybe we can find another parish."

"We're in the most liberal parish in this city," I said sadly, "Or we were until Father Ignoramus came. It bothers me so much that the kids are running into the same kind of prejudice I ran into as a kid. I assumed things had changed."

"Maybe it's just kids."

"I don't think so. It's entrenched conservatism and, with regard to school, elitism. I've been thinking that I could maybe ignore the anti-abortion stuff, but it's more than that. Women are the workhorses of this church, and they're completely disenfranchised. I've been reading feminist theology with Suzanne, but now I don't see anything but pushback and a return to the 1950s church. More and more, it's like Vatican II never happened. It's preferential option for the penis all the way."

"I have to admit that I despise how the church has handled clerical abuse. I'm appalled at how the hierarchy continues to lie about it."

"I know. And every time the Pope or American Council of Bishops speaks publicly, I want to vomit."

"You sound done," said Noel, taking my hand and lacing his long fingers through my shorter ones.

"I'll miss the ritual, especially the Eucharist."

"Other churches have communion."

"Yes, but it's not the same. I actually believe in the Real Presence, but I don't want to raise our children in a church where I'll always be criticizing and hoping they don't believe what they've heard from the pulpit."

After the twins finished their sports season, I met with Father Gerald and was honest with him about our reasons for leaving. When I told him about the twins' experience with their teammates, he shook his head sadly and said, "I wish these things would change. I hate to think it's just the way kids are. I was the only kid in my parish whose parents were separated. Everyone knew. I had a couple of friends, but the other kids treated me like I had a contagious disease."

10

He promised to pray for me and asked me to pray for him. As we parted, he said, "You know, Marcia, after Vatican II, we used to say that for every person who left the church because it was changing, ten people left because it wasn't changing fast enough."

"Back then, the church was actually trying to change," I replied sadly. "Now it's digging back into the past. That's not just bad news for women. It's bad news for everyone."

I spent the next few months visiting churches in our area. Although I realized how deeply I loved and depended on the ritual of the Mass, I finally had to admit that I would never find this particular comfort outside of the Catholic church.

In talking with Noel, I realized that we wanted a community of faith in which to raise our children. Once I recognized and set aside my historical and ritual prejudices, I found a progressive Presbyterian church with a robust program for children and youth. After attending several services, Noel's only comment was, "The music is so much better!"

On their first visit, the twins discovered several school friends in the congregation who immediately invited them to their Sunday School classes. The pastor and one associate were women, and it never grew old for me to hear their voices from the pulpit.

I reflected now on how prescient the gift of the Guatemalan cross had been—not a crucifix but a cross—as if I had known the Catholic Church were not the final destination but only a stop on my spiritual journey.

"I hope memory is a form of prayer," I thought and with a last look at the cross, gave up my attempt to pray.

I put the files away and went downstairs to sit in the living room where my feeling of impending doom reminded me of the days and nights I had spent at my mother's bedside during her last illness. For so many hours, I had sat trying to pray, both wanting and dreading her final release. When I told the Hospice chaplain about my inability to pray, she replied, "Prayer isn't just words. Right now, your loving presence is your greatest prayer."

Part of me wanted Noel to come home and talk to me, explain, soothe my hurt, answer my suspicion and doubt, but another part knew that no explanation was possible and I might as well lock the doors against both him and his words.

This was not a movie or book where the child would end up belonging to some shiftless cousin or brother. This could only be deep, heart-breaking, long-term deception. Yet as I looked out at the bright yellow jonquils that marked the end of winter, the words of Psalm 130 continued to echo through my mind: "If you, O Lord, mark iniquities, / Lord, who can stand? / But with you is forgiveness…."

I met Noel at a dinner party when he had been in town only a few months. I immediately noticed his clear gray eyes which had a distinctive, darker rim around the iris. As we stood talking, something made him smile, and I realized how attractive I found this tall, fair, soft-spoken man. Now I had to ask: when he invited me out for dinner that first time, was he still with her?

When I heard the front door open, I quickly wiped away my tears.

"Marcia?"

"In here."

"Thank God. I was so afraid…." His voice broke and he knelt beside my chair.

I drew back, but he put his arms around my waist, burying his head in my lap like a small child, and saying, "Oh, God, Marcia, I'm so sorry. I love you. You've got to believe me! I've always loved you."

I could feel his tears dampen my jeans.

"Please don't leave me. Promise me you won't leave me."

I looked down at his blond hair, now mixed with silver, and caught myself before I stroked it.

"I searched your office," I informed him flatly. "I found the files and checkbook."

He drew back, looking shocked.

"Under the circumstances, I thought an invasion of privacy was warranted. And, believe me, if I ever systematically deceive you for twenty years, you have my permission to search everything right down to my underwear drawer."

"I deserve that."

"And I deserve the truth."

"Okay." He stood up. "Let's talk in the kitchen. I need something to drink, and this is going to take some time."

12

"Before we start, how old is that boy?" I asked harshly.

"Tommy will turn nineteen in December."

"He's only four months older than the twins," I gasped. "My God, Noel! You were fucking her while I was planning our wedding?"

"Not exactly." He ran his hand through his hair and looked at me with pleading eyes.

"I can't believe this! I was having wedding showers, and you were fucking someone else!"

Furious, I stomped into the kitchen. Noel followed, opened the refrigerator, and stood staring blankly. He finally brought out the milk, poured himself a glass, and put the carton back.

"I'm sorry. I didn't offer you any," he said, sitting down at the table.

I shook my head impatiently, refilled my coffee cup, and sat down. We faced each other in silence, and his hand trembled as he reached for the glass and took a sip.

"I'm waiting," I finally said in a low, nasty tone.

"Please," he pleaded, reaching across the table.

Drawing my hand back, I snapped, "Go ahead! Explain. It had better be good.

III

"I met Consuela when I was a senior at UCLA. She was waiting tables at a Mexican restaurant in the valley where some friends and I used to go for happy hour. She was very beautiful, and one of the guys bet me that I wouldn't ask her out. So I asked her out, and I was amazed when she said yes." Noel paused and swallowed hard. "She was putting herself through a two-year college, taking a course or two a semester and living at home. From the beginning, when she met me at the movie theatre for our first date, she told me that her father didn't want her dating anyone, but he especially did not want her dating an Anglo.

"We fell in love. Because of her, when I graduated, I stayed at UCLA for my master's degree. That's when I began asking her to marry me. She had met my mother, brother, and friends who all liked her, but I had never been to her home or met anyone in her family except Teresa, her older sister. We would fight over this and break up because I was sick of lying and sneaking around, and then a few days later, we'd talk, and we'd be right back where we started. She was convinced that if she married me, her father would disown her and she'd never see her family again." He fell quiet.

"So what happened?"

"I was close to finishing my master's and knew that I would probably be moving away for work. Consuela always swore that she wanted to marry me. So one evening, when I knew she was at work, I went to talk with her father and ask his permission to marry her." Noel paused for a long moment and then said, "My God, I was completely naïve. I thought that my love for Consuela and recognition of his authority would persuade him. I had rehearsed everything I wanted to say in Spanish. I even thought that he might like me. I was such a complete fool!" Noel looked down and shook his head sadly.

"Did you see him?"

"Oh, yes, I saw him! For about five minutes on their front porch. After I told him I wanted his permission to marry Consuela, he threatened to kill me if I ever saw her again."

"What did you do?"

"I went to find Consuela at work. I pleaded with her to elope, but she kept telling me that if she did, she would never see her family again. She was furious that I had gone to her father and told me that she never wanted to see me again. Two days later, her sister called to tell me that their father had beaten Consuela, and if he suspected that she was seeing me again, Teresa warned me that he might hurt her even worse. I pleaded with her to help me, but, like Consuela, she just kept saying that I didn't understand and begged me to stay away.

"I even went to the police station near where they lived, and this white cop explained to me that there was nothing I could do. Only Consuela could complain, and even if she did, the cops probably wouldn't do anything because, and these are his exact words: 'We take care of our business and the, the…'--he used a really pejorative expression for Mexicans—'take care of theirs.'"

"How horrible."

"Even now, I can hardly bear to think about that time in my life. I delayed finishing my master's and hung around for another six months just in case she might change her mind. The week after I saw her father, I wrote to her. I addressed the letter to Teresa, but I have no idea if Consuela got it because I heard nothing.

"I was so desperate that I called a bunch of Mexican restaurants in the valley trying to find her, but none of them would give out any information. Two or three times a week, I would drive over the hill and eat at a different Mexican restaurant, just hoping that I would run into her or run into someone who knew her. I even tried the two-year college she was attending, but, of course, they wouldn't tell me anything. Finally, I gave up. I accepted a job in San Diego and thought that was it. I kept telling myself that I had to accept the fact that she had made a choice, and I wasn't it."

"Did you start dating other people?"

"After I'd been in San Diego a few months, I started going out a little, but I didn't meet anyone I could be serious about. Over the next few years, Mom retired and moved back to Connecticut to live with my aunt, and my brother took a job in New York so I didn't have any family to keep me in California. Somehow I never felt at home in San Diego, and so, when the headhunter contacted me about the job here, I was ready to make a big change. I came for the interview on a beautiful fall day and simply fell in love with this city." He smiled at the recollection. "So I came here and after a few months, I met you. I was so happy with you. I felt completely alive for the first time since I'd lost Consuela. Marcia, you've got to believe me."

"Until today," I said, swallowing hard, "I would never have doubted you."

"I'm such a fool," he said. "I'm so sorry. You have to believe me. I'm just so sorry."

"Go on," I said coldly, bracing myself for what was coming.

"The year we got married…," he began and stopped. I waited, and he finally spoke again, saying, "Remember that conference I went to in Los Angeles? It was in March. It was a hassle for me to go because the wedding was coming in May, but it was important. The company needed me to be there. I had also just started consulting on the side and thought I might pick up a client or two."

"I remember. It's that conference you go to every year, isn't it?" I asked and suddenly stopped as if I had just admitted to believing in Santa Claus.

Noel saw my expression and frowned, saying, "Actually, I *do* go every spring, and it *is* a real conference. It's not something I've made up. Everyone goes to it. It helps the company but has also brought me consulting jobs over the years."

"I guess so. Looking at that checkbook made me realize that I had no idea how lucrative your business has been."

He looked down, and I found myself wishing I could take more pleasure in hurting him.

16

"At that first conference, I went to the banquet and found Consuela waiting tables. She asked me to have a drink so later I met her in the hotel bar. I told her all about you, how much I loved you and how happy I was that we were getting married. Her father had died the previous winter. Teresa had gotten married and had a little boy with another baby on the way. They all lived together, and it was getting crowded so Consuela had just moved out. She had been forced to drop out of school and work two jobs to pay off her father's funeral and help her mother keep the house, but things had gotten better so she was planning to start taking courses again.

"I drove her home to her apartment, and she asked me in to see the place. She also wanted me to taste some Tequila her cousin had brought her from Mexico. So we did some shots and finally talked about what had happened to us." Noel sat silent for a long time. "We had a lot to drink." He paused, took a deep breath, avoided my eyes, and said flatly, "We ended up in bed."

"So why didn't you just tell me that you were still in love with her?" I demanded angrily.

"Because it wasn't like that. I was in love with you," protested Noel. "The minute I realized what I had done, I felt like the biggest fool in the world."

"So you drunkenly fell into bed with your old love in a fit of momentary amnesia about our impending nuptials?"

"It sounds stupid. It was stupid. I was stupid, but I'm telling you the truth. I was drunk. Drunk and stupid."

"Thank God every walk down memory lane doesn't end this way."

"I'm trying to tell you the truth without any excuses," Noel replied with unusual sharpness. "Immediately after we had sex, I realized what I'd done and started to leave, but Consuela stopped me because I'd had so much to drink. She made me stay. I slept on the sofa."

"Gosh, that makes me feel so much better. You didn't just fuck her five or six more times for old times' sake, but you slept on the sofa. Great!"

"You're not making this any easier," Noel said, his face flushing with irritation.

"I don't mean to make it easy for you. Jesus, easy for you! How the hell do you think this is for me?" I shouted. "Do you think I ever dreamed that my life would suddenly become the stuff of a trash novel or tabloid article? How the hell do you think I feel?"

17

"I can't imagine how you feel," he said softly, shaking his head.

"No, you really can't!" I began to cry. "Don't touch me!" I snapped when he tried to embrace me. The picture of misery, he sat back down on his side of the table.

I wiped my eyes and blew my nose.

"Okay, tell me the rest."

"I came home, and we got married."

"Did you think about her?" I asked, watching his eyes to see if he would tell me the truth.

"Occasionally. But whenever I thought about her, it was because I was ashamed of what I had done and terrified that you might find out. When Consuela and I said good-bye, I made it clear that I would never see her again. She said that maybe now that she knew I was in love with someone else, she could move on with her life."

"You're sure you weren't still in love with her?"

"Absolutely not. Please believe me. I cared about her, but I wasn't in love with her. I didn't want to be with her. I only wanted to be with you." He paused and took a deep breath. "The next year I went to the conference. The same company was handling the catering so I looked for Consuela." He saw my look. "No, it's not what you're thinking."

"Please tell me that you weren't planning to cheat on your now-pregnant-with-twins wife?"

"I just wanted to say hello. I actually hoped she had moved on and met someone." He saw my skeptical look and added, "I will swear on whatever you want me to swear on."

I nodded and held my tongue.

"I asked one of the servers about Consuela, and he said that she had quit after Thanksgiving because she was expecting a baby, and her doctor had said that she couldn't be on her feet all the time. He told me to talk to a friend of hers who was working in the kitchen. I did, and she said that Consuela had moved back in with her mother. She gave me the address and a phone number."

"So you went and found her," I said after a long pause. "Why did you do that?"

18

"I wanted to be sure she was okay. I tried to call, but the number didn't work. That worried me. I had an afternoon free before I flew home so I drove out to the valley. When she came to the door, she was holding Tommy. She told me that he was mine, but she didn't want anything. Her mother was taking care of him, and she was back to waiting tables. Originally, she had planned to have an abortion and gone to Teresa to borrow some money, but Teresa told her mother, and together they convinced her to have the baby. They promised to help her raise him." Noel took several deep breaths and finally looked at me pleadingly, "You can't imagine how I felt."

"Probably I can," I replied sharply, "Probably better than you can imagine how I feel right now." He started to speak, and I cut him off, "Did it occur to you that the baby might not be yours?"

"It did, but Consuela swore to it."

"And you took her word for it?" I sneered. Entitlement to my anger warred with shame at my sarcasm, but being nasty was keeping me from howling out my pain.

"I believed her because she had never lied to me about anything," Noel said quietly. "I also talked to Teresa who assured me that Consuela had never looked at another man. A few years ago, I had a DNA test on Tommy."

"Why would you do that if you were so sure?"

"When we made our wills before our trip to Europe, I wanted to add a codicil to mine that left some money to Tommy. I felt like I had to have proof."

"That was ten years ago! Didn't you think about telling me then?" I demanded incredulously.

"I've always been afraid that if you found out, you'd leave me." He spoke the words earnestly with an undertone of pleading.

I stared at him for a long moment, wanting to say, "Well, you got that right!" Instead, I managed to say, "Tell me the rest of the story."

Noel looked at me hopefully for the first time since he had arrived home and started to say, "Do you think you...?"

Horrified at the idea of being asked for anything, I said impatiently, "Just tell me. I need to hear the rest of the story."

19

"I could tell that Consuela and her mother needed money so I gave them what cash I had. Consuela kept telling me that she didn't want money, but I felt if the baby were mine, I needed to support him and help her, for his sake."

"How noble of you!" I sneered, and he flinched. "Did she try to get you to stay with her? To leave me?" I asked the questions in a flat, matter-of-fact tone.

"She was very happy that I would help them and kept saying it was only until she could finish school and get a better job."

"That's not what I asked."

Noel swallowed hard and studied his large, elegant hands whose touch I had always loved.

My anger surged again as I waited him out.

"Yes," he finally said, looking up to meet my eyes, "She wanted me to leave you, but I told her that I loved you and we were going to have twins in May."

"So that's why you stayed? The twins?"

"No, that's not what I'm saying! Marcia, you've got to believe me! I never thought for a moment, not even for an instant, of leaving you."

"So why'd you look her up? Another quickie? At that point in my pregnancy, you weren't getting much."

"No, of course not! I don't know why I looked her up. When the guy said that she'd had a kid, I asked, and he didn't think she was married. I was concerned. I didn't love her—not like I love you—but I'll always care about her. It never crossed my mind that the baby might be mine until she told me."

"So what did you tell her when she asked you to leave me?"

"I told her that if she ever mentioned that again or if she ever tried to contact you, I would never speak to her again. I would pay the money for Tommy to her mother or Teresa, and I would never see either him or her again."

"Okay. You expect me to believe this. Let's just pretend that I do."

"But, Marcia, it's the truth!"

I stared at him pointedly, and his pale skin flushed a dark red.

"I changed my flight to the next day and called you to say that I was working on a consulting deal. The irony is that when I got back to my hotel, I ran into someone I'd just met who was starting his own company, and I ended up with what's been my most lucrative consulting contract. I spent the evening trying to work out how much money I could give Consuela and how I could do it so that you would never know about Tommy." He swallowed hard. "I already had the consulting company incorporated and had begun to make pretty good money so I decided that I'd pay myself a regular salary, put it in a separate account, and send Consuela money from that."

"And you thought I would be too dumb to notice?" I was both incredulous and offended.

"You've always pretty much left the finances to me."

"I pay all the bills."

"I mean taxes and investment. I always did the taxes, and you never paid much attention."

"Here I just thought that you worked all the time in the evenings and on the weekends because you loved your work," I said sarcastically, momentarily angrier at my own stupidity than his deceit.

"I do love my work, but sometimes it's been hard to manage to do as much consulting as I needed to do in order to pay for Tommy," he admitted. "I didn't want to use any of my salary so out of the money I take each week for expenses, I've saved as much as I could. I wanted to send Tommy to a private elementary school, but I couldn't afford the tuition. Fortunately, he ended up in decent public schools and got into a very good high school. He's like Dana and Will in so many ways. He's such a smart kid, and he works hard. I've been paying his community college tuition and hoping that he gets a scholarship to UCLA."

"You love him," I said, the jealous words leaping out of my mouth.

"Marcia, he's my son. I love him like I love Dana and Will. I want what's best for him just like I want what's best for them," Noel said defensively. "None of this mess is Tommy's fault."

I felt ashamed and admitted, "No, it isn't his fault. He seemed very nice and polite." I made the concession reluctantly, asking myself if I would have preferred he were an ill-mannered delinquent.

21

"I told Consuela that I would send her money each month, and I took out a personal loan to help her finish school."

"A loan?"

"From the bank where I have the other account," Noel explained. "When Consuela finished her degree, she got a job as an x-ray technician, but things have always been tight because she's had to support her mother. Teresa and her husband don't make much, and now they have four kids."

"She didn't marry?"

"According to Tommy, she's always said that she's too busy to have another person in her life."

"Do you believe her?"

"No, I think…," Noel stopped and looked away.

"You think she's still in love with you."

After a moment of silence, he shrugged, saying, "I don't know. We never talk about that kind of thing."

"But you know she is." When he did not answer, I quelled my desire to shake the answer out of him and asked, "So how often have you been seeing the boy?"

"The two trips to California each year. One in the spring and one in the fall. Occasionally, I've had to go out on business and worked in an extra visit."

"Consulting." I spit the word out.

"Actually, it's true. I go to the conference for my company in the spring, but I stay an extra few days to do some work for Jim Bowden's firm. That's the contact I made that first year I was out there. Jim's also brought me some other business. I always add a day or two to spend with Tommy. In the fall, I work, but I've always tried to go when he had days off school so I could take him places."

"Have you told him about us?"

"When he went to kindergarten, he began asking questions about why I didn't live with them. Consuela and I decided that it was best that he know the truth so he's grown up seeing pictures of you and the twins and hearing stories about you. When he was small, he was always begging me to take him home with me so he could play with Dana and Will, but as he got older, he understood."

22

Noel's voice was sad, but instead of sympathy, I felt violated as if a spy had lived among us.

"Consuela's a good mother, and Teresa and her family have been very good to Tommy. His cousins are like brothers and sisters."

"So when you'd go to California, you'd see her?" I forced myself to ask the question.

"Yes, but the only time we've been alone together has been when we've had to talk about Tommy, and I swear that our conversations have all been brief and business-like."

"You swear," I said, raising my eyebrows. "*You...swear?*" The irony was mean-spirited, but I could not stop myself. Noel looked as if he had been slapped, and I did not care. Had he been on the rack, I would have called for the torturer to turn the wheel even though I felt each twinge of pain in my own body.

I got up and made more coffee, furiously banging and slamming my way through the process. Noel came up behind me and put his hands on my shoulders.

"Marcia?" he spoke gently, pleadingly.

"Please don't touch me."

He stood back and watched me put coffee into the basket of the maker. As I flipped the switch, tears splashed off my hand and I realized they were sliding silently down my cheeks. I kept my face turned away and went to get a tissue from the bathroom.

"Honey, are you all right?" He was standing outside the bathroom door.

"Go back in the kitchen. I'll be out in a minute," I said gruffly and heard his retreating footsteps.

It was a few more minutes before I could stop the tears which seemed to have their own sad life. I bathed my face in cold water and took several deep breaths before I went back and sat down across from Noel. Back to business.

"She's never called here. Does she call you at work?" My hurt had turned once more to anger, and I wanted to pounce on each detail and devour it, force it to reveal its secret until there would be no more secrets. "And then what?" I asked myself. "Does the pain just go away? Does it just stop? Do we just wake up in a new world?"

23

"I used to call Tommy once a month. Now we FaceTime once or twice a month. It's always a night when I have to work late anyway."

"Oh, yes, all those nights working late," I said bitterly.

"I was not lying," Noel began insistently, and then stopped.

"You used your work computer?" This surprised me, as much as I could still, under the circumstances, be surprised. Noel had always been scrupulously honest about anything related to work. "Scrupulously honest." I smiled grimly over the phrase.

"Of course not!" He immediately saw the folly of his indignation. "I used to buy calling cards and use my laptop to Skype," he muttered, "But now I have another phone. Now we also text."

"Where do you keep this other phone?" I got up and poured myself a cup of coffee. I felt self-mockery overtake me as the journalist in me stepped up to frame compelling questions.

"Locked in my desk at work."

"So you don't think I'm completely stupid?"

"For God's sake, Marcia, I never thought that!"

"Really? You assumed that you could get away with this deception, and I'm supposed to believe that part of your assumption wasn't that I was stupid? Please!"

Noel buried his face in his hands, and I could tell he was fighting for control. Finally, he looked up and demanded, "Can't you understand at all? Fear does this! I never had a big plan. I was so terrified of losing you that I just figured out each thing as it came up. Can't you just for one moment believe that I love you so much that, from the beginning, the idea of losing you was overwhelming? Only something so terrifying would ever have made me lie to you and do these things."

"Very romantic."

Stung by my venomous tone, Noel drew back, but I fought any feeling of sympathy.

"So why is the boy here now?"

"Consuela is dying."

"What?"

"She has cancer. They operated for the second time last week, but when they opened her up, it was everywhere." Noel's voice broke.

24

"Oh, my God!"

"Teresa has almost run out of sick time, and there's no one to take care of Consuela. Tommy is desperate so he borrowed the plane fare from his friends and came. He's just a kid! He has no idea how to handle this, and I think he's so upset that he had no idea...," Noel's voice faded. "He didn't mean to cause trouble, but he didn't have anywhere else to go for help. He was afraid that if he called, I wouldn't believe how bad things are." Noel paused and met my eyes. "This is what he says, but I think he came because he needs me. Not just my help, but *me*."

"Poor kid! Where is he now?"

"I got him a room at that motel out by the expressway. I've gotten him a flight home for tomorrow, and I feel like I have to go with him."

"I hope you got a double room," I said softly and stood up. "I think you should   go   now.

IV

After Noel packed his bag and left, I walked numbly from room to room and realized that it was late afternoon and I had not eaten all day. As I stood in front of the open refrigerator, my phone rang: Dana.

"Hi, sweetie! How are you?"

"I'm fine, but you sound kind of strange. Is anything wrong?"

"No, of course not. Dad has to go to California early tomorrow to handle an emergency for one of his clients."

"Wasn't he just there?"

"He was, but something came up so he's flying out again."

"Is he home? Can I talk to him?"

"No, he's working late. Try his cell." I was amazed at how casual I made the quick lie sound and wondered if this is how it had been for Noel all these years—each lie creating a premise from which other lies easily flowed.

"It's nothing. I just wanted to tell him that I got the highest grade on that project in my programming class."

"That's wonderful!"

Although Dana looked like me, except for Noel's gray eyes, she was a math whiz like her father and had decided to major in computer science. She was a first-year student, but she had gone in with college credits and was already taking advanced courses.

"Dad made a couple of suggestions about how to debug the program, and everything worked great after that!"

"Good for you! So how's Will?"

"Gross but fine. Honestly, Mom, he's such a slob that I'm not sure we can live together next year. His room is a disaster area just like when he was living at home! He never picks anything up."

"I talked to him over the vacation, and he said, 'Uh-huh' in that half-listening, dismissive way," I reported with a sigh, wondering if Tommy treated, or used to treat, his mother with the same in-one-ear-out-the-other attitude.

"I know you tried, but it's hopeless. He just doesn't see the mess he's making, and I don't intend to be his mother," she said resentfully. "Rita asked me to live with her next year, and, much as I love my brother, I'm thinking that it might be a good idea not to live together."

"Have you talked to Will?"

"Yeah. He sulked and acted hurt so, of course, I told him I'd give him another chance to stop acting like a pig."

I had to smile. The twins had never been able to stay mad at each other.

"See if you can work it out. Maybe the three of you could share a place."

"It's a possibility as long as Will doesn't expect maid service. Rita and I looked at this four-bedroom house close to campus. It's coming open in July so we might have to pay an extra month, but the lady who owns it liked us. Four of us could live there. Maybe if there were three women, we could form a coalition to beat Will into picking up his own stuff!" laughed Dana.

"I'm sure it will work out, dear," I said and realized that I had been drifting, wondering how the twins would cope when they met Tommy. From there, my thoughts had drifted to what they would do if anything happened to me. I snapped to attention and asked, "Anything else new?"

"Dr. Briggs gave me some interesting computer stuff to do on her project, but that's more news for Dad," laughed Dana.

"Right."

"Mom, are you sure you're okay? You sound weird."

"I've been writing all day," I lied, adding, "I'm a little out of it. Too much coffee, not enough food. I was just looking in the fridge when you called." Half-truths flowed easily, and I again thought of Noel: There's a client in California…There's a conference in California…I just need an extra day or two to finish this job…I have to work late tonight….

"Well, get yourself some dinner, and I'll talk to you this weekend," said Dana.

"I love you," I told her.

"I love you too," she replied and hung up.

I found the open bottle of Nero d'Avola, and poured myself a hefty glass.

"Not a good idea on an empty stomach," I heard myself saying out loud. I drank two quick swallows of wine and found some cheese and crackers to take into the living room.

I sat facing the French doors into the backyard, watching twilight come and thinking how it would have been if Noel had told me about Consuela either when it happened or later when he found out about Tommy. I sipped my wine and tried to remember who I had been at thirty, working as a reporter, married for less than a year, and carrying twins.

I had loved my job. Out of college, after an internship, I had been lucky enough to land a job on my hometown paper. I had bounced around for a few years and eventually became a lead reporter with a reputation for covering tough stories and doing investigative reporting. I remembered my intense surge of pride the day I overheard a veteran reporter, whom I admired, tell a younger colleague, "Go talk to Marcia. She'll tell you how to get it. She might even help you."

There had been men along the way, even one engagement, but by the time I turned thirty, my family and friends had begun to assume that I would never marry, or, more accurately, that I had married my work. Obsessed with my work, I did not question the long hours until I fell in love with Noel, and we began to plan a life together. Perhaps before Noel I had been afraid to imagine a different life for myself, but as I fell ever more deeply in love with him, I realized that I wanted a family. His tech work would provide enough income and benefits so that my earnings would always be secondary. One of the gifts of our relationship was that I could consider doing free-lance writing.

"Are you sure you're ready to have children?" Noel had asked me one evening as we opened wedding gifts together. "You love your work so much! Are you sure that you're ready for that big a change?"

"I think so. What about you?"

"I definitely am, but my work won't change the way yours will. Your job is so important to you," he said, turning his cool, gray gaze on me.

"I love my work, but I'll have time to adjust. I'm sure it will take us a while to get pregnant," I replied.

"Let's go practice," he said, leaning in to kiss me.

We decided to stop using contraception on our wedding night.

I took down our wedding album from the shelf. It held pictures from the entire time around our wedding. I opened it to the backyard barbecue Simon and Julie, friends from the paper, had thrown us in late April.

"A month after he impregnated Consuela," I said to myself, thinking how Noel's secret had provided a new timeline against which I would forever view the events of our life together.

I went through the pictures and studied Noel's face, looking for signs of preoccupation, anxiety, or disenchantment, searching for clues that all was not well. In one candid photo of us, I was talking, with my usual animation, to someone outside the frame of the picture, and Noel was watching me, a small smile on his lips. I had to admit that this man was in love with the woman he was watching. There was no other way to interpret his expression.

On that mild, spring day, what if he had told me about Consuela? What would have happened? I tried to imagine the scene.

We were driving home in his car, and he said, "There's something I have to tell you. I'm afraid that it will make a difference. I'm afraid that you'll never be able to forgive me, that you'll stop loving me. I'm terrified that you'll leave me."

I could see myself smiling and thinking, "What could possibly be that bad? What could ever make me stop loving him?"

"I hope you haven't committed a crime," I would have said, laughing. He might have laughed nervously with me. I would have felt my anxiety growing and said, "Just tell me!"

"When I went to California last month," he would have begun because Noel was always precise in his recounting of events, "I ran into Consuela." I would have recognized the name because he had told me about her and how long it had taken him to get over her. He might have then fallen silent.

"Okay. So what happened?" I would have prompted him.

29

"We had too much to drink and…." He might have had trouble saying the final words so I might have been forced to fill in the blank.

"And you fucked her?"

No matter how I ran the scenario, I went ballistic, yelling and demanding that he stop the car. No matter how I tried to imagine that moment differently, my pain and fury, my sense of betrayal and humiliation made it final.

Perhaps I would have missed him. Perhaps we would have realized that we were deeply in love and managed to reconcile, but I did not believe it. To my thirty-year-old self, cheating would have meant that I could never trust him again. Every business trip, late workday, and unanswered phone call would have filled me with suspicion. I knew that I would not have chosen to live that way. So what did infidelity and deception, now joined to over twenty years of marriage, mean?

I pulled down the next photo album: the first year of our marriage. To our surprise, I had gotten pregnant barely four months after we were married. We documented my pregnancy with hundreds of photos. "Two months pregnant!" the caption read. I studied my former self and marveled. Was I ever that young? Was I ever that thin? Someone had taken a picture of the two of us on a brief trip to the Smokies. I was showing then, and Noel had his hand resting proudly on my belly. There were pictures of me in bed, on the sofa, in the recliner during the last three months of pregnancy when I was on bed rest. Photos showed me resting a cup, a book, a pile of notes on my burgeoning belly like a convenient table. Beached whale that I resembled, I was radiant--my happiness palpable even in those last difficult months when we were trying to keep the twins from coming early.

I flipped through the pages and carefully studied the pictures of Noel, trying to remember if he had seemed distracted or worried, but we were both distracted and worried about the twins who eventually came a month prematurely and spent two weeks in the neonatal intensive care unit. There were pictures of us, masked and gowned, holding our tiny, precious babies. Our eyes crinkled with proud smiles, but I could see the stress. How would I have been able to tell that Noel was anxious about anything other than the twins?

Aware that I was drinking too much but sure that it was the only way I would sleep, I went back to refill my wine glass. I put the empty bottle into the recycling and pulled another from the wine rack. Noel, thoughtful as always, had bought a case of my favorite wine on his recent trip to the liquor store. His thoughtfulness made my eyes fill with tears. I brushed them away, uncorked the bottle, and topped off my glass.

It was almost dark now. I closed the drapes, switched on a couple of lamps, and ate more cheese and crackers. I took down another album and studied pictures of Noel during the first months of the twins' lives. In the home-coming photos, I studied his face intently like a cipher, looking for signs of his secret. All I could see was the joy, pride, and fascination that parenthood had always seemed to hold for him.

I got down another album and flipped through to the following March, when Noel had found out about Tommy, and the following months when he was living with that knowledge. The twins' first birthday. I scrutinized the photos carefully and saw nothing out of the ordinary as my quiet, patient, loving husband helped celebrate this milestone.

At that point, if Noel had come in one evening and said, "Honey, there's something I have to tell you, but I'm terrified you'll leave me," I would have laughed and said, "Talk fast before one of the babies wakes up!" But then, seeing how serious he was, I would have taken his hand, saying, "I can't imagine anything that would ever make me leave you."

He would have replied, "I hope so," and then said, "I have a son by Consuela."

Right then, before we got into dates, I would have been off like a rocket, demanding, "Why didn't you tell me?"

He would have agonized for a moment and finally said, "Because I didn't know. I just found out."

Okay. That would have made it better. Quickly calculating from his break-up with Consuela, I would have asked, "How old is he? Five or six?"

He would have had to reply, "No. He turned one in December."

Would I have ended things? Would I have thrown him out? As a journalist, I had covered many stories about single mothers and their struggles. Would I have resigned myself to raising the twins alone? As it was, my parents, Noel's mother, and various friends had taken turns visiting the first six months to help us with the twins. That first year remains a blur of nursing, diaper-changing, doctor visits, and baby events—first smiles, rolling over, sitting up, making sounds, crawling. Aside from filling in their baby books, I did not write a word for the first eighteen months of the twins' lives. What would I have done if I had been forced to support the three of us? Even with Noel's financial help, I still would have been alone with two babies.

Perhaps my hurt and anger would have carried me through. And later? I had never made good money either as a journalist or a free-lance writer. How would I have paid for two infants in daycare? Who would have helped me with the day in/day out tasks of caring for two babies? Would I have moved in with my parents? What sort of life would I have been able to provide for the twins?

Or would I have swallowed my sense of betrayal and allowed Noel to stay? Would he have wanted to stay? What kind of marriage would we have had?

I began to feel not less but more confused. I walked into the kitchen and poured another glass of Nero D'Avola. The rich, dark red wine slid down my throat. I found my phone and called Suzanne.

"Marcia! How are you? I'm just fixing us a very late dinner so I can talk."

"I'd like to drive up tomorrow and spend a few days."

"Of course. I have an early class tomorrow, but I can take the afternoon off, and I'm free on Wednesday. Can Noel come with you?"

"No, he's out of town. Can I stay with you?"

"Of course. Why don't you plan to stay for Shabbat?"

I usually loved celebrating the Sabbath with Suzanne, her husband Ben, and Joshua and Sarah, their two children, but I was not sure how a family celebration would feel to me at this point.

"Can I wait and see?"

"Sure. No problem. Are you all right?"

"Why?"

"You sound kind of strange. Distant or worried."

"I've had some news today that I'm still trying to make sense of."

"Oh, my God! You don't have cancer, do you?" This reaction would seem strange from most people, but Suzanne has dealt with cancer in those she loves throughout her life.

"No! Of course not! It's just a situation. I can't talk about it over the phone."

"Okay. Do you want to meet me out for lunch tomorrow?"

"Can we just eat at home?"

"Sure."

"Good. I'll see you around noon."

"Marcia?"

"What?"

"Be careful on the drive up. You know I love you, don't you?"

I choked up but finally managed to say, "I love you too, Suz."

I poured myself another large glass of wine which I sipped as I sat and watched the night close in. Then I turned out the lights and went upstairs to pack for Cincinnati. As I pulled a small suitcase from the closet shelf, I realized that the room was in motion. I lay down on the bed and closed my eyes.

The next thing I knew I was awake and thinking, "Where's Noel?" Then I remembered. I looked down at my rumpled clothes and realized that having fallen asleep (or passed out, I thought wryly) on top of the bedspread, I had awakened because I felt cold. My eyes were burning, probably from all the crying I had done the previous day. I squinted at the clock: four in the morning.

I got up, took off my clothes, put on a nightgown, and then realized that I was fully awake. I pulled on my robe, picked up the empty wine glass, and went down to the kitchen where I drank two large glasses of water and took some acetaminophen. I knew that I would not be able to go back to sleep so I went into my office and began writing the article that I had planned on writing the previous morning.

Two hours later I printed out a rough draft and packed up my laptop to take to Suzanne's. I went into the kitchen, drank a glass of milk, set my phone alarm for nine, and went back upstairs to bed. I was not sure that I would be able to go back to sleep, but the intense concentration of the last

33

two hours seemed to have soothed my mind, and I drifted off, vaguely wondering when Noel and Tommy would leave for California.

V

When the alarm went off, the gut-wrenching memory of the previous day assaulted me and then quickly turned into a hysterical voice saying, "What am I going to do? WHAT AM I GOING TO DO?"

I forced myself to lie back for a moment, close my eyes, and pray, as I did each morning. This peaceful routine immediately turned problematic since I always prayed first for Noel and then for Dana and Will. I settled for saying a general prayer for all of us, ending, "God, please help me! I don't know what to do!"

Then I lay there thinking that perhaps I did not need to do anything. Perhaps I could just let life go on. An appealing strategy but ridiculous--there was no way to ignore this situation.

I forced myself to get moving. After I drank my coffee, I went up to Noel's office, pulled the three Rodriquez files, and packed them in my messenger bag. Clearly I had chosen knowledge.

As I got on the road to Cincinnati, I realized that I was in no shape to drive the interstate so I decided to cruise along the river and hope the clear spring day would work its healing magic. I hate being vulnerable even to those closest to me so, although I was eager to talk to Suzanne, I dreaded having to tell the story.

As I drove, I thought about her. She had majored in English literature, gotten her doctorate, and written her dissertation on the representation of Jews in nineteenth-century British literature. The introduction to her dissertation, which she had published in a respectable academic journal and then re-written for a popular Jewish magazine, was a brilliant essay on images of Jews in the English tradition back to the Middle Ages. Her interest in nineteenth-century fiction, which she referred to as "those big, baggy novels," led her to George Eliot and finally a specialty in women's literature.

Her university appointment was a dream job where she taught for both the English and Women's Studies departments. Suzanne was originally from Cincinnati, and, like me, her work had unexpectedly led her back home. She had met Benjamin Spivak, a professor of dentistry, when they served together on a committee. They often joked that they were still serving together on a committee, but now it was called "family." Joshua was fifteen and Sarah almost eighteen. Our children had spent time together since birth, including many family vacations.

Each year the Spivaks came to us to share Christmas Eve dinner although they stopped short of attending the candlelight service at our church; however, we did exchange gifts on Christmas morning. We usually visited them one of the nights of Chanukah for the lighting of the candles and sharing of gifts, and we had been in their home often for Shabbat.

I thought this intimate experience of another religion might have fueled Will's interest in religious studies. He had always been full of questions and had avidly read the books on Judaism Suzanne and Ben had given him over the years. Now he was talking about wanting to spend time in India studying yoga and Hinduism. I sighed over the gulf between his intellectual development and housekeeping skills.

I stopped at Big Bone Lick State Park to use the restroom and buy a bottle of water, something I had forgotten to pack. Looking at the deserted park, I thought how I had always intended to spend more time here where mastodons, ground sloths, and bison had come to drink from the mineral springs. I was strolling toward the car, sipping water, when my phone rang: Noel. I let it ring several times before deciding not answering would be childish.

"Where are you?" he asked in a worried voice. "I stopped by the house on the way to the airport."

"I'm on my way to see Suzanne and Ben."

"I wondered if you would," he paused and awkwardly cleared his throat, "need to talk to her and Ben."

"Yeah. I'm going to spend a few days with them."

"Damn. We're in the boarding line and it's moving. I'll call you when I get to California."

"I thought you'd be gone by now."

"This was the earliest flight I could get. I need to hang up. I love you."

"I love you too," I started to reply automatically and stopped, shocked to realize that if I had said it, I would have meant it—I did still love Noel. That had not changed.

Instead I mumbled, "Talk to you soon."

When I arrived at Suzanne's, I let myself in and got settled in the guest room. In a short time, I heard the front door open.

"Marcia, where are you?"

"In the guest room."

Suzanne quickly came up and gave me an enormous hug, saying, "I've been so worried about you. You sounded so upset, and after we hung up, I began to worry that you had not told me the truth and that you really are sick!"

"Mental illness aside, I'm fine."

"Okay, so there's nothing new," she joked and hugged me again. Then she stepped back and studied me with her wide blue eyes, her freckled brow wrinkled in concern.

"You look terrible."

"I had a broken night of sleep, and I drank a couple of glasses of wine beyond my limit last night. Then I woke up at four and wrote an article that I should have written yesterday."

"You've been up since four?"

"No, I went back to sleep for a few hours, but I'm a mess."

"Come in the kitchen, and I'll make lunch while we talk."

She linked her arm through mine, and I suddenly felt tears well up and spill down my cheeks. Suzanne glanced up at me, stopped, and hugged me hard. We stood together, as I cried with huge, aching sobs for the next few minutes.

I finally backed away, saying, "I'm okay. Let me just wash my face and I'll be right down."

In a few minutes, feeling embarrassed, I made my way to the kitchen.

"Sit down. Is grilled cheese with tomato soup okay? I have good bread," said Suzanne, looking at me with concern.

"That's great. I'm sorry."

"For what?"

"For being such a mess."

"Marcia, you are a fool," she said, putting her hands on her wide hips. "If after more than thirty years of friendship we can't cry on each other's shoulders, where are we going to go for sympathy?"

"I know," I said quietly and watched her make the soup and sandwiches as she asked after Dana and Will and chatted about Joshua and Sarah, including the college acceptances Sarah, a high-school senior, had received in the past few weeks.

"She's leaning toward MIT, but...," she paused as she set the food before us and sat down. "We can talk about all this later." We held hands and bowed our heads as Suzanne said the traditional Hebrew blessing.

"Now, tell me what's going on. No, first eat a bit, and then talk!"

"Jewish mother!" I said accusingly, and she laughed.

I had not realized how hungry I was, but, hung over and eager to get on the road, I had skipped breakfast. I finished the sandwich and began sipping soup out of a thick, ceramic mug.

"I'm relieved to see your appetite is undiminished," Suzanne said, smiling. "Now, tell."

"I don't know where to begin."

"Just begin at your beginning," she said, so I began with Tommy's knock on the door. Somewhere in the story, she cleared the dishes, poured us cups of coffee, and put a plate of cookies on the table between us, but for the most part, she sat listening patiently, her chin resting on her hand, her eyes sympathetic.

"So I told him that I hoped he had gotten Tommy a double room so he would have some place to stay, and he left."

"So that's it?"

"No, he called me this morning. He was in the boarding line at the airport so we only talked for a moment."

"What did he say?"

"That he'd call from California. He said he loved me."

38

My voice quavered, and tears suddenly filled my eyes. I wiped them away, saying impatiently, "I've got to stop this."

"Not for a while," said Suzanne with a sigh. "You have a lot to mourn in this mess." She shook her head. "Poor you! Poor Noel, but poor Tommy and poor, poor Consuela."

"Yes, I know. He's the same age as the twins," I said, my voice breaking.

"And he's losing his mother to a horrible disease." Suzanne spoke from experience—her mother and aunt had both died of ovarian cancer when Suzanne was in her twenties. "You know that Noel had to go with him."

"Of course. Given all the other stuff, Noel's making this trip to California doesn't bother me at all. It's the right thing for him to do for his, his...," I swallowed hard, "His son. It isn't the boy's fault."

"It isn't. I'm so glad you see that. Tommy would never have come if he had not been desperate."

"The worst part of this is that I've been living a lie all these years, and I was too damn stupid to figure it out."

"What do you mean 'living a lie?'?" Suzanne asked with a puzzled look.

"Here we were playing happy marriage and happy family while he had another family, a whole secret life."

"Marcia, I'm not sure that's accurate."

"What do you mean?" My voice had an edge to it.

"He didn't treat Consuela and Tommy as family. He supported Tommy, but he told you that he had no relationship with Consuela."

"That's what he said," I replied, my voice heavy with suspicion.

"You don't believe him?" asked Suzanne.

"Well, since he's been lying to me for twenty years," I said bitterly, "It's a little hard to believe anything he says now." I saw Suzanne's sad look and demanded, "What's wrong?"

"I'm trying to see how to help you with this."

"You've already helped me by letting me cry my eyes out and unload on you."

"I have broad shoulders," Suzanne laughed, and then frowned thoughtfully. "You aren't going to do anything hasty, are you?"

"You mean like file for divorce?" I asked. She nodded. "No. I'm clear on only one point: I feel completely at sea. At thirty, I would have had a lawyer and changed the locks by now, but I'm not thirty, and I've realized that I still love Noel."

"Can I tell Ben?"

"Of course. I'd prefer not to have to go through the whole thing again, but you can't tell Joshua and Sarah because of Dana and Will! That's a whole other problem that I've barely begun to think about. I've been completely wrapped up in my own misery."

"You don't need to tell the twins anything now. They're at school. You and Noel probably need to decide together what to tell them."

"They always wanted us to have another baby," I said bitterly, "But I'm not sure a brother their same age by a different mother is exactly what they had in mind."

"Why didn't you?"

"What? Have another baby?"

Suzanne nodded, saying, "In spite of how hard the pregnancy and birth were, I always thought you and Noel might have more kids. I know you thought about it."

"We did, especially when the twins were three or four years old. When you had Joshua, you know how much we wanted another baby. We talked and talked, but we finally decided that we just couldn't take the risk."

"Having twins or even triplets?"

"Not just that and not just the one baby naturally and one by cesarean which was a bitch to recover from!"

"But you got a great article out of it! Just thinking about that article still makes me laugh!"

"I got more emails and even letters about that article than anything else I've written. If I had simply recounted what happened as a childbirth story, no one would have had a problem, but when I recounted it as an example of human expectations (so to speak) gone awry, a lot of women wanted to argue. I was damned for not being properly serious about childbirth."

I smiled and sighed at the memory which had long ago ceased to upset me. The article had been my first foray back to work, and, at the time, the backlash had stung. It had made me realize how thin my skin had become in almost two years away from the rough and tumble of journalism.

"Being on bedrest was not great, and the birth was awful, but the real deal breaker for both of us was the anxiety. We worried every hour of every day until the twins hit each developmental milestone and then finally learned to read. Even though, thank God, the twins turned out fine, neither of us wanted to go through that again."

"Nothing really prepares us for parenthood, does it?" asked Suzanne with a smile.

"No, but after yesterday, I'm beginning to think that nothing prepares us for any relationship," I replied bitterly.

"You look so tired."

"I suddenly feel exhausted."

"Why don't you go lie down? I have papers to grade and a class to prepare."

"Let me help with the dishes?"

"No. I'll just put them in the dishwasher. Go lie down," Suzanne insisted.

I stood up and walked around the table to hug her, whispering, "I'm so glad to be here."

"I'm always glad to have you," she replied, hugging me tighter.

When I got to the guest room, I took off my clothes and slid between the fresh sheets, shivering as the cool cotton touched my warm skin. As if talking with Suzanne had drained away the emotions of the last twenty-four hours, I felt nothing. I closed my eyes, and the next thing I knew Suzanne was sitting on the side of the bed, rubbing my shoulder, and saying, "Honey, aren't you getting hungry?"

"I slept so hard," I said, rolling over with a groan. "What time is it?"

"Six. Dinner's about ready. Ben's home, and we're having a glass of wine. The kids have gone out to eat with some friends."

"Have you told Ben?"

"Yes. You can talk about it or not talk about it. No pressure from us," she assured me.

"Okay. I appreciate that. I'll get dressed and be down in a minute."

When I walked into the living room, she and Ben stopped talking, and he jumped up to give me a hug, his short black beard tickling my cheek.

"My God!" he said. "What a mess! I'm so sorry."

"Thanks!" I said as he pressed a glass of wine into my hand, his dark eyes sympathetic behind his glasses. He smiled at me, and I raised my glass, saying, "To friends!"

"To friends," Ben and Suzanne replied, raising their glasses.

After a brief silence, during which we sipped our wine, I said, almost to myself, "You know what bothers me. I keep wondering why he went out with her and then took her home if he didn't, at some level, want to have sex with her." I looked up and met Ben's eyes.

"Noel is a good man," he said evenly. "At this distance, does his motive matter?"

"It matters a helluva lot to me," I replied bluntly.

"So you need to ask him, but if he tells you he didn't intend for anything to happen that night beyond an exchange of news between him and a woman he once cared for, you need to believe him," said Ben. As always, he spoke slowly and thoughtfully, the rabbi he had once thought of becoming never far from the surface.

"Believing him is hard with all the lies he's told me."

"For what it's worth, here's what I think. Noel is a good man who made a mistake, but, Marcia, he loves you."

"Okay," I said, "So why didn't he confess? Just tell me when it happened."

"He told you that he was ashamed of what had happened and terrified that if he told you the truth, you would leave him."

"So he says," I muttered cynically.

"I think he's telling the truth," Suzanne interjected. "If he had confessed, what would you have done?"

"I've thought about that." I shifted uneasily. "It's hard to reach back and know what your younger self, your foolish, impulsive, vulnerable, younger self would have done."

"That's true," replied Ben. "I bet the Noel of today can hardly figure out how he came to make such a mistake."

"He was in love with her," I said flatly. "I'm willing to admit that it's possible to love two people at once." My voice broke, and I took a sip of wine. "Maybe he just thought it would be too complicated to stop the wedding."

"That's just silliness," replied Suzanne quickly. "Noel loved you then, and he loves you now. I don't want to blame the woman, but maybe she seduced him, and he just doesn't feel right about presenting her in a bad light."

"And a seduction has two participants. Admitting that he was seduced would be just another way of making himself look stupid," said Ben flatly. "He also knew that you wouldn't let him get away with blaming the woman. I think he's telling the truth when he says that they had too much to drink and lost their inhibitions."

"So anytime a man has a drink with an old flame, there's a chance that they'll kiss and history will repeat itself?" demanded Suzanne. "Now, that's stupid, if anything is! Is that honestly what you're saying?"

"It is, but old flames are admittedly not my field of expertise," Ben said, holding up his hands in a defensive gesture.

"I think that he was still in love with her at some level. Their relationship never had a proper resolution." I paused while Ben refilled my glass. "I just wish to hell I were reading this in a book instead of discussing my husband."

"Okay, so what if he still had feelings for her?" Ben asked. "Didn't he tell you that he clearly ended things and was even more emphatic later when she suggested that he leave you?"

I nodded miserably.

"He chose *you*, Marcia, no matter what feelings he might have had." Ben spoke in a firm, quiet voice. "He chose you when he married you, and he chose you again when he discovered that he had a son by this other woman. He made a clear decision, and I think maybe that choice is the most important evidence of his feelings."

"Okay, so I can just let go of the twenty-year deception? Gee whiz, I feel so much better!" I said sarcastically, hanging onto my anger and not wanting to admit that Ben's argument moved me.

"Maybe he thought that you would never have to know about Tommy and the rest of the story," suggested Ben.

"Okay, so Noel, God forbid, dies, and my first knowledge of Tommy is when the will is read, and I discover my husband has, without my knowledge, added a codicil about his other child," I said angrily. "What a thoughtful gesture from beyond the grave!"

"Remember Pietro Delvecchio?" Suzanne asked in what seemed a strange conversational detour.

Irritated by the interruption, I frowned at her and said, "He was one of your colleagues, wasn't he? The womanizer?"

"Yes. That's him. He died almost a year ago, and I went to the memorial service. His widow--her name's Maria--asked me if I would come to see her after the service. Delvecchio was only in his late fifties and died of a massive coronary so it was quite a shock. Maria and I chatted for a bit, drank a glass of wine, and then she said that she had always like me so she hoped that she could trust me to keep her confidence. I was beginning to get nervous when she brought out an envelope and handed it to me, saying, 'I need to know who this person is.'

"The envelope was full of letters from someone named Angelina. Maria admitted that she had always known that her husband had affairs and had decided a long time ago to ignore them, but this one was different. She thought that this Angelina had once been his student and was now an academic so she wanted me to find her. When I asked her why, she said that she wanted to return the letters. She wanted this woman to know that she had found them the week after her husband's death, and they had made her detest him."

"Oh, my God! It's like something out of revenge tragedy. Were you sure that she wasn't going to kill this woman?"

"I hoped not."

"And, if she knew he was always screwing around, why did this particular affair trigger such a response?"

"I think it's because it wasn't a casual affair but a relationship that had lasted twenty years."

"Did she check his email?"

"There was nothing in his university email, but I suspect he had another account somewhere. Anyway, I agreed to help her. I guessed that the woman was in her forties. I had a hunch that he might have directed her dissertation so I had to get Maria to let me look through his files until I found copies of his curriculum vitae that went back that far. That's how I found this woman's last name. From there, I googled her."

"I can't believe you didn't tell me about this!"

"I meant to, but we always have so much to talk about that I kept forgetting."

"So what happened?"

"I decided to call Angelina before I told Maria anything. It was one of the strangest calls I've ever made. She's a professor at a small liberal arts college, and when I told her about Maria Delvecchio finding the letters, she began to cry. She felt terrible. She had repeatedly told Delvecchio to destroy her letters and delete her emails so this would not happen, but the saddest part was her grief. Whatever his feelings were, she had loved him. When I explained what Maria had asked me to do, Angelina asked for a day or two to think about it. She called me back the next day and said to go ahead and give Maria her contact information. I didn't hear anything until about two months later when Angelina wrote to thank me for putting her in touch with Maria. She said that they had met and talked. She hoped that she had made Maria understand that Delvecchio had loved his wife, not her. He had never intended to leave his marriage."

"So you're saying that if Noel, God forbid, had died and I had contacted Consuela, she might have made me understand that he loved me more?" I asked in a skeptical tone.

"Maybe so," said Suzanne, smiling. "Noel was with her once."

"Once that I know of."

"Once," insisted Suzanne. "I believe him. Once. And he's been with you for over twenty years. Delvecchio had been with Angelina whenever they could meet for years. Just a few months before he died, he had met her at a research forum, and they had spent the night together. But whatever drew him to Angelina or any of the others, the lasting bond was with his wife."

"So you're telling me it could have been worse!"

"I don't know what I'm telling you except the last time I talked to Maria she said that she had forgiven him, but she is very angry at how he 'ruined' Angelina's life."

I laughed at the irony, studied the wine in my glass, and tried to feel grateful that at least I had found out while we were both alive and some resolution might be possible.

"You want me to forgive him," I snapped at Suzanne in an accusing tone. "That's why you told me this story."

Ben and Suzanne exchanged wary looks.

"We aren't in the business of telling you what to do," Ben began slowly, "But we love you, and we love Noel."

"It's easy to stand outside a situation and see how to fix it because you have no emotional stake. You can be rational because you don't know how it feels to be inside it and have it inside you," I said angrily. If my best friends could not understand, who would? Just as self-pity and despair overwhelmed me, a timer went off in the kitchen.

"Dinner's ready," said Suzanne, getting to her feet.

"Can I help?" I asked.

"No need. It's all done."

We went to the table, and Suzanne brought in a huge, steaming casserole full of chicken and wide, home-made noodles.

"You made my favorite," I said, forgetting my earlier irritation. "How good of you!"

"Hey, I'm a Jewish mother. You need to eat in a crisis," laughed Suzanne.

The three of us joined hands, and Ben said the blessing.

We were clearing the table when my phone rang: Noel. I briefly studied his picture, remembering how he had laughed at my efforts to take a good picture of him with my new phone. I could not refuse to answer.

"Hello."

"Hi. Marcia, I need to talk to you." He sounded very upset.

"Okay." I walked upstairs to the guest room and sat on the bed.

"I'm at the house. Actually, I'm sitting on the back steps. God, it's awful. Consuela's dying." He paused, and I could hear him taking a deep breath, trying to regain control of his voice. "They've called Hospice, but Teresa has to go back to work, and Consuela needs full-time care. There's no way Tommy can handle this."

My heart went out to Tommy as I replied quietly, "He shouldn't have to. He's just a kid." I had done plenty of nursing during my mother's final year, but by then, I had already had two children and was in my forties. Nothing prepares you for the process of someone dying, but I could not imagine facing it at such a young age.

"What are you going to do?" Before he could answer, I rephrased my question, asking, "What do you *need* to do?"

46

"Thank you. I love you. You've got to believe that." He paused, and when I could not say the words I knew that he was hoping to hear, he continued, "I need to hire caregivers for the nights. I've talked to Hospice, and they've given me some names. I need someone who speaks Spanish because Consuela's pretty out of it, and sometimes she doesn't seem to know English anymore."

"What about Tommy? What about school?"

"We're going to talk with an advisor and get him withdrawn from his classes, but he's going to keep his job. He needs to go somewhere and get away a little bit, and Tommy says the owner of the restaurant where he works is a very nice guy. We're going to talk with him and his wife tomorrow to make sure they understand the situation. I need to help Tommy have that conversation. He can hardly talk about what's going on without losing it."

"I want you to do what you need to do to help him and to make Consuela comfortable."

"Hopefully, Hospice can help. She's in a lot of pain." He paused. "You're sure you're okay with this?"

"I know it's going to cost money. Is that what you're asking?"

"Yes, I guess so."

"I'm fine with your doing whatever you need to do."

"Thank you." There was another long pause as if he expected me to say something else. He finally said, "I'm going to fly home Sunday night. I know that I'll probably have to come back soon."

"I'm staying with Ben and Suzanne until sometime this weekend."

"I'll call you Monday morning. My plane doesn't get in until after eleven Sunday night."

I knew that he was waiting for me to say that he could come home. I felt neither the desire nor the obligation to invite him, but I relented enough to murmur, "I need time, Noel."

"I know," he said, and I could hear the relief in his voice. "I know. I'm just so grateful that you haven't...that you aren't...." The torrent of words stopped. "I need you. Marcia, I love you." I could hear the desperation in Noel's usually calm voice. "Can I call you?"

"Yes, but don't call on Shabas."

"Thank you. Oh, honey, thank you." There was another long pause. "One more thing."

"What?" I asked in a wary tone.

"Would you please pray for Consuela and her family, and especially for Tommy?"

I remembered my attempt to pray that morning and thought ironically of Jesus' words about "loving" one's enemies, but then I realized that these people were not my enemies. They were people with whom I was connected not only by a biological "accident," but also by the sense of responsibility and, I had to admit, the goodness of the man I had married.

"I'll   do   my   best,"   I   promised.

VI

The next morning, I awoke at six-thirty to the sound of Joshua and Sarah's whispered squabble over the bathroom. I heard Ben shush them as I snuggled deeper under the covers. I thought back over my conversation with Noel. How would it feel to know you were dying and leaving your child? At nineteen, some people are out on their own or already parents, but most of the young people I knew, no matter how independent, still needed their parents. I prayed for all of us, especially Consuela, Tommy, and their family.

I thought back to losing my father suddenly the year after the twins were born, and then losing my mother gradually just after they turned fourteen. My mother's painful battle with cancer had made me bless my father's quick passing. I still missed them both, and there were still moments when I needed them. Having been an only child added to my heart ache for Tommy and Consuela.

I found myself thinking about the Lord's prayer: "Forgive us our trespasses as we forgive those who trespass against us." Some traditions translate "trespasses" and "trespassers" as "debts" and "debtors." In contrast to what we owe or are obligated to provide or return to others, I had always thought trespassing evoked more clearly the accidental, unintentional, inattentive quality of so many of our sins against others.

Suddenly uncomfortable with where my reflections were leading, I threw back the covers, put on my robe, and went downstairs to the kitchen where Joshua and Sarah were packing their lunches as they ate their breakfasts. After they each gave me a quick good-morning hug and went back to their tasks, I poured a cup of coffee and went into the living room.

"I didn't expect to see you so early. I hope the kids didn't wake you!" said Suzanne, looking up from her tablet where I knew she was reading the *New York Times.*

"Not really."

"Sleep well?"

"Actually, I did. Where's Ben?"

"Early meeting. I was thinking that we could go to Eden Park after breakfast and walk. We can have lunch out, but I need to work this afternoon."

"Sounds good. I also have some work to do," I said, remembering the three fat files awaiting my attention.

Knowing from long experience that neither of us is a morning person, I sat down and began reading the *Courier-Journal* and *New York Times* on my phone. Josh and Sarah went off to school. Only stirring to get more coffee, Sarah and I read in companionable silence for the next hour.

"Shall we have omelets?" Suzanne asked, setting her tablet aside.

"That sounds good. Can I help?"

"You can set the table and make the toast."

The early morning sun streamed in the kitchen window, promising a clear, bright day and setting off the red highlights in Suzanne's dark, curly hair.

"I always envied your curls," I said.

"And I envied your straight hair," she replied, smiling. "But now I like my hair. It's easy."

"And when I cut mine short, I discovered it was actually wavy, if not curly. I just wonder who will win the race to go gray?" I asked, and we both laughed.

"It's still pretty cold," said Suzanne. "Did you bring a coat?"

"No," I admitted, "Just a windbreaker."

"Of course, you can borrow," she said, smiling.

We had been wearing each other's clothes since college.

I put the heavy, whole-grain bread in the toaster, watching as Suzanne poured the eggs into the skillet. She added a twist of pepper from the grinder and a sprinkle of salt. Finally, she slid chopped parsley off the cutting board. She let the eggs set, skillfully tilting the pan and sliding the spatula gently under the edges to let the uncooked egg run toward the hot, buttered pan. She finally added a handful of grated white and yellow cheese, waited a bit, and folded the omelet neatly.

"You're such a good cook," I said, admiring the grace she always exhibited in the kitchen.

"I like to cook, especially when there's time to think about it and, like this morning, someone to share it with."

"I know what you mean. Since the twins left for college and I have more time, I find myself cooking much more interesting meals. For the first time in years, I've been trying new recipes. I was in such a rut when the kids were in high school. I just made whatever was fast and easy or could be reheated later because we were always running in so many different directions."

"You think that little kids take a lot of time and attention, but I swear teen-agers require just as much, if not more," Suzanne commented, sighing as she slipped half the omelet onto each waiting plate.

The toast popped up, I buttered it, and we sat down at the table.

"You say the blessing," said Suzanne, and reached across the table to grasp both my hands.

I closed my eyes, savoring the smell of the food and the warmth of Suzanne's hands in mine, and said, "Thank you, God, for the food we have before us. Bless the hands that prepared it and please be with those who are hungry this day."

We said, "Amen" together and began eating.

"So what did Noel say?" Suzanne asked.

Exhausted and feeling talked out the previous night, I had gone to bed right after his call. I summarized our conversation.

"It's good you were generous," said Suzanne.

"I suppose so."

"When will he be back?"

"Late Sunday night." I met Suzanne's eyes and added, "I didn't invite him home. We'll talk on Monday, I guess. I told him it was all right to call me."

"Did he say why Tommy came instead of calling or writing? It seems strange that Consuela would not have told Noel that she was sick."

"I don't know. He was out there a month or so ago. As far as I know, he had no idea that she was sick."

51

"Maybe she just didn't tell him or didn't want him to know," suggested Suzanne. "He might not have even seen her if Tommy met him someplace. Don't you wonder if she told Tommy?"

"She had to, but I honestly don't know." I sighed. So many questions, so few answers.

We finished breakfast and cleared the dishes in companionable silence. Twenty minutes later, we were headed to Eden Park where we left the car in a lot and began to follow the path that led around Mirror Lake and toward Krohn Conservatory. The sunlight glinted off the buds and light green leaves and grass. It was cool enough that I was happy my borrowed coat had deep pockets.

Suzanne smiled up at me, saying, "Isn't this a treasure? I usually come here to walk on the mornings I don't have to be at the university early."

I nodded, noticing how pink her freckled cheeks had turned in the brisk, morning air.

"The parks are one of the things I love about Louisville. I forget how unique they are until someone comes to visit and is astonished by all that green space in the city."

We stopped by the lake and stood studying the reflective surface.

"Why did you tell me that story about the Delvecchios?" I asked, turning to Suzanne.

"I had been meaning to tell you because I thought you'd be interested, but suddenly yesterday it seemed like a story you needed to hear."

"Why? So I'd feel lucky to learn about this mess now?" The anger in my voice surprised me.

"That's part of it, but maybe it's also to help you realize that Noel is a good man who made a mistake. He isn't like Pietro Delvecchio who was routinely unfaithful throughout his marriage."

"So he was also unfaithful to Angelina?"

"When he died, he was having an affair with one of my younger colleagues in another department. Of course, there were always grad students. His grad assistant was always a smart, attractive female and probably assisting him with more than research, but no one complained. We all knew, but you can't do anything about this kind of thing if no one complains." Suzanne sighed and added, "The guy was handsome and charming. He was smart—a good scholar. It was hard not to like him even if you knew about the womanizing."

"Do you think Angelina knew?"

"Good question, and I don't have an answer, but I assume so. Loving him must have been hard for her in so many ways."

"She chose it," I said.

"She did, but he was a very persuasive, powerful man. When it started, she was just a kid—a first-year graduate student, only twenty-two."

"And it's been going on for years?"

"She's in her forties now."

"Maybe being in a relationship that was not full time…maybe that's what she wanted."

"I don't know. It's hard for me to imagine loving someone and not wanting to be with that person all the time," said Suzanne thoughtfully. "I also can't imagine being willing to share your partner."

"Well, until day before yesterday that would have been hard for me to imagine too," I said ironically. I stopped and met Suzanne's bright, blue eyes. "You told me that story so I'd know that some people can learn to live with a betrayal much larger than mine, didn't you?" I asked in an accusatory tone.

"Maybe so. I just don't want you to do something you'll regret." She put her arms around me in a tight hug, and I could smell the slight lemon scent of her shampoo.

"I know," I finally said, pulling away. "Honestly, I'm trying not to be a hot-head about this, but one moment I'm hurt and the next I'm angry and the next I know that I love Noel and the next I never want to see him again."

"Can you just give it some time?" asked Suzanne. "Just ride the waves for a little while and not do anything."

"That's pretty much what I've been doing."

"Actually you've already done something positive."

"What?"

"You've been compassionate. You told Noel to do what he *needed* to do, and, perhaps more important, you answered the phone when he called."

I shrugged and said, "He's my husband. We've been partners for over twenty years. Maybe it was just habit," I added, laughing.

"Take the compliment," replied Suzanne, nudging me and making us both laugh.

We had lunch at a small Italian restaurant tucked away in the hills around Eden Park. When we got home, Suzanne retired to her office, and I sat down at the desk in the guest room. I pulled the three files out of my messenger bag and sat looking at Noel's neat, clear printing on the tabs.

Why had he saved these letters and pictures? Had he wanted me to find them? Did he think that they would constitute proof that Tommy was his son? Or were they mementos he had secretly returned to again and again? I hesitated. Earlier I had flipped through the files casually, looking at the pictures and not reading much. What if I now found that they contained love letters?

I closed my eyes and sat quiet for a few moments, asking myself: How much do I need to know? How much do I want to know? How much can I stand to know? Can I just decide not to know?

No bolt of lightning struck, but when I opened my eyes, I knew that I had to read the files because imagining their contents would drive me crazy.

Noel filed forward to put the most current material at the front, so I took out the bottom folder, turned to the back, and began reading.

"Dear Noel,

When you came to our house last week, it was the answer to my prayers, proof that Our Lady is looking out for me and our son. I know that you were shocked to find out about Tommy. Believe me, I never meant to tell you, but now I am so happy that you know. It's not just because you are going to help us, but now my son will know his father.

Thank you so much. I want to say that you are the best man I ever hope to meet. I will love you until the day I die.

I will not write such things again because I know that you do not want to hear them."

She had enclosed two pictures of Tommy: one was a hospital picture from the day after he was born and the other a studio picture from when he was eight weeks old.

I sat holding the letter and feeling my heart pound as I wondered whether Noel had replied. Had he told her that, although he was married to me, he would always love her? I suddenly felt sad for all of us. I almost decided not to read on but then realized again that my imagination would probably be harder to live with than whatever was in the letters.

At the end of two hours, I had read through the contents of the three folders and looked at all the pictures of Tommy from infancy to high school graduation. Consuela was either true to her promise and never wrote another word about loving Noel, or those letters were not in the file. She often thanked him for his kindness in notes full of news about Tommy. She reported how he was doing in school, what extracurricular activity he was doing, what sport he was playing, and what the doctor said about how he was growing. She included some family news, mostly about her mother whose failing health was a constant concern. There were no photos or notes about her except when she finished her degree and became an x-ray technician.

She sent a snapshot of herself in her cap and gown. It was a close up, and I saw a young Latina with a heart-shaped face, delicate cheekbones, olive skin, and large dark eyes. Her curly hair was pulled back from her face, and she was beautiful. It was not the healthy prettiness of youth, but genuine beauty. The back of the photo read: "Thank you! I could never have done it without your help!"

I sat quietly staring at the photo and wondering why her beauty should be such a blow, but I knew the answer. I was smart and talented, but I never had been and never would be beautiful in the way Consuela was.

There was a knock at the door, and Suzanne came in, saying, "Want a glass of wine before dinner? What are you doing?"

I suddenly realized that the room was growing dark. At a loss for words, I handed Suzanne the photograph.

"That's her, isn't it? She's so beautiful," she murmured and then saw my expression.

"Yes, she is," I said and began to cry.

VII

Over the next few days, I managed to re-write the garden show article and e-mail it to my editor. For something written under bizarre, distracting circumstances, it had turned out well. I tried to read, walked, slept, fretted, and talked to Suzanne who listened with the endless patience of a true friend.

We celebrated Shabbat on Friday evening, and, as always, the lighting of the candles and prayers moved me. Celebrating with Suzanne always made me feel how the roots of our faiths were as deeply intertwined as the roots of our lives. To thank them for having me, I took the entire family out to dinner on Saturday evening.

On Sunday morning, I awoke early and went out to walk. On impulse, I went into a church close to Ben and Suzanne's house. I had not attended Mass in eleven years. The church was old and small, an almost perfect reflection of its sparse, aging, and infirm congregation. The celebrant was probably eighty years old, used a cane, and needed the server's help to get up the steps to the altar. At the beginning of Mass, he introduced himself by saying that he was retired and helped out where needed because of the shortage of priests. I had to make a conscious effort to set aside the suspicion I now had of all priests.

After the opening greeting and prayer, he began the Confiteor, so-called because in Latin, this prayer begins "*Confiteor*" or "I confess." I found myself intensely aware of the words: "I confess to Almighty God and to you, my brothers and sisters, that I have sinned through my own fault, in my thoughts and in my words, in what I have done and in what I have failed to do, and I ask blessed Mary, ever-virgin, all the angels and saints, and you, my brothers and sisters, to pray for me to the Lord, Our God."

The words made me consider both Noel's transgression and my reaction. I thought of Jesus' call to forgive "seventy times seven." I had always thought that it meant you might need to forgive many sins, but what if it meant that you would have to forgive the same sin over and over again? Was there an end point? Would forgiveness bring amnesia? I found myself praying fiercely for a change of heart that would ease my hurt and anger.

The gospel reading was about the shepherd who leaves his flock of ninety-nine sheep to seek out one lost sheep. The priest's homily was canned. I have never discovered where these homilies with their polished superficiality come from, but I suspect there is a weekly digest for priests that is meant to educate and ensure orthodoxy but ends up serving as a kind of clerical Cliff's notes. When I was younger, I saw this lack of originality as evidence of ignorance and laziness, and it infuriated me. Now I found myself thinking how beautiful it was that this old priest still volunteered to do the work to which God had called him. The homily (which he was clearly reading) had one line that caught my attention: "The shepherd's care in seeking the one lost sheep reflects God's extravagant care and love for each of us, His eternal desire that no soul be lost no matter how far it has wandered from the flock."

The priest stopped reading and looked out at the congregation for the first time since he had begun his homily. He cleared his throat and said in a flat, dispassionate tone, "The Holy Scripture tells us today that we can be like God in seeking to forgive, even if it takes us away from the comfort of what we've known. There's a risk, but instead of using that risk as an excuse, we should take it and trust that God's love will work through us."

After Mass, I knelt and prayed to find a way to forgive Noel. On my way out, I stopped in front of the statue of Mary, lit a candle for Consuela, and prayed that she be comforted. As I walked back to Suzanne and Ben's, I reflected on how much I still loved the ritual of the church yet how little desire I had to go back.

After lunch, when I got ready to leave, Suzanne, Ben, and I stood silently by my car. I wished that I could run back into the house, jump into the guest-room bed, pull up the covers, and never come out.

"It will work out," Suzanne said, almost as if she had read my thoughts. She gave me a hug and said, "Call."

I nodded.

"Tell Noel to call me if he wants to talk," said Ben. "You know there aren't sides in something like this."

"I know, and I appreciate your wanting to help. Noel isn't close to a lot of people, but he's always considered you a good friend."

"I am, but I don't want you to doubt that I'm your friend too," Ben said and hugged me.

No sooner had I crossed the bridge into northern Kentucky than my phone rang. I decided not to answer: whoever it was would just have to wait. As I pulled up to the house, my phone rang again: Noel. I debated for a few seconds and then answered.

"Marcia! I'm so glad you picked up." He paused, and I knew that he wanted me to say I was glad to hear from him, but, even though I was, I held back. "Punishing him," I thought uncomfortably. So much for forgiveness.

"I had to go to the market. I'm in the parking lot, and I just wanted to talk to you for a few moments while I have some privacy."

"How are things?" I asked after another awkward pause.

"It's awful. My God! It's just awful!" His voice broke.

"I'm so sorry."

"Now she's turning orange because her liver's failing, and she's so thin. She barely eats."

I thought of the beautiful young woman in the photo.

"Do you need to stay longer?" I asked.

"I can't. I have project meetings this week that I can't miss." He sounded weary, pressured, desperate. "But I promised Tommy I'd fly back out on Friday."

"How's he doing?"

"Actually, he's better since Hospice got Consuela on the morphine pump. Her pain was so hard for him." He paused. "It was hard for all of us."

"I can only imagine."

"I know. I keep thinking about your mother and what you went through with her. I wish I'd understood better."

I said nothing.

58

"You know, Consuela's had cancer for well over a year and never told me," Noel continued nervously with an undertone of anger. "She didn't tell Tommy either. She told Teresa that she didn't want to spoil his graduation and first year of college."

"I can understand that," I said softly.

"I can too, but if she'd told me, maybe I could have gotten her into a better treatment program or just…," his voice broke, and I could hear him crying softly. "Marcia, I love you. This is just so awful, and, on top of what's happening to Consuela and trying to help Tommy, every minute I'm terrified that you're going to leave me."

"I can't promise anything, but I haven't left yet," I said. I took a deep breath. "Why don't you come home from the airport? I'm sure we can fight just as well at home as over the phone."

"Thank you, dear. Oh, thank you so much."

"Don't thank me," I replied sharply, "Thank God."

Noel chuckled, saying, "So I have God on my side?"

"I don't know why someone you aren't even sure you believe in should be on your side, but I think God might be," I replied tartly although I found myself smiling.

"I need to get the shopping done and go back. Thank you for picking up."

"I'm praying for all of you," I said softly.

"I love you," he said.

I swallowed hard because the words he wanted to hear still stuck in my throat.

"See you later tonight," I said and ended the call.

I unloaded my bags, opened the front door, and listened to the silence of the house. It felt good to be home, and I was glad Noel had called. I was even glad that he would be home later although I avoided thinking about the complications this posed. I took my suitcase into our bedroom and was beginning to unpack when my phone rang again: Dana.

"Mom, I've been trying to get you! Where have you been?"

"I was driving home from Suzanne and Ben's. You know how I hate talking on the road, and I forgot to check my missed calls."

59

"You are just hopeless," sighed Dana in exasperation. "Listen, I have the most amazing news. There's a show of Bettina Lowe's quilts here at the university."

"You're kidding!"

"I saw a flyer yesterday and went to see them. They're fantastic! They're in this small gallery on campus. The show is due to come down in three weeks. Do you think you and Dad could come up next weekend on Saturday and maybe spend the night?"

"Dad's probably going back to California later this week."

"Again?"

"They're having a lot of trouble with this project."

"Well, can you come?"

"I'd love to." I thought quickly. "I'm going to call my editor tomorrow and see if I can do an article on the quilts. I would love to write about Lowe's work."

"Can I talk to Dad?"

"He doesn't get home until late tonight. I'll talk to him about next weekend, but I'm pretty sure he's going back to California. I'll let you know, okay?"

"Sure," said Dana and added, "I really want you to come."

"Is something wrong?"

"No, I just want you to see the quilts. I've never seen anything quite like them."

"I'm definitely coming. I'll call you tomorrow, sweetie. I love you."

"I love you too, Mom."

I sat thinking about how Dana had sounded and decided that article or no article, I needed to go up and see what was going on. I knew she had been dating someone, but I had not thought that it was serious. Worried, I sat for a moment and prayed for my children, surrounding them with light and love. As they moved into adulthood, sending light and love was often the only thing I, a helpless, frightened by-stander, knew to do.

After unpacking, I went into my office and opened my messenger bag. I stared at the three Rodriguez files for a moment. I opened the oldest one and looked again at the graduation picture of Consuela. I tried to imagine this vibrant, beautiful young woman now emaciated and dying. I could not. I had no image of the older woman she had become. Had she gained weight? Had she cut her hair? Was her hair still dark? Did she wear glasses? I realized that the real question I wanted answered had nothing to do with her looks. I wanted to know if Noel had had sex with the woman in the picture because he loved her. I wanted to know if he still loved this woman. Even if he knew the answers to these questions, I did not trust him to tell me the truth.

I put the picture in the top drawer of my desk under the pencil tray because I knew that I would have to look at it again.

"If he misses it, too bad!" I thought as I climbed the stairs and suddenly realized that his missing the photo would be too bad in ways I could not bear to consider. I put the folders back in the file cabinet.

I took a long walk in the afternoon. Sally Bryan, a good friend and neighbor, called around five.

"Is Noel gone?" she asked. "I haven't seen his car."

"Yes, he's been in California on business. He parked at the airport. I've actually been up in Cincinnati with Suzanne."

"Chuck has a dinner tonight. His department is trying to hire someone. Would you like to go out?"

"Sure. Vietnamese?"

"Sounds good. Want me to drive?"

"I can."

"No. Just come over around five, and we'll take my car."

I hung up and began to have misgivings. Sally and I had been friends for years. I did not want to talk about what was happening, but I distrusted my ability to dissemble to my closest friends. I began to feel stupid for having accepted her invitation, but, at the same time, I knew that I did not want to spend the evening alone, obsessing over what would happen when Noel walked in the door.

I took a long shower and put on casual clothes. Reading was hopeless so I sat down and tried to knit but found myself thinking of Tommy and wondering how he was doing. It sounded like his aunt and her family were close to him, but still…to be twenty and have your mother dying before your eyes….

My mind wandered to Noel, and I thought about how methodically he had worked to deceive me. I wondered how many times I had excused his absent-mindedness or preoccupation as evidence of how hard he was working. I had to laugh--he had been working hard but not on any project I could have imagined. I tried to think back over his trips to California, but so much of our life together had been so busy. Maybe I had been too preoccupied with the twins and my work to see the signs that something was going on. I realized that I had been holding the knitting needles motionless while I tortured myself.

I thought back to the homily and readings at church. How does one get from a deep sense of anger, hurt, humiliation, and betrayal to the desire to forgive and from there to the act of forgiveness? Is there some trick like Hamlet's advice to "assume a virtue if you have it not"? If I pretended to forgive Noel, would I then begin to feel forgiveness? But even pretending to forgive him seemed impossible. I looked at the time and forced myself to put my shoes on to walk over to Sally's.

She opened the door and hugged me tight, saying, "I'm so glad to see you! We haven't been out in ages!"

My misgivings fell away and I smiled, saying, "It's good to see you too! I should have let you know that I would be gone, but it was a sudden decision."

"No problem. If the house had burned down, I'd have called you," she said, laughing as we got in her car.

"So, how are you?" I asked. "I like your hair." She had cut her perfectly high-lighted blonde hair shorter than usual.

"Thanks. I'm just running like a rat in a maze as usual," she said, and then added with a frown, "Chuck's been approached about a job."

"Here?"

"Actually not. Texas."

"Texas?" I could not keep the surprise out of my voice. "Did he apply for it?"

"Not exactly. He gave a paper at a conference, and some guy talked with him about it. Then he was invited to submit his credentials."

"And he did?"

"Worse than that," said Sally with a frown. "He did it without saying anything to me."

"What?" I tried to sound genuinely astonished although it was a stretch after the week I had been through.

"I know. He says that he didn't think it would go anywhere, but it has. He's one of three candidates they've invited to visit and give a talk."

"Is he going to do it?"

Sally parked, and we walked into the small restaurant. She did not answer my question until we were seated with menus in front of us.

"Everything depends on how his meeting with the Dean goes this week. He wants to use this job in Texas for leverage to get a raise and more funds for his lab."

"So what if the Dean says no?"

"Given recent budget cuts, I think that's a pretty good bet," she said sadly.

We ordered dinner, and the server brought us jasmine tea and egg rolls.

"Do you want to move?" I asked.

"Texas? Are you kidding?"

"Where in Texas? I've heard Austin and San Antonio are great."

"College Station, the totally Texas part of Texas," she said with a groan. "I can't even think about it. We finally get the last kid off to college, and now this!"

"Well, maybe it won't happen," I said, trying to sound soothing.

"I hate the idea of moving and looking for a new job."

Sally was a social worker.

"You're talking like you think this is serious."

"Chuck is very frustrated. He never wanted to be department chair, but there was no one else. Now he's got major problems with his lab equipment. It's gotten so out of date that he can't do the research he wants to do. If the Dean doesn't give him any hope and he gets offered the other job, I can't stand in his way," she said, sounding sad, frustrated, and resigned.

"But you don't want to go?"

"No, I don't! But his work is so important to him, and I can find a job anywhere—you know, the poor are always with us," she said with a grimace.

I ate my egg roll in silence thinking how men always seem to define themselves in terms of their work so women often allow them to make work-related decisions that the women find neither pleasing nor in their best interests. I had, at least, been lucky in this regard.

"How do you think the boys will take it?"

"Not well! They don't want to see us all the time, but the idea of home moving elsewhere would certainly upset them. Charlie's doing so much better that I hate the idea of his having to deal with a major change."

Charlie, their twenty-four-year-old son, had recently, on a third try, completed a rehabilitation program for drug and alcohol abuse. He had found a job and seemed stable. He was even talking about finishing college. I knew that Sally constantly worried about him. The two younger boys were away at college within a two-hour drive of home.

"Maybe it will all work out," I suggested.

"And even if it doesn't, maybe Chuck will come to his senses," laughed Sally. "Let's talk about you for a while. I'm sick of thinking about this!"

I quailed inwardly but smiled and said, "Dana called this afternoon to get me to come up for a quilt show. Bettina Lowe has her quilts on display at the university."

"Didn't she win the grand prize at the State Fair a couple of years ago? You sent me to see her quilt." I nodded. "The color was breathtaking. Are you going up?"

"I'm going to talk to my editor tomorrow and see if I can do an article on the show. I'd like to write about her, but Dana sounded kind of upset or something so I think I probably need to go up and see her."

"Is Noel going?"

"No, he has to go out of town again."

"Why is he travelling so much?"

Sally's question was casual, but its directness caught me off guard.

"There's some problem on a consulting project in California." For a brief moment, I thought about confiding in Sally and wondered what she would say about the situation. In her job, she dealt with the family trauma of cancer, and she might have also encountered a family surprise like mine. With a start, I realized that I had lost track of the conversation.

"…surprised that Noel kept consulting."

"I'm sorry! I kind of drifted off into my own thoughts," I apologized, adding, "I think I'm worried about Dana."

64

"I was just saying that Noel has such a high-powered job that I'm surprised he's kept up his consulting work."

A perfect opening to confide in Sally, but my wounds felt too raw and new, the situation too unresolved for me to confide in her. Perhaps I was just talked out. "She clearly has problems enough of her own," I told myself.

"I know. I thought when he moved up in the company that he might stop consulting, but he finds the work interesting—it's very different from what he does day in and day out—more technical, less people management. Besides, he's very loyal to his clients," I explained easily while thinking that he certainly had been "loyal." I had barely avoided describing his work as "stimulating." I was glad I had resisted saying something dreadful like, "He's had an intimate relationship with some of his clients for years."

"Workaholic men," snorted Sally.

"Amen to that."

I got home about eight, got ready for bed, and then sat in the living room with my knitting and a book. When I could not seem to pay enough attention to make progress on the sweater or follow the book's plot, I began looking for a movie to watch. I wasn't up to a streaming search so I looked over our DVD collection and noted that every film seemed to involve some form of betrayal in love. I finally chose *Plenty*, thinking that Meryl Streep's riveting performance, as the young woman who has been part of the Resistance in France and cannot adjust to post-war England, would hold my attention. Nothing, in reality, could hold my attention, but the time passed until I heard the door open.

"Marcia?" Noel called quietly, and I heard him set down his suitcase.

I went into the hall as I had a thousand times before, but instead of embracing, we stood there awkwardly gazing at each other, waiting, trying to figure out what to do. He looked terrible: he was thinner, needed a haircut, and had large circles under his clear, gray eyes.

"How are you?" I asked with genuine concern.

He shook his head, saying, "I'm beat." He looked at me, and I could see there were tears in his eyes. "I was so afraid that you'd change your mind and wouldn't be here."

I moved closer and put my arms around him, murmuring, "I said I'd be here."

"I just wasn't sure," he said in a choked voice. "I wouldn't blame you if you did change your mind. I love you. You have to believe that I've never wanted to be with anyone else."

I drew back, involuntarily thinking, "That wasn't true at least once!" but bit back the words and asked, "Are you hungry?"

"I'm so tired that I don't know, but I think I am."

"I just got home today and haven't gone shopping. I can open some soup and make you a sandwich. Turkey okay?"

An almost unbearable hope flooded his face at this small gesture.

"Sure. I'll take a shower first, if that's okay."

I nodded, turned away to go to the kitchen, and realized that I did not know how to keep my distance from my husband.

VIII

Noel barely spoke as he ate his soup and sandwich, murmuring "Thank you" when he had finished.

"I'll sleep in the guest room tonight," I said quietly.

"No, I'll sleep in there. Just let me get my clothes for tomorrow."

"It's after midnight. Let's talk tomorrow, okay?" I sounded more conciliatory than I wanted to, but I was concerned about how tired he looked, and also, I had to admit, how sad he seemed. I could not help wondering if he was sad because of me or her. Then I judged myself for my pettiness and lack of compassion.

"Okay. Sure," he said. "I'll be home by seven." He looked apologetic. "I'm so far behind that I can't get away any earlier."

"It's okay."

He got up to leave the room and turned back.

"Promise me that you'll be here when I get home," he said quietly.

"Okay."

"No, I need you to promise, or I'll be a wreck the entire day."

"I promise that I'll be here," I said, adding, "And I might even fix dinner."

He smiled. Habits of a lifetime die hard, and we had always teased and bantered with each other.

"I'd offer to take you out," he began, but I shook my head.

Although it was almost one when we got to bed, at six the next morning, I heard Noel passing quietly by the bedroom door. I did not get up. I did not want to see him and perhaps start something it would impossible to finish. I grimaced, thinking, "As if that will not be true this evening!" I turned over and tried to go back to sleep, but when I heard his car start, I got up.

I felt numb until I saw the note lying by the coffee pot. It simply said, "I love you. You've got to believe me." I cried for twenty minutes.

I had no idea what to do so I did normal things—drank coffee, read the paper, and finally called my editor.

"This is pretty early to hear from you," Larry said with a chuckle.

"Glories of freelance work," I replied archly.

"What have you got for me?"

"Bettina Lowe is an extraordinarily interesting quilter. She's having a show at IU, and I'd like to write an article about her."

"What's the hook?"

"This is Kentucky. Everyone loves quilting and quilters!" I laughed.

"Come on!"

"She hand quilts in an age when a lot of quilters, especially arty ones, are machine quilting. She is originally from somewhere in the Deep South but went to art school so her quilts are an interesting blend of traditional and original design. She's won several prizes at the Kentucky State Fair and won the grand prize two years ago."

He did not respond, but I could hear him rummaging through papers on his desk.

"Okay, I found something. I thought the name sounded familiar. She's going to have a quilt hanging in one of the local galleries starting in June."

"Really?"

"Yup. I got an invitation to the opening. Someone also sent a press release. I'll forward it to you. You do your bit, and then we'll see if you can do something later as a follow-up. Can I have it by next Monday?"

"That's tight. I'm not going to Bloomington until Saturday."

"Go sooner! You're a free-lancer!"

"I can't."

"Okay. Tuesday morning at the latest, and I mean in my e-mail when I come to work at eight!"

"Sure. Thanks a lot, Larry."

"Take care."

I had not wanted such a tight deadline and began thinking that I might go to Bloomington on Friday. Although I had been a news reporter, I now liked to let my writing sit before I did the final editing. I might have become soft and spoiled, but I now wrote better, more considered prose than I ever had as a front-line reporter. "Work: the antidote to anguish!" I thought as I sat down to begin researching Bettina Lowe.

She was born in Marks, a small town in the Mississippi Delta, famous as the starting point of the 1968 Poor People's March. When she was four, her father deserted the family, and her mother moved with the children to her sister's place in rural Georgia. After her mother died when Lowe was thirteen, her aunt raised her and her three siblings. Her high-school art teacher recognized her talent and helped her apply to college. She never thought to show any of her college art teachers her quilts until her senior year when she made a quilt as a gift for her mentor. In an interview, Lowe quoted the teacher as saying, "To graduate, you have to do your portfolio like everyone else, but this quilt is the work you should be doing!"

After finishing her undergraduate degree, Lowe received a scholarship to a prestigious Atlanta art school and began working on a graduate degree. She dropped out after a semester, and the only explanation I could find was a single comment she made much later: "The program had little to do with my work, and I just couldn't afford any more school."

She then moved to Louisville and held a variety of jobs, none of them remotely connected to art. When she was nearly thirty, she married and moved to Hopkinsville, her husband's hometown. They had two children. She joined a quilting circle at her church and "found her way back to making art," as she put it. She had entered many quilts in the Kentucky State Fair over the years and gradually found a market for her quilts at art fairs and in regional craft centers. I finally found a phone number and decided to call her.

She was a soft-spoken woman, and when I explained to her what I was doing, she became very excited, saying, "This show is a big deal for me. The professor who arranged it teaches textiles—you know, weaving and design—and she got several people to loan their quilts for individual shows. I'm the first in the series, and I've never had such a show before! I feel so honored."

"I haven't seen the show yet, but my daughter is a student at IU and went to see it. She loved your quilts. I plan to go up later this week. I'll probably have a lot of questions for you after I look at the quilts. Do you mind if I call you again?"

"Of course not. Call me any time you want! It's so exciting that you're going to write about my quilts!"

Energized by Lowe's excitement, I spent the rest of the day doing research on quilting and studying the quilts on her website. The information was not all new to me. I had always loved quilts and, through the years, gone to many quilt shows. The work distracted me from my own problems until I looked at the clock and realized it was almost four. I then distracted myself further by planning dinner, going to the grocery, making preparations, and laying the table so everything was ready when Noel, looking relieved to see me, walked in just before seven.

"I've opened a bottle of wine and put cheese and crackers in the living room," I said.

"Just let me wash up."

He soon joined me in the living room. I had already poured the wine which we sipped in awkward silence as we sliced cheese and arranged it on crackers.

"How was work?" I finally asked. A stupid, mundane question, given the circumstances, but it was what came to mind. In our other, "before" life, it was the question I would have asked.

"It was okay." He frowned. "I'm swamped. I can't take any more time off this week, but I have to go back to California next weekend."

"Okay." I took a deep breath. "Tell me about it."

"How much do you want to know?"

"As much as you want to tell me."

Noel sighed deeply, took a sip of wine, and began, "I finally got a chance to talk to Teresa alone. It seems that Consuela knew about the cancer and didn't tell anyone—not even her."

"Why?"

"She works in a hospital, and she told Teresa that after the first surgery, as soon as she got the diagnosis, she knew she was going to die."

"What?"

70

"I thought it was just crazy talk, but by the time she had surgery, the cancer had already metastasized."

"Where did it start?"

"Her ovaries, they think."

"That's often bad news."

"It's a very aggressive cancer, and by the time they did surgery last year, it had spread throughout her abdomen and was in her liver and pancreas. They got as much as they could and hoped the chemo would do the rest, but...," his voice broke. He swallowed hard and continued, "Teresa said that the oncologist told her that neither she nor the surgeon had ever seen such extensive metastasis with so few symptoms."

"She didn't have any symptoms?" I asked in amazement.

"Not quite. I've done some reading. Teresa feels awful that she didn't force Consuela to go to the doctor sooner, but she had some common symptoms that make it easy to think they're something else. She often had indigestion, but she thought it was just indigestion. She had back pain, but she insisted it was just from work because she often has to help people move for x-rays. She started having occasional shortness of breath, but she had gained some weight and insisted that was it. Just before she got diagnosed, she began having irregular bleeding, but she told Teresa that it was probably just menopause."

"So what happened?"

"When she fainted at work one day, they insisted that she see a doctor for a complete physical before they would allow her to return to work. When her doctor found out about the bleeding, she sent her to a gynecologist who ordered an abdominal ultrasound. When they operated last year, she didn't tell me and downplayed it to her family."

"I can't believe that she didn't tell anyone."

"No, she finally told Teresa after the operation because she had to do chemo, but they didn't tell Tommy until the chemo made her so sick last fall that she couldn't work. Then they had to tell him. Her boss at the hospital has been wonderful, and Consuela even went back to work part time for a couple months." He paused and buried his face in his hands. "I can't believe that I didn't realize she was sick. She seemed tired last fall when I saw her, but I had no idea. When Tommy told me about the surgery, I tried to ask her about it, but she put me off with some vague reference to female problems which she would not talk about. When I was out in March, I didn't see her. Tommy came to my hotel."

"If you had known, what would you have done?" I forced myself to ask.

"At first, I thought maybe I could have helped her find a different treatment program or clinical trial, but her oncologist is part of a research group at UCLA. She's had great care," he said, looking up to meet my eyes and read the suspicion in my face. "For God's sake, Marcia, you don't think I'm in love with her! It's always been you. You have to believe me," he added, in a desperate, pleading tone.

"I want to believe you," I said quietly. "I want with all my heart to believe that what happened that night was simply a passing moment of lust, and not evidence of love or regret. And I want to believe that it was only that one night, but…."

"It's the truth. I swear to God it's the truth!"

"So why did you try to find her the next year when you went back?"

"I just wanted to know that she was all right."

"But you didn't have any other communication with her in that year?"

"No. In fact, I called her from the airport right before I got on the plane to fly home. I wanted to make sure that she understood that I would never see her or communicate with her again."

"How did she take that?"

"She was very upset, but she knew that I was in love with you, not her."

"Did you blame her for what had happened?"

"No. She accused me of that, but I didn't blame her. It was *my* fault. I had been drinking and should never have gone up to her apartment. When she brought out that bottle of Tequila, I should have said no thanks and left."

"But you sought her out the next year."

We both sipped our wine in silence for a few long moments. I found the wine going straight to my head and, remembering how little I had eaten, I sliced more cheese and placed the wedges on the half-moon of crackers on the cutting board.

"I'm trying to figure out how I knew there was something wrong," Noel said slowly. "I just knew. Maybe it was something about the way her friend reacted when I talked to her. I might have been imagining something, or maybe she was just worried because Consuela had had to quit her job and now had a baby. Maybe it was the way her friend pushed me to get in touch with her."

"So what did you think?"

"I don't know. She was pregnant, unmarried, had been forced to quit her job, and had moved back home even though she loved her apartment. I thought she might need help. I never dreamed...," his voice trailed off, and we sat munching cheese and crackers in silence.

"Have you heard from the kids?" Noel finally asked.

"Dana called yesterday. She wants us to come up next weekend to see a quilt exhibit."

"I can't do that," Noel began.

"I know," I interrupted him. "I already told her that you might have to go back to California on business, but I'm going up. I may go Friday and stay over so I can look at the quilts twice. I talked to Larry, and I'm writing about them."

Noel nodded, and we sat in silence. I wondered if he had begun thinking, as I had, about what we were going to tell Dana and Will. The timer on my phone went off and I got up, saying, "Dinner's ready."

We ate the pork tenderloin, rosemary potatoes, and asparagus in almost total silence, occasionally passing the bread basket or refilling a wine glass. We were both drinking more than usual. It was a simple but perfect meal that we would have celebrated if we had not each been locked in our own thoughts.

"I'll clear the dishes," said Noel, glancing at the clock which read nine-thirty.

I nodded and went to sit with a book which I tried vainly to read as I listened to the mundane sound of some dishes being loaded in the dishwasher and others being washed by hand. He had talked. I had asked questions. He had told his story, but I did not know how to begin the real conversation: the one about if and how we were going to go on in our marriage. At ten, I heard the dishwasher start and then the ring of Noel's phone.

"Hi, Tommy," I heard him say as he walked upstairs to his office.

73

It was as if a meteor had landed in the backyard. The landscape I had known with Noel was still there somewhere, but the most compelling feature was now this foreign object that had plunked down from nowhere and rearranged everything around it. Consuming waves of resentment and jealousy in me alternated with pity for Tommy and Consuela.

I found myself playing "what if." What if I could forgive Noel? What if I could accept this other child and woman, as a feature of our landscape, not just the buried treasure in Noel's landscape or the meteor in mine? How would my acceptance and their presence rearrange our life as a family? How would it affect Will and Dana? How would it change their relationship with Noel? And with me?

I looked up to find Noel standing before me.

"That was Tommy," he said, sitting down on the sofa.

"So I gathered."

"He's having such a rough time. I told him to call me every evening because I want to know how his mother is doing. Actually, it gives him a chance to talk. I'm so worried about him."

"I know. It must be incredibly hard for him."

"Because she's home, he's exposed to the pain and so much of the physical stuff." Noel shook his head. "It was hard for me to be around so I can't imagine how hard it is for him. For her, too."

"Death is a messy business," I said quietly.

Noel reached out to take my hand, and I let him.

"I'm sorry I have to go this weekend, but…," his voice trailed off.

"It's okay."

"Please talk to me," he said after a long pause. "I have to know what you're thinking. You've hardly said anything about how you're feeling."

"I don't even know where to begin."

"I'm so sorry."

"I know you are, but just saying you're sorry doesn't make it okay for me. I feel angry and humiliated and…," I started to cry, and Noel put his arms around me.

"I don't know what else to say," he murmured. "Please, please forgive me."

I pulled away from him, wiping my eyes.

"The truth is that I love you and I want to forgive you, but I don't know how   to   begin.

IX

I spent Tuesday and Wednesday going to both the public and university libraries to consult books on quilting. I took long walks and felt numb. Tuesday night Noel came home at eight. As we ate dinner, I found myself considering the nature of silence: is it a fixed state or can it increase? Perhaps silence is not a state but an organism, and that's why the silence between us felt like it was growing.

Noel had a dinner meeting on Wednesday so he did not get home until almost nine. I felt relieved that we did not have to figure out how to deal with each other. He sat with me for half an hour watching the end of a completely mindless movie. Just as we might have begun talking, his phone rang. While he was talking to Tommy, I went to bed.

On Thursday morning, I was awakened by my phone: Suzanne.

"Suzanne?" I mumbled sleepily.

"Marcia, are you still in bed?" demanded Suzanne. "It's almost eleven."

"I didn't mean to sleep so late."

"Are you okay? You haven't called so I started to worry. How are you?"

I sat on the side of the bed and thought for a moment. I still felt numb.

"I honestly don't know how I feel."

"Why don't you fix yourself a cup of coffee and call me back? I'm working at home."

"Do I want to talk?" I asked myself as I washed my face and went downstairs. As the coffee maker hissed and bubbled, I looked out the window at another brilliant, spring day. I stood thinking about where I would go if I could go anywhere and realized that where I wanted to go was back in time. I wanted to go back twenty years and move that stupid conference to any state but California. I wanted to go back and rewrite our lives so that Noel never again saw Consuela and was, therefore, never tempted to make love to her. I wanted to go back and make Noel the man I had always thought he was.

I poured myself a cup of coffee and took it in the living room to watch the sparrows and robins gathering around the feeder. It would soon be time to fill the birdbath. Life goes on. I sighed and called Suzanne.

"What's going on?" I asked her before she could say anything.

"Not so fast, my friend! Are you awake now?" I grunted. "Tell me how you're doing."

"I feel like I've been run over by a steamroller. I just can't seem to see my way through this," I said, and my voice broke.

"How's Noel?"

"He's a wreck. He's exhausted and came back to a lot of work, and now Tommy calls every night at ten. I know that he can't sleep after that because I hear him moving around."

"You hear him?"

"He's sleeping in the guest room."

"Are you talking at all?" Suzanne sounded concerned.

"We did some talking Monday night, but not really. It's hard to know where to begin, and I'm not even sure what to say."

"Have you forgiven him?"

"Good question." I started to say something flippant about forgiving and forgetting but was suddenly overcome by tears. "I don't know how to forgive him," I admitted in a choked voice. "I want to. I love him, but I'm just so angry and hurt that I can't see how to do it. I feel totally humiliated."

"This is a big one," Suzanne said softly. "It's not like forgetting an anniversary."

"It's not just the fact that he had sex with her," I said. "It's all the lies he's told me. What's worse is I keep thinking that maybe he didn't have to lie that much because I wasn't paying attention. I just trusted him."

"None of this is your fault," she said firmly. "Don't start blaming yourself."

"I feel bad in so many ways. I have a moment when I think I'm doing okay, and then this anger or jealousy or hurt just possesses me. Sometimes it's humiliation. I've always thought of myself as an intelligent person. A perceptive person. How could I have been so blind?"

"I'm sorry. Is there any way I can help?"

"I don't know."

"Have you thought about talking to a therapist?"

"Do I need to remind you that I just got out of bed?"

"Are you praying about this?"

"Of course, I'm praying about this!" I snapped.

"Can you pray honestly?"

"Now that's a different question," I conceded. "I've been trying."

"Can you talk to your pastor? You've always liked her."

I loved the pastor of my church, but the thought of re-telling my story made me want to either scream or go back to bed.

"Maybe you and Noel need to see a marriage counselor."

"Right, but first Noel and I would have to agree to do it and then find time. He has to go back to California this weekend." I sighed. "It's just a tough, confusing time right now."

"I understand, and I don't mean to push you," Suzanne said gently.

"I know you don't, but everything is just so raw. It's like any place you touch me, it hurts."

"I'm sorry."

We chatted for another few minutes about the article I was going to write on Bettina Lowe's quilts. After we hung up, I realized that after my first question, I had not asked Suzanne anything. The call had been all about me. Were my problems turning me into a lousy friend and total narcissist? I thought for a moment that maybe I should begin keeping a list of "Things to Feel Bad About," but who needs a reminder, I thought glumly, when material comes so easily to mind.

I texted Suzanne a quick apology which she immediately dismissed as unnecessary. I forced myself to eat breakfast and dress. Hoping the spring sunshine, fresh green landscape, and clear blue sky might cheer me, I decided to take a walk. I was headed for the park when I saw Father Gerald coming toward me. He was using a cane and walked with slow, careful steps. In the eleven years since I had told him that I was leaving the Catholic church, he had aged a lot.

"Marcia?" he said with a smile as we approached each other.

"Father Gerald. How good to see you," I replied, taking his outstretched hand. "How are you?"

"Old and getting even older," he muttered with a chuckle. "I have the noon Mass most days and always take a little walk afterwards to see my old neighborhood and sometimes meet neighbors."

"You don't live in the rectory anymore?"

"No, I live not too far from here with several other retired priests." There was a brief silence and he said, "I've missed having a critic in residence, Marcia. Over the years, I've often thought of you and your family. How are you?"

I met his kind, interested gaze and, instead of saying, as I had intended, "We're fine. The twins are at IU," tears spilled down my cheeks and I said, "I need help."

Father Gerald handed me a clean, white handkerchief, took my arm, and said, "Let's go to the rectory and talk."

As we slowly walked the two blocks to the rectory, he gave me time to regain my composure by remarking on the wonders of spring around us.

He unlocked the front door to the rectory, and we went into the small sitting room immediately inside. He opened the blinds and asked, "Would you like a drink of water?"

I nodded, and he returned a few moments later with a glass of water.

"I'm fine now," I said, taking a sip. "I don't want to keep you from things."

"I'm retired," he said, smiling. "Not much to keep me from. Tell me what's wrong."

"I've found out something about Noel," I began and the whole story spilled out of me.

At the end, he was silent for a long time, looking down thoughtfully at the tent of his gnarled fingers.

"I'm sorry," he finally said, looking up and frowning. "I'm so sorry for all of you. Poor Noel. What a burden he's been carrying! And that poor woman and her son and her family. I'm so sorry."

For a moment, I felt cheated, as if Consuela had stolen my suffering, and then I felt bad for resenting a dying woman.

"But what can I do to help you, Marcia?"

"I love my husband," I said, beginning to cry again, "He's so sorry for all of this."

"I'm sure he is. He's always seemed to me like a deeply good man. If he were not, he would not have taken care of this other child."

"I know," I finally managed to say. I took a deep breath, willed myself not to cry, and said, "I want to forgive him, but I don't know how…I don't know where or how to begin. No one has ever wronged me in this way before."

"The first step is to pray."

"I've been doing that! I've read all the Scripture passages about the lost sheep and forgiving seventy times seven," I said impatiently. "I know what I'm supposed to do and I know why and I know that I don't want to go on feeling the way I do, but I don't know how to begin!"

"Actually, I'm wrong about the first step," Father Gerald said. "The real first step is to admit everything you're feeling no matter how ugly or painful or humiliating."

"I think I've done that. I've done nothing but think about this situation since Tommy came to our front door. I've talked endlessly to my best friend about it, but the emotions just keep coming up. I'm like a hamster running in a wheel, and I hate feeling this way. I know that the only way I'll have any peace about what's happened is to forgive Noel, but I can't seem to get there. My brain goes there, but my heart…." I stopped. Was my heart broken? Had Noel's deception damaged me in some irreparable way? Would I heal but be like a broken vase, leaking at the place where the pieces joined? Or would this kind of healing be like broken bones knitting stronger around a stabilizing pin? Or could it even be like porcelain mended with gold to make it more valuable?

"This may seem like simple-minded advice, Marcia, but you may just need to be patient."

"Patience," I muttered derisively, "Definitely not my strong suit!"

Father Gerald chuckled and said, "So perhaps that is part of the lesson here. You need to pray for patience both with yourself and with Noel."

80

"Have you ever had someone betray you like this?" I asked. "Of course, I don't mean exactly like this, but…."

"I would have to say I haven't," Father Gerald replied quietly. He regarded me for a few moments as if weighing his words, and finally added, "But that wouldn't be quite true." He studied me for another long moment before he spoke.

"My parents separated when I was eleven. My three younger sisters went with my mother who took them back to Pennsylvania to live with her family. I was the oldest--the only boy. She left me here with my father who was an alcoholic."

"I can't believe she did that!" I exclaimed, and he held up his hand with a small smile.

"This might not happen now, but when I was a boy, there was much less concern about children, especially poor children." He paused, I nodded, and he continued, "My father was not abusive, but let's just say that he was not an attentive parent. He worked, and when he wasn't at work, he drank. The priest at my parish church where I went to school looked out for me."

I must have raised my eyebrows because Father Gerald said angrily, "I know what you're thinking, but he was a good man. He did not abuse me but hired me to do odd jobs at the church, made sure I got a few good dinners each week, found me hand-me-down clothes, and insisted that I pay attention to my schoolwork so I could get a scholarship to Catholic high school. When I did, he paid for my books and other expenses. He gave me an allowance and taught me how to save. His example and kindness is why I became a priest, and one of my greatest joys is that he lived to see my ordination.

"I could not forgive my mother for abandoning me. There wasn't money for me to go visit her and my sisters. The months after they left were probably the lowest point in my whole life. I decided that I hated her and didn't want to see her. She would write me each week and make my sisters write. She would send small sums of money. Occasionally, usually on my birthday, Easter, and Christmas, she would call, but my anger and resentment made those calls a misery for her.

"When I was in seminary, I had a spiritual director who asked, as a starting point for our relationship, that I write my autobiography. This was

81

probably the most painful writing assignment I have ever had because it forced me to look at and begin to feel all the emotions from my childhood that I had buried. At that time, my father was still alive and still drinking. I blamed my mother for his drinking because I thought if she had only stayed, if she had only been more patient, he would have stopped. I had to begin to confront my feelings about my mother. I'm an old man now, but it's still hard to talk about this." He stopped for a moment and seemed to be gathering himself.

"My spiritual director, Father Terence, suggested that I pray every day for the forty days of Lent to forgive my mother. It was not a penance, he said, but an 'opportunity for spiritual growth.' He used to say this so often that we called him 'Father Opportunity' behind his back." Father Gerald chuckled, making me smile. "He also said that if I could not learn to forgive her, I would not be able to help others learn to forgive or ask for forgiveness."

"So did you do it?"

"I tried to do it. Just like you're trying to forgive Noel. I'd kneel and try to pray and, just like you said, all these emotions would come up in me. I probably cried more tears in those forty days than I had before or have since. Then, at the Good Friday service—which used to last three hours!--I prayed to leave my hurt and hatred and all the other emotions toward my mother at the foot of the cross, and something happened. My load somehow lightened when I asked Christ to help me carry it. Of course, I immediately told Father Terence about this miracle and was relieved that the lesson was over, but," Father Gerald paused to smile, shaking his head, "After the Easter Vigil mass, Father Terence found me and handed me an envelope. Inside I found a card, some money, and a round-trip bus ticket. The card said that he would take me to the bus station on Monday morning, and my mother would pick me up when I arrived."

"How did you feel?"

"Furious at his meddling. At that point, I hadn't seen my mother since my high school graduation where I'd made it clear that I didn't want to see her again. I didn't even go to my college graduation because I was afraid that she might come. I could forgive her in theory at a distance, but I still wasn't sure how I would feel in person, and I didn't want to find out."

"So did you go?" I asked.

Father Gerald chuckled, saying, "You don't know much about seminaries, do you? It's all about obedience! Of course, I went."

"So what happened?"

"I got off the bus, saw my mother, and totally broke down. I spent three days with her and got to know my sisters again. The day before I left, I finally asked her why she had abandoned me." He stopped and wiped his eyes. "She said that she was terrified of having more children. She was a good Catholic woman and wouldn't deny my father so she had to get away from him. She hoped her leaving would shock my father into getting sober so they could go back together. I was the oldest, the only boy, and she thought that a boy needs a father, but her real reason for leaving me behind was that my father adored me. She hoped that I could save him."

"But you were a child!" I protested.

"True, but back then, kids used to grow up faster than they do now. My mother said that every night for the first year she cried herself to sleep worrying about me. Understanding that she had done the best she knew to do helped me forgive her even though facts are facts, and she had, in fact, abandoned me."

"So how did you finally forgive her?"

"I worked at it in prayer and then was blessed to hear her story with an open heart, I guess. But that's not the end."

"Don't tell me your parents reconciled and everyone lived happily ever after?" Father Gerald laughed.

"Not at all. Until she died--God rest her soul--I visited my mother every year and talked to her frequently. My father never stopped drinking. He— God rest his soul--died while I was in seminary. No, it was not happily ever after at all," he said. "But when I got back, Father Terence met me. He heard the whole story and was very happy. Then at the end, he asked if I had ever abandoned anyone assuming they would be better off or could manage without me? Had I ever made this sort of decision for someone without asking how that person felt, just assuming that I knew what was best? He told me to think about it and then said something I've never forgotten: 'We have the hardest time forgiving acts that reflect what we ourselves have done.'"

"So what did you figure out?"

"I had abandoned my father. As I grew up, I worked. I studied at friends' houses or the rectory. I ate dinner and visited with Father O'Connell. I stayed away and let my father drink not only because I couldn't stop him but also because I thought that having me there when he was drinking shamed him. I never asked him if I should stay or if he wanted me to stay. I left him to his own devices just as my mother had left me to mine."

"I have to say it again--you were only a kid!"

"I know. That's an excuse and an explanation, but the reality is that I abandoned him. In my heart, I know that. I know that, especially as I got older, I looked for ways to escape being with him. When I realized what I had done, I was finally able to forgive my mother."

"'Let the one who is without sin cast the first stone,'" I murmured, and he nodded.

"It helps to remember that none of us is without sin."

"But I've never cheated on Noel. I've never lied to him."

"Yes, but have you ever done something that you could not admit to? Have you ever avoided telling someone the truth because you were afraid of what that person might think or what you might lose? From what you say, that's what Noel's been doing. He's been afraid of losing you so he got trapped in this complicated web of lies."

"Thank you for telling me your story. You've given me a lot to think about," I said, rising.

Father Gerald stood up and held out both hands, saying, "Let's just pray silently for a moment for whatever help we both need."

We stood holding hands for a few moments. I have no idea what form his prayer took, but mine was a wordless plea for help. Our prayer ended, and I hugged him.

"Thank you."

"I'll keep all of you in my prayers," he assured me, "And if you need to talk or if Noel would like to talk, I would be happy to help in any way I can."

"I appreciate your generosity more than I can say."

He walked me to the door and said quietly, "You know, Marcia, you can always come back."

"I know, but I love the church we go to, and if I hadn't run into you, I would have gone to see my pastor. I may still go talk to her."

"It's good to know that you've found a spiritual home," he said, squeezing my hand.

I went from the cool, dark rectory out into the blinding sunlight and walked slowly home pondering Father Gerald's story and his final question. Had I ever lived out a series of lies to cover up something I had done and was afraid to admit to? Had I ever done anything that would mirror Noel's unfaithfulness and deception?

My first response was, "Of course not!" But as I walked through the park, I tried to set aside my sense of moral superiority and outrage.

X

Beneath our polite silence, I sensed Noel's impatience to get back to California. I struggled not to feel jealous by arguing that at least he was sharing the nightly news from Tommy. When I called Suzanne Thursday night, she asked, "What stick are you beating yourself with today?"

She made me laugh but forced me to see the emotional pattern I seemed unable to break. I told her about my talk with Father Gerald and how his questions nagged at me.

Friday morning, I got up early and packed. I had kissed Noel good-bye and told him to call me if he wanted to talk. He was still sleeping in the guest room, but I had begun to miss having his body beside me.

As I drove north to Bloomington, through the greening fields and trees unfurling their fresh leaves, I found myself singing Marty Haugen's version of St. Francis' hymn to creation: "The heavens are telling the glory of God/And all creation is shouting for joy!"

I also found myself asking Father Gerald's questions again. Had I ever done something so shameful that I feared owning up to it? Had I ever lied and then continued lying because I feared the consequences if I confessed? Nothing leaped to mind so I began reviewing my life from fights with my best friend in elementary school to the casual cruelty of middle school to the shifting ins and outs of high school. I considered the busy pattern of work and study in college. Looking back, I could see that on occasion there were sins of commission and omission but no act so shameful that I had been afraid to own it.

I thought about my close friendship with Suzanne. I had started out mistrusting her because I had never known either an observant Jew or someone so serious about religion, but she had spotted my ignorance immediately, and, as we grew closer, she never held my mistrust against me but helped me grow out of it. In high school and college, there had been guys, but no one serious until after college. The image of Lionel Carstairs and the moment of revelation were simultaneous. Even all these years later, my cheeks burned with shame.

As part of a follow-up article on what previously-profiled new lawyers were doing, I had interviewed Lionel. He came from a long line of lawyers and had graduated at the top of his class. He looked like old money—tall, blond, piercing blue eyes, whip smart, charming, witty, and thirty-one to my twenty-five. Lionel was about to become the youngest partner ever in the city's most prestigious corporate law firm. After my article appeared, I was flattered when he asked me out.

Even at the time, I was not quite sure what he saw in me. He came from a wealthy, conservative family, and I was a liberal whose father had been a union steward. We argued constantly about politics. I was a reader, as always, but he was an avid movie-goer and loved theatre. He introduced me to opera and ballet. In the eighteen months I dated him, I was probably exposed to more culture than I had been in my entire previous life, and I loved it.

Because of family connections and his status as the protégé of a prestigious older partner in the firm, he was invited everywhere, and he took me along. The people I met and places we went enhanced my connections in and knowledge of the community; in other words, they were potentially useful to me as a reporter. As long as we avoided politics, Lionel was interesting and fun to be with. He was also a good lover.

After eighteen months of dating, on Valentine's Day, in an exclusive downtown restaurant, with the chef and servers eagerly awaiting my reaction to the beautiful engagement ring at the bottom of my gin and tonic, he proposed. It would have been hard to say no, yet as soon as I said yes, somewhere deep inside, I knew that I had made a mistake.

Until he proposed, I had thought I might be in love with Lionel, but once I said yes, I began to quail at the prospect of spending the rest of my life with him. On the surface, he was a "great catch" and the "right man" for me as everyone, but Suzanne, was quick to tell me. Her response to the news of my engagement was to ask first, "Do you love him?" and then, half-jokingly, "So how are you going to handle politics at home?"

Both questions angered me because, unsure of my feelings, I had to admit that I could overlook Lionel's politics when we were dating, but the prospect of life in the company of those values and their continuous articulation bothered me. It was fun to enjoy the privileges of his position when we were dating, but did I want this pattern of privilege to define the rest of my life? Did I want to pass these conservative, upper-class values on to our children? His family had welcomed me, but I doubted they would tolerate much deviation from their values and life style.

As the plans for the wedding moved forward, I felt more and more uncomfortable. It seemed that Lionel began every conversation "When we're married…" which made me want to scream, but I did not know how to stop the train and get off. It seemed like time for me to settle down, and part of me was afraid that if I did not marry Lionel, I would never marry or have children. Who would ever love me as much as Lionel did?

I could not sleep or eat, not because I was a "nervous bride," but because I did not want to be Lionel's bride at all. I felt so confused and ashamed that I avoided talking to Suzanne. When my mother remarked, "You don't seem happy," I began to avoid her too. I worked overtime to avoid spending time with Lionel as it became more and more apparent to me that I was living a lie and, worse yet, about to commit to a lifetime of living that lie.

Four months before the wedding, my mother, Lionel's mother, Lionel, and I met at the stationer's to finalize the invitations. On an earlier visit, Lionel and I had narrowed the choice to two or three invitations we liked. Although printing was cheaper and looked fine to most people, Lionel's mother insisted that the invitations be engraved. Actually, she did not insist. She simply said, "Of course, you'll have them engraved" in a tone that rendered any objection unthinkable. My parents, bless their middle-class hearts, were so intimidated by Lionel's family that they ponied up whatever was required without question, simply wanting their only child to have a dream wedding and live happily ever after.

We made the final choice and would see a proof later, but the salesperson had quickly run a mock-up of the invitation. When it came around to me, I sat looking at the elegant, Italianate script announcing that "Marcia Marie Holmes, daughter of James and Helen Holmes" would marry "Lionel Ellington Carstairs III, son of Lionel Ellington Carstairs, Junior, and Amelia Darlington Carstairs, on the twenty-first day of June." I stared at it for so long that Lionel finally asked, "Is something wrong?"

I looked into his eyes and said, "I'm so sorry, Lionel, but I can't marry you. I just can't. I'm sorry." I met my mother's eyes across the table and caught a fleeting look of relief.

"What do you mean?" Lionel's fair complexion had gone white.

"You're a good man, but I can't marry you." I took a deep breath and said, "I don't want to marry you."

I placed the engagement ring on the table, ran out the door to my car, and never looked back. Later, I wrote notes of apology to the salesperson and Lionel's parents.

A few days later, I finally accepted Lionel's call. I told him that I did not want to talk, but he replied, "You, at least, owe me this!"

The quiet downtown bar he chose for our meeting, with its dim interior, comfortable private booths, and men's club atmosphere, was the kind of place I would never again frequent.

"You owe me an explanation," he began angrily when we were seated. "Did you have to humiliate me publicly?" His adding, "Marcia, don't you know that I love you?" did nothing to undo the sense of entitlement behind his first words. We argued, and he bullied me, asking variations on the question, "If I'm such a great guy, why don't you want to marry me?"

Anger finally overcoming guilt, I blurted out, "I don't love you. That's it! That's all! I've just been too chicken to tell you. I never should have said yes when you asked me to marry you!"

It was messy, dishonest, painful, and ugly in every possible way. I could look back and think, "I was young," but I was not that young, and youth was not a sufficient excuse for my inability to be honest. From our first date, I had known that we were not compatible, but I had ignored the signs and indulged myself, having fun, enjoying his attention, using his connections, and luxuriating in his privilege. Then I was trapped because I had never stopped to consider how Lionel felt.

When he proposed, I had not had the courage to turn him down publicly, but, later that night or the next day or on any of the days that followed, I could have pleaded for more time or told him that I could not marry him. As the wedding plans rolled forward, my shame made it harder and harder to speak until finally the words had escaped without regard for Lionel's feelings or propriety. I had inflicted a much greater wound by my failure to be honest with myself and Lionel from the beginning.

I had met Noel four years later and never told him the story in any detail. By thirty, everyone has a history. Just as he told me that he had been in love with someone and it had not worked out, I told him that I had been engaged and broken it off because we were not a good match. He had accepted at face value what I told him--one of the few instances where I had been less than honest with him. I now had to admit that I had never shared the details because I was ashamed of how I had treated Lionel.

As I drove into Bloomington, I was almost laughing at myself. Finding my failing that, in some part, reflected Noel's had not been difficult, and I felt more sympathy for Noel's plight than I had at any time since I opened the door to Tommy. I remembered the lies I had told about work to avoid being with Lionel: "I need to work late...," "They need me to cover this story...," "I have to do this interview this evening...." What if I had married Lionel? What lies would that situation have led to? I could find ways to explain but no way to excuse my behavior. To Noel's credit, his lies had been in the service of supporting his son.

I found a parking place downtown and walked to the Thai restaurant to meet Dana. She had gotten us a small table in the window of the converted house and waved to me as I came in. We hugged, and I felt happy to see her.

"How are you?" I asked, sitting down and noting the circles under her gray eyes. She shrugged her shoulders, and then her eyes filled with tears. I took her hand. "Honey, what is it?"

"This is so embarrassing," she finally stammered, fumbling for a tissue in her backpack. "I'm sorry, Mom."

"No, don't be embarrassed. What's wrong?"

"Didn't Will call you?"

"No. Should he have?"

"I didn't want him to, but he threatened that he was going to call you."

The server came to get our order, and we each pointed absent-mindedly to one of the lunch specials.

"Tell me what's wrong."

"I was dating this guy. I thought he really liked me," said Dana, her eyes filling again.

"How long did you date him?"

"I know that I mentioned him to you when I was home for spring break," she said, flicking her long, dark hair back over her shoulder impatiently.

"I know you did, but I wasn't sure it was serious."

"We've been seeing each other all the time since January."

I read between the lines and knew that she had been sleeping with him. "What's his name?"

"Chad Shearer. I know I told you, but it doesn't matter."

Our soup and spring rolls came.

"Eat, honey. You'll feel better."

"That's such a mom-thing to say," she said, smiling for the first time.

"Hey, I'm your mom so I get to say mom-things!"

We both laughed and then ate in silence for a few moments.

"So what happened with Chad? Did he dump you?" I asked.

"No, I actually dumped him after I found out that he bragged that he was only dating me to get help with that computer course we're both taking."

"You're kidding!"

"I wish I were," she said, shaking her head and wiping away fresh tears.

"What an asshole! How did you find out?"

"He was at some bar with a bunch of guys. He didn't see Steve who is also in the class, but Steve heard him. Someone was talking about how hard this course is, and he said that he had figured out how to get through it in a pretty painless way. Someone asked him how, and he said 'by going with the smartest girl in the class.'"

"Maybe he was just joking," I began, but she shook her head vehemently.

"No. He was serious."

"That's awful!" I exclaimed, adding, "But at least he knows you're the smartest girl in the class."

"Actually, I'm the smartest *person* in the class," she said, adding bitterly, "Small consolation for such a huge humiliation."

91

"At least Steve is a real friend," I offered tentatively.

"I never much noticed him except to say hi. Last week he came and found me where I usually study in the library. We went and had coffee, and he told me. He felt so bad. He had known since before spring break, but he wasn't sure that he should tell me. He just kept hoping we'd break up, and he wouldn't have to say anything."

"So what did you do?"

"I tried not to cry and thanked him. Then I called Will who wanted to kill Chad." She managed to smile. "I got him to settle for coming with me to confront Chad. That asshole tried to bluff his way out by saying that he might have started out dating me for that reason but now he really cares about me. I told him that was bullshit, and Will just towered over him and glowered and told him that if he gave me any trouble, he'd kick his ass."

"Not really!" I was genuinely alarmed but also amused.

"Yes, really! I made Will promise to be non-violent, but he told me that I didn't make him promise not to threaten violence! So he came and sat with me in class for the next couple of meetings and glowered at Chad."

I was hard pressed not to laugh at the vision of my tall, thin, blonde, usually mild-mannered son trying to intimidate someone.

"You're well rid of Chad."

"I know," she said slowly as the server brought our heaping plates of pad thai. "I know, but it was nice to have someone." She brushed away two large tears and sniffed.

"There are lots of guys…," I began.

"I know, but Chad's the only one who's shown any interest in me, and it was nice."

I tried to think what to say. Dana was not one to define herself in terms of male attention. She had been a science and math whiz her whole life. Although she had dated a few boys in high school, there had not been anyone special, and she had looked forward to the larger social world of college.

"I feel so lonely," added Dana. "I had hoped college would be different for me because guys would be smarter and interested in the things I'm interested in. Will has a girl, and Rita has a boyfriend, and everyone but me seems to have someone!"

92

This was the first I had heard about Will and a girl, but I had known her best friend Rita was going with someone. This was also the first time I had ever heard Dana complain about not being paired off, and it bothered me. I thought we had raised her to be strong, sensible, and independent, but I had to admit that we all want to be loved. I thought again of my relationship with Lionel Carstairs and looked into the face so like my own except for Noel's gray eyes.

"What are you doing outside of your classes?" I asked, deciding to take a practical rather than philosophical approach. I knew that Dana was in no mood for being told that "a woman needs a man like a fish needs a bicycle," especially from her long-married mother.

"Is this going to be a lecture on getting involved?" she asked in a morose tone.

"No, but you may just need an activity that gets you out of your normal courses and in touch with some other sorts of students."

"The Honors program is supposed to do that," she replied, rolling her eyes.

"You don't like it?" I was surprised.

"I like the courses, but I haven't gone to much of the social stuff," she admitted. "Will has, and he likes it, but I'm usually too busy studying." She met my eyes with a guilty look. "Will's been after me to start doing other stuff, like playing co-ed volleyball, but my courses are so hard...," she said, her voice trailing off.

"You're obsessing over your work," I said gently, knowing my perfectionist daughter.

"I know, I know." She frowned. "It's so embarrassing that Steve and all those other guys know about this. I just feel humiliated."

"You didn't do anything wrong, Dana. Think of Chad's grade from here on as your revenge. Has anyone said anything?"

"No! Steve's been very nice. He sits with me in class, and we've had coffee a couple of times, but it's just so humiliating that anyone knows how stupid and gullible I was," she said bitterly.

I thought of Noel for the first time since I had entered the restaurant. How would I feel when everyone knew how I had spent twenty-some years in La-La Land? I could hear the comments, "How could she be so *stupid?*" "How could she *not* have known?" "Maybe she just didn't *want* to know?"

"Let's stop talking about me and talk about something else," Dana said impatiently. "I'm actually getting sick of my own drama."

"That's a surprise!" I replied, laughing.

Dana tried to look offended, but finally giggled, saying, "Come on! We are growing up a little bit. Will is bringing Fernanda to dinner tonight so you can meet her."

"Do you like her?"

"Aside from their insistence on speaking Spanish all the time, she's great!"

"Is she from here?"

"No, Colombia."

"Do you think it's serious?"

Dana was quiet for a few moments before saying, "I'm not sure. I think it may be too early to tell, but Will seems very happy when he's with her."

We finished lunch talking about my research on Bettina Lowe and then walked across campus to the art gallery. Dana and I moved around the exhibit together, but before I got to the last quilt, she had become impatient with my taking photos and making notes.

"Mom, I'm going to sit outside in the sun. Take your time!"

The twelfth quilt was hung separately. When I rounded the corner, I stood transfixed by one of the most beautiful objects I had ever seen. The quilt was a twelve by twelve square. On a flat black background, Lowe had quilted many concentric circles of petals ranging in exact gradations of color from blood red at the outermost petals through a range of ever lighter reds and pinks to a blinding white at the center. The flower, a stylized lotus, seemed to rise so vividly out of the black background only as a vehicle to move your eyes from the blood red petals toward the bright center.

I stood for a long time lost in contemplation. The center of light drew my eyes inexorably. I finally moved forward to read the text posted next to the quilt, which was called "Forgiveness." Many of the other quilts had commentaries on their meaning, the thought process or experience behind them, or the tradition that informed the design, but not this one. This commentary was purely technical: "Lowe herself dyed the fabric for this quilt in order to have exact gradations of color moving from red through pink to white. Silk on a cotton background."

I stepped back and realized that looking at this quilt directly was like falling into the light. The pattern was irresistible: the bright, dark red rising out of the flat darkness and each shining tier of petals moving along the spectrum toward a blinding whiteness.

I found myself wondering what that light center represented—was it forgiveness itself, the peace of forgiveness, or the transcendent grace or love that fosters forgiveness? Was enlightenment literally and figuratively at the center of forgiveness? And what blood red deed or emotion came from darkness to begin or make necessary that move toward the light?

I went outside and found Dana, telling her, "I want you to come back in and look at something."

After getting up from the bench, picking up her backpack, and pocketing her phone, she smiled indulgently and came with me to stand before the last quilt.

"What do you think this is about?" I asked her after a few moments.

"It's called 'Forgiveness.'"

"Okay, but what do you think is at the center?"

"Love of God," she said, a little uncomfortably. "You know, inner peace. Perfect harmony."

"Do you like it?"

Dana did not answer for a long time.

"I like the contrast in texture between the flatness of the cotton background and the silk of the flower."

"Is that all?"

"I find it powerful in a disturbing way."

I looked at her, and she shifted uncomfortably before adding, "It's weird, but it makes me think about Chad. I hate him, but I know I shouldn't. When I first saw this quilt, I started thinking about that."

I hugged her tight.

The quilt haunted me for the rest of the day.

Will brought Fernanda to dinner, and she turned out to be delightful. Dana even seemed happier. Late that night, before I drove her back to her dorm, we sat up talking over a final glass of wine. She admitted that she understood why Chad had dated her. He had talked his way into the course without adequate preparation. She had spent much of their time together helping him learn what he should have come into the class knowing.

"He's not dumb," she explained, "Just arrogant. I first started helping him because I felt sorry for him. I realized in the first lab session that he didn't have a clue."

"And it was probably easier for him to go after someone pretty and sympathetic rather than admitting to another guy that he was so far behind," I suggested, and Dana nodded thoughtfully.

"I don't want to hate him because it hooks me in. It keeps me from moving on. I think that quilt was trying to say that if you forgive someone, you get a kind of clarity that can free you."

"Well put," I said. "Can I use it for my article?"

Dana laughed, saying, "Whatever!" Then she added, "Chad actually taught me something."

"What?"

"I'm good at teaching, and I enjoy it. I might like to be a professor someday."

"Clarity out of darkness," I said. Dana rolled her eyes, and we both laughed.

The next day I went back to see the quilts again. I spent a long time standing before "Forgiveness" and taking in every detail, but it was inevitable that my eyes would move back to that bright center. I thought that the quilt was about coming to peace by recognizing and letting go of emotions in order to rest in God who is both at the center of the universe and our beings. The quilt traced the trajectory from raw emotion to a clear tranquility.

When I got home late Saturday afternoon, I sat down and wrote my article on Lowe's quilts. It was a matter of putting down the words I had been thinking and re-thinking during the drive home. I ended with a paragraph on the "Forgiveness" quilt. After I finished writing, I decided to call Lowe. She was home so I told her how the exhibit had impressed me, but when I mentioned that "Forgiveness" was the work I had found most powerful, she grew silent.

"The text on this quilt didn't give much information except to say that you dyed the fabric yourself in order to get the color gradations," I said. "There wasn't anything about where the idea for the quilt might have come from or its meaning."

Lowe did not reply but laughed uncomfortably.

"I was going to ask if you've studied any Eastern religion. The flower looks like a lotus," I offered tentatively.

Lowe laughed again and said, "I've been asked about the flower every time I exhibit that quilt. I'm just a plain, old Christian, but I might have seen that flower somewhere. I honestly don't remember where, though."

I waited for her to continue, but she said nothing further.

"I have a situation in my own life where I'm trying to forgive someone," I said tentatively, "And, in a way, your quilt helped me begin to see and feel the process."

"I'm glad," she replied, and another silence fell.

"I'd like to e-mail you a draft of my article."

"That would be great, but I'm sure it's fine."

She gave me her e-mail, promising to read the article and call me the next afternoon. I usually did not share my writing with subjects, but I was hoping that reading what I had written might lead Lowe to tell me more about the "Forgiveness" quilt. I did not want the information for my article as much as I wanted it for myself.

I went to bed that night feeling uneasy that I had not heard from Noel.

XI

Sunday morning, I slept late and had to rush to get to church. I thought about not making the effort, but later, I was glad that I had because an hour filled with scripture readings, music, and other people speaking helped quiet the voices in my head. When I turned my phone back on, I found a message to call Bettina Lowe. I hoped that this did not indicate that she had objections to my article. Given my state of mind, I was not up for re-writing at short notice.

Lowe answered the phone, and after exchanging pleasantries, I asked her how she liked my article.

"I like it! It's very good. I appreciate all the research you did! You almost know more about me than I know about myself," she chuckled.

"I love your work, and it has certainly repaid my attention in ways you'll probably never know."

"When you called yesterday, you asked me about the 'Forgiveness' quilt, and I kind of put you off."

"You've been more than generous with your time," I assured her.

"No," she interrupted, "I *was* putting you off. I don't like to talk about that quilt, but I've seen that you take my work seriously. I think you deserve an explanation, but you *can't* write any of this. It's just between you and me."

"Of course. You have my word."

"I lived with a man I met in college, and he was abusive. Very jealous and controlling. He had slapped me a few times, and I finally left him after graduation. I moved in with a friend across town. I started working on my master's and thought I was safe, but he came after me." She paused for a long moment before saying, "He beat me up and raped me which is when I finally got help in getting away from him. That's why I dropped out and never finished my master's degree. Because of him, I couldn't stay in Atlanta so I went to Louisville where I had a friend who helped me get on my feet. I didn't even try to go back to school because after what happened, I had so many problems."

"I'm so sorry."

"Later, even though I married a good man, I carried my hatred and anger with me. I did therapy and read books, but it just kind of sat inside me like this huge dark place that was always waiting to suck me in. I asked the Lord to help me lay down this burden. I prayed and prayed. Nothing seemed to happen, but one morning I woke up, and I had dreamed that quilt. Just as it is. I didn't know what it was called—I could just see the design and colors, but as I worked on it, I gradually came to know that it was about forgiving him so that he would no longer possess me through my hate. Then one day it came to me that the quilt was not only about forgiveness but also about God's love being at the center of forgiveness. It's by God's grace that we forgive. It wasn't just about moving away from the rage and violence, all that stuff that comes out of darkness. I knew the darkness that was in him, but I finally saw the darkness was also in my hate. It was about choosing to dwell in that white light at the center."

"So it just came to you one day to forgive him?"

"No. Not at all. I would block him out of my mind for months, but anytime I would think of him and what he did to me, anger and hate and fear would fill me. I hated him for ruining my education. He was always jealous of my work and by what he did, he kind of took the heart out of me. I saw other women break free of their abuse, but I still felt imprisoned in mine. I finally realized that I would never be free until I found a way to forgive him. So I prayed harder and harder."

"And it just happened?"

"Not all at once, but gradually. Nothing seemed to be happening, and then I saw that quilt in my dream, and as I began to work, I kind of poured my hatred into the dark area and my sense of violation and bitterness and hurt into the red and gradually as I dyed the fabric and quilted the petals, I began to be able to turn it over to the Lord. It was pure grace. Every stitch of that quilt is a prayer to be released from the burden of hate. I always pray when I work, but that quilt is special. I finally understood that even my enemy was a part of the flower and that even he might someday find the light."

"Thank you for sharing this," I said softly. "I've been struggling to forgive someone, and I just can't seem to find the place to begin. It's like looking for a toehold on a smooth wall."

"Exactly. I know how hard it is, but you got to pray. The good Lord promised us 'Knock and it will be opened.' Sometimes I swear you gotta pound on that door with both fists, but that's all I know to do," she said with a sigh. "It took me years."

"I understand, and I've been trying to pray, but you've inspired me to try harder and not give up."

"I'll pray with you if you want."

"Thank you. I'd like that." I felt comforted. "If you come into Louisville, please call me. I'd love to take you to dinner and talk."

"And if you get over by me, you call. And let me know how your problem works out," she added. "I trust in the Lord, but I always like a progress report."

She laughed in her low, warm voice, and as we said good-bye, I knew we would stay in touch.

I went over the article again, did some minor editing, and e-mailed it to Larry with "Hahaha! I'm early!" in the subject line. Thirty minutes later, I got an e-mail that said, "Hahahaha! I like it!"

I made the minor changes he suggested, sent the article back, closed my laptop, and turned to the rest of the day. Noel was supposed to be home on the late flight. Just as I was wondering why he had not called, my phone rang.

"I was just thinking of you," I said by way of greeting.

"Telepathy. I've been thinking of nothing but you all day."

"Where are you? On your way home?"

For some reason, this conversation felt easier, more like old times.

"That's what I called to tell you. I can't come home tonight. I need to stay."

"How is she?"

"Much worse. In and out of consciousness, but she's not in too much pain. She's confused, but that may be the drugs. I can't say enough good about Hospice. They've been wonderful."

"I'm glad. How's Tommy?"

"Terrible. He's afraid to go to work for fear she'll die while he's gone. He's been staying home and mostly sitting by her bed, holding her hand."

"I feel so sorry for him." I hesitated. "And for you too."

"Thank you, sweetheart." After a long pause, he said, "I need to ask you something."

"Okay."

All bets were off, I realized, as I tried to imagine what he was going to ask. Now I will always have this sense of foreboding, I thought sadly. Whenever he says, "I need to ask you something" or "I need to tell you something," my heart will stop and mind go blank, fearing the unforeseen will rock my world again.

"It's a huge thing to ask. I know that," he began, and I could hear him taking a deep breath. He cleared his throat.

"Just ask," I said impatiently. I heard him take another deep breath, and I knew he was rubbing his hand against his chin, his typical nervous gesture.

"Marcia, could you...uh, would you come out here?" He quickly added, "I know it's a lot to ask, but...." He fell silent.

"But what?" I asked and could not keep the anger out of my voice. So much for forgiveness--how could he ask me to do this?

"It would help me. That's all. I know I'm being selfish, but it would really help me, Marcia. I need you."

His desperation made me angry. So what was I supposed to do when I got there? Play Florence Nightingale to the mother of his other child? Minister to his mistress?

I tuned back in to hear him saying, "I'll understand if you can't come. It's okay. I know I'm asking a lot."

"I'm glad you understand," I said coldly, "Because I don't think I can do this."

"I see."

I wanted to reply, "No, you *don't* see...," and scream on from there, but I checked my anger, asking instead, "When are you planning to come back?"

101

"I've got a flight that arrives late Wednesday night."

We chatted for another few moments about Dana and Will and said good-bye.

After his call, I walked around the house feeling angry, forlorn, bitter, used, and lonely. I dreaded spending the rest of the day alone, but who could possibly understand this mishmash of emotions? I was the one who had been wronged, yet I felt guilty for turning down Noel's request. I wanted to forgive him, didn't I? I thought that I did. I had decided that I loved him and wanted us to stay together. I thought that I had dismissed the fantasy of going back to the way things were, but I suddenly realized that I had not committed myself to dealing with the way things were going to be. His request, a plea for help, had triggered a blaze of self-righteous anger. I thought of Bettina Lowe carrying the burden of her abuse and rape for years and shuddered. I stood looking out at the daffodils blooming in the garden and tried to pray but could not quiet my emotions.

I finally did something that I had not done in years. I went upstairs and knelt by the bed. I leaned into the softness of the spread, closed my eyes, and rested my forehead on my folded hands. I just let myself babble, "God, I don't know what to do. I don't know how to begin forgiving Noel, or maybe I've begun forgiving him and don't recognize it, but I feel horrible about everything. About Noel. About myself. About Consuela and Tommy. I'm scared of telling Will and Dana. I feel angry, guilty, and resentful about everything. I hate his asking me to go to California. I hate myself for not saying yes. What am I supposed to do? Please help me."

I rested in an uncomfortable silence for a long time. Nothing happened. I said, "Amen," and rose.

The house seemed oppressive. I tried to call Suzanne and got no answer. I sat thinking about my other friends. Who could I trust with this secret? I tried Suzanne again. Still no answer. I left a message and then dialed Robin Carver. Three years earlier we had met when we were both reading at a writer's workshop for local college students. We had connected in a way that guaranteed a long, happy friendship. We usually had dinner or lunch once a month although we texted or e-mailed each other more often. After Suzanne, whom I counted as my sister, Robin had become my closest friend.

"Hi, Marcia! Where have you been? I've texted you several times in the past week or so, and you didn't reply. I even called and left a message. I was beginning to worry."

"I'm sorry. I've been having a crisis, and I was on deadline." Actually, I had noticed her texts and call but forgotten them minutes later. I wondered what else I had forgotten lately.

"Are you okay?"

"Not really. What are you doing today?"

"Laundry, but I can come over. Should I do that?"

I suddenly felt embarrassed, fearful that if she walked in the door now, I would wail and blubber like a six-year-old. I had trouble speaking.

"Marcia, what's wrong?"

"It's complicated," I said, my throat constricting with tears.

"I'm coming over now. I'll see you in about twenty minutes."

"Okay." I was crying and felt horrified at how I had exposed myself. It was one thing to cry all over Suzanne whom I had known for years, but to let Robin in was much scarier.

I closed my eyes and lay back on the sofa, almost wishing that I were sick so I could drift on the sensations of my body with a perfect excuse for not thinking or feeling.

"Excuse me. Since I'm feeling feverish, I can't possibly feel wretched emotionally as well," I could imagine myself saying, holding one hand dramatically to my forehead--Lady Marcia, swooning on her daybed, garnering sympathy and attention, excused from dealing with reality.

I had to smile at my naked plea for sympathy. I was acting like Dana and Will who, when they were small and had gotten in trouble, would complain of a stomach ache, headache, or, my favorite, leg cramp.

When Robin rang the bell, I dragged myself out of my fantasies and off the couch to open the door. As soon as she hugged me, I began to cry.

"What on earth is wrong?" she asked when I finally stopped.

"I'll tell you, but let's fix some coffee."

"I brought donuts," she said, pulling the box out of her large, straw purse.

"Why did you bring donuts?"

"You sounded so sad on the phone, and I always think donuts make people feel better!"

I began to laugh, admitting, "What I mostly feel now is embarrassed."

"Why?" Robin watched me with concern as I put the coffee on. "I thought we were friends."

"We are!"

"So sit down and start talking," she said bluntly, "But have a donut first."

I did and then told her the whole story, ending with Noel's request.

"He actually had the nerve to ask you to go out there?" Robin sounded both angry and astonished, a perfect reflection of how I had first felt.

"In his defense, I have to say that he's stressed out and probably not thinking clearly."

"But still, what nerve!" She eyed me for a moment, and then said, "You aren't going, are you?"

"I told him no, but…"

"You want to go?" The question was genuine.

"'Want' is too strong a word. I keep having the feeling that I gave him the wrong answer. Even if I don't feel happy about it, I keep thinking that I should go."

"Can I just say that I think it's crazy?"

"Maybe. But I keep thinking that if I asked Noel to do this for me, he would."

"But what about the other things he's done?"

"It isn't 'things,'" I said quietly. "It's one mistake that's had a lot of consequences."

"So you believe him?" Robin asked, arching her eyebrows skeptically.

"I've realized that I do. He's been stupid and deceitful, but I do believe that he was only with her that once." My sudden clarity on this point surprised me.

"So you're not going to leave him?"

"No. I love him. I can't imagine my life without him," I replied honestly.

"Are you sure that this won't always be between you?" Robin asked bluntly.

"That is the question, isn't it? I don't have an answer, but we both want to figure it out. Neither of us wants a divorce."

"I envy you," Robin said with a sigh.

"Well, that's bizarre!" I exclaimed, and we both laughed.

104

"I don't mean this situation, but the relationship. In the past, I've never felt that way about any of the people I've been with. So far, there's always come a day when it seemed better to be without them than with them, especially that loser I married in my misguided youth!"

"I just feel so confused."

"I don't think you're confused at all," said Robin sharply. "You've made the most important decision—you want to stay with Noel."

I realized that she was right and said, "But the more I think about it, the less clear it becomes how all this is going to work. Consuela's going to die, and what's going to happen to Tommy? Dana and Will have to be told about him, and how will they feel?"

"You're not mentioning the real concern."

"What?"

"It may have been only that once, but I think you're worried that Noel is still in love with her."

I studied the table, not wanting to meet Robin's dark eyes, willing her not to see how this question pierced the heart of the matter. I finally nodded, saying, "It's romantic and stupid. Noel's assured me that he loves me, that he chose me, but...," my voice trailed off. "Let me show you something."

I went to my study, returned with Consuela's graduation picture, and handed it to Robin who examined it carefully.

"She's very beautiful," she finally said, and I nodded, not daring to speak.

Robin looked at me expectantly until I said, "Even on my best day, I never looked like that!"

"Me neither!" agreed Robin. "Fucked by Fate!" We both laughed. "But you have to remember that love is about a lot more than looks. Noel chose you."

"What if he was sorry for me and just stayed because of the twins?" I asked forlornly.

"What does he say?"

"He insists that he wanted me and was terrified that I would leave him if I found out about his...," I swallowed hard, trying to find the right word, "His infidelity."

"'Infidelity' makes it sound like a whole series of events. It was more like a mistake, a momentary lapse, an indiscretion fueled by liquor. God, men!

Especially young men!" Robin snorted and stood up. "Let's take a walk! I think it would do you good to get out, and I could use some exercise, especially after these donuts. Let's go walk in the park and see what's blooming. Then we can come back and eat the rest of the donuts."

"You're not going to tell me what to do, are you?" I asked with a small smile.

"I wouldn't be your friend if I were! I'm willing to play devil's advocate, but what you choose to do is up to you."

"And God?" I asked mischievously.

"I guess if you want the Old Guy on your team, you can have Him!"

"Might be an Old Lady—a Wise Woman!"

"Cut the theology and put your sneakers on!" laughed Robin.

We walked up into the park and took a trail through the woods, pointing out newly blooming flowers and fresh green plants to each other, trying to remember the names, and delighting in the sunshine. The fresh air and exercise gradually worked their magic. By the time we got home, we were both hungry. Instead of finishing the donuts, we decided to go eat at a small Persian restaurant that had just opened.

We spent dinner talking about our work, especially Robin's new collection of poems. Her previous publisher had gone bankrupt so she was looking for a new one without much success. As always, she urged me to work on a collection of my articles, and for the first time, I considered her suggestion seriously, thinking that it might be time for this project.

"Are you going to write about your situation?" she asked, and I laughed.

"Initially I thought that I was supposed to be writing about this, and it definitely *wasn't* supposed to be happening to me!"

"Memoir? The market's hot now."

"I know that I've always argued that everything is grist for the mill, but not this," I said firmly. "I'll never write about this."

"Never say never," replied Robin saucily.

"So how's your love life?" I asked, changing the subject.

"Did Dana tell you that she came to hear me read at IU?"

"No, but when I saw her, she was having man, or should I say boy, problems so don't blame her for not reporting."

"I only mention it because I met a very interesting woman. She's actually a professor of Comparative Literature, and she's coming to spend next weekend with me. I'd like you to meet her."

Robin's adventures in love were based on serial monogamy, fueled by an attraction to both men and women. She had turned forty the previous summer and begun talking about settling down.

"Serious?"

"Serious attraction, but maybe something else. She's my age. After the reading, we talked at the reception, and then we went to dinner."

"And?"

Robin smiled, flashing her dimples, and admitted, "I was supposed to stay at the Student Union, but I ended up staying with her."

As we were saying good night, Robin hugged me and said, "I'm touched that you called me."

"I'm very glad I did. It helped talking to you, and I think that I've made a decision."

"And?"

"I won't be meeting your friend this coming weekend. I'm going to California. It's the first step toward figuring out what Noel and I have to do now."

"Is that all?"

"No," I admitted. "Maybe you're right. I think in the back of my mind I'm wondering if he still loves her. It's a chance to see."

"You're brave."

"Sometimes you don't get a choice," I replied, sounding grimmer than I felt.

After Robin left, I called Noel who, happy and relieved, insisted on staying on the phone while I made my reservation.

"I'm so grateful you're coming," he said, a tremor in his voice. "I can't tell you. I know it's selfish, but I need you."

"We have to begin figuring this out," I said, trying to sound more reasonable and hopeful than I felt.

"So you're going to stay?" he asked softly, and the fear in his voice touched my heart.

"Yes. What about you?"

"Of course!" He sounded shocked. "I never thought of leaving you. Not ever. I love you!"

"I don't think this is happily ever after," I could not resist adding drily, "But I believe that we can make it work."

"Of course, we can. You know I'm not a praying man, but I've been praying for this. For us, Marcia. I can't imagine my life without you."

"And I can't imagine mine without you."

Before ending the call, for the first time since Tommy had appeared at our door, I told Noel that I loved him.

XII

The next morning, Robin drove me to the airport. After going through security, I called Will and Dana to tell them my plans.

"This must be some project Dad's got going out there!" said Will, echoing his sister's words almost verbatim.

"He's been gone a lot!"

"I think things are slow at his job. He wrapped up a couple of big projects so they've been able to let him have some time off," I said, giving Will the same story I had given Dana.

"I hope you get to have some fun while you're out there!"

"I hope so too. I'll text you both when I get in, but I won't call for a day or two. You know you can call or text if you need anything."

"I need a week in California and no finals or papers!" laughed Will.

Standing in the airport bookstore, I realized how far behind I had fallen on my murder mystery reading. Marcia Muller's latest was already out in paperback so I purchased it, along with the latest from J.A. Jance and Laurie King. I had been reading Muller for years and two books into her Sharon McCone series, I realized that I was reading more for the characters than the mystery.

I found my gate, sat down, and began to read. Given my lack of concentration for the past few weeks, I was glad to find myself immediately engaged with Muller's story. My flight was soon called. On the plane, as soon as I was seated, I buckled my seat belt and opened my book. I did not have the energy to be more than superficially polite so for the duration of the long flight west and our brief layover in Phoenix, I lost myself in Muller's fiction.

When the pilot announced that we would soon be landing in Burbank, I realized, with a sense of panic, that I had no idea what Noel expected of me. Before my anxiety became full-blown, we were leaving the plane. I turned on my phone and saw a text from Noel: "Call me when you are on the ground." I walked into the airport which, though small, was very busy.

When I arrived in a big city like Los Angeles, it always felt strange that there were so many people everywhere. Noel claimed that it had not always been this way and had shown me a book of historical photographs to prove his point, but I still found it hard to imagine the less busy LA of his childhood. I stood at the outdoor baggage carousel—a tribute to the famous sunshine—and called Noel.

"Hi," he said. "I'm just coming around the loop again. I'm in a gray Toyota Camry."

"Okay. I think I see my bag."

"Just walk to the curb and go to your right. You'll see the loading zone."

"Got it." I grabbed my bag and headed out into the blinding sunshine just as Noel pulled up to the curb. He got out and hugged me tight.

"I'm so glad to see you," he whispered.

We stood for a moment, and it felt good to be in his arms.

"Hey, buddy, can you give me some room?" a young man yelled. He was trying unsuccessfully to pull a pick-up truck in behind Noel. I glanced over at the family of four he was trying to pick up. Noel opened the trunk and put my suitcase in. I smiled and waved as I got in the car, and the man yelled, "Thanks!"

The volume of traffic in Los Angeles was another shock that always took some getting used to. Noel also claimed that there used to be much less traffic, but that was impossible to imagine because it now took so much time to go anywhere no matter what hour of the day or night you were on the road.

I sat back and closed my eyes.

"Tired?" Noel asked.

"I think so, but it's that funny sort of tired from flying. I haven't done anything but read a book."

"I know. It's only five o'clock here, but I thought we could grab some dinner."

"That would be nice. I haven't eaten since breakfast."

"Mexican, okay?"

"Of course. I've been looking forward to great Mexican food!"

After a few minutes of silence, Noel said, "This last week or so, Teresa and her family have been staying with friends in the neighborhood. They said it was to keep the house quieter, but I think Teresa and Jorge didn't want the kids exposed to everything that's going on."

"Understandable," I said, "Especially if they're young."

"Yes, but everyone still comes over every day, and they sometimes spend the evening, but they leave fairly early. I'm sure they're getting more sleep."

The restaurant was filled with comfortable booths and quiet music. When the chips and salsa came, I dug in, realizing that part of my fatigue was probably hunger.

"Do you want a Margarita?" Noel asked, and I shook my head. "Beer?" I nodded, and he ordered us each a Dos Equis. He leaned back and sat looking at me.

"What's wrong?" I finally asked.

"Nothing's wrong. I'm just so happy to see you." He stopped and swallowed hard. Seeing tears fill his eyes, I reached out and took his hand.

"I have no idea how I can help," I began.

He cleared his throat and said, "Just having you here helps me."

"You haven't said anything about work. By the way, I told the twins that you weren't busy at work and had a project out here that needed attention. When do they expect you back in the office?"

"I got them to let me take two weeks. I told them that a family member was dying."

"It's almost the truth," I said and then immediately regretted my ironic tone. "I'm sorry. I didn't mean it to come out that way."

"It's okay. I didn't tell you about using the vacation because I was afraid that you would be mad. It means I can't take much vacation later this year," he stammered.

"It's okay. I'm not sure you had any other choice."

"I didn't. I'm Tommy's father, and I need to see him through this." He sipped his beer in silence, and then added, "It's so awful."

"How is Consuela?" I asked, forcing myself to say her name.

"She's sleeping more and more, and when she's awake, she's not very lucid."

"Does she still recognize everyone?"

"Thank God, she does. I don't know what Tommy would do if she didn't know him. It would break his heart."

"How can I help? What do you want me to do?" I had finally steeled myself to hear the answers I was dreading.

At that moment, our food came. Noel sat looking down at his enchilada, beans, and rice, and shaking his head.

"What's wrong?" I asked, assuming it was something about the food.

"I don't want you to *do* anything. I just want you to *be* with me. I've got a nice motel with a pool on Ventura Boulevard, about ten minutes from the house. I told you to bring a bathing suit, didn't I?" I nodded. "Just *be* with me, Marcia, and that will be enough. It will be more than enough. Certainly more than I deserve."

I looked at his tired face and smiled, saying, "I may find something to write about," but then added more seriously, "Do you think two weeks will be enough time?"

"God only knows. There have been moments this past week when I didn't think she'd live another hour, but she's a tough lady," he replied softly, and I tried not to feel jealous of the admiration in his voice.

The first two days I read, swam, explored Ventura Boulevard, watched a few movies, and thought about a couple of ideas for articles. It felt like a bizarre vacation. Noel would leave in the morning after breakfast and return around six to take me to dinner. He had arranged for a caregiver to stay at night so he, Tommy, and Teresa could rest, but Tommy insisted on sleeping on the sofa near his mother's hospital bed.

Noel told me the second day that he had tried to get Tommy to come to dinner with us, but he was too embarrassed by all the trouble he felt that he had caused. Sooner or later, I would have to deal with the reality of Tommy, but the ambivalent feelings Noel's invitation aroused made me realize how unprepared I still was to deal with his son.

"We're going to have to figure out how to tell Dana and Will," Noel said as we were getting in bed that evening.

"I've been thinking about it. I think we should wait until the semester is over, and they're home for the summer. They'll have questions and may need some help dealing with this. I think they should be with us when things come up."

Noel rubbed his forehead tiredly.

"Jesus Christ what a mess I've made. What are they going to think of me?" he muttered and looked at me with real despair.

"They're going to think what I think," I said softly.

"What's that?"

I felt his tension as he waited for my answer.

"That you're a good man who made a mistake and dealt with the consequences as best you could."

He sat up in bed and turned to look me full in the face.

"Is that what you believe?"

"Yes, it is," I replied, and he embraced me with the desperation of a drowning man.

I realized that I had spoken honestly. I believed neither the children nor I should presume to punish Noel with our anger, disappointment, jealousy, or grief. I hoped that I could help Dana and Will see that nothing about Consuela or Tommy's existence changed the facts of our lives: Noel had always been a loving father and husband.

I held out my arms and as he came into my embrace, I felt at peace for the first time since Tommy had told me his name.

Two days later, when Noel and I were finishing dinner, he said, "I have something to ask you."

My stomach dropped, and I could not help thinking, "What now?" as I said, "Okay. What?"

"Consuela was much more alert today. She was awake most of the afternoon. She asked Tommy to show her pictures of when he was little."

"That's good," I said, "Especially for Tommy."

"She wants to meet you," he spoke quickly, not meeting my eyes.

"She said that!"

"Tommy must have told her that you were here. I didn't. As I was leaving tonight, she asked me to bring you to the house."

"Tonight?"

Noel nodded. I realized that we both knew about a period of clarity preceding death. The day before my mother died, after two weeks of not recognizing anyone but me, she had known everyone from the chaplain to the nurses to Noel and the children.

"Are you absolutely sure that she wants to meet me?"

"She said, 'Bring your Marcia to me,' and she said it twice in English. She never speaks English now, so she was making sure that I understood."

"I'm not made for sainthood," I said to Noel, my eyes filling with tears.

"I know it's a lot to ask, but she's...." He could not finish the sentence.

I hesitated for a moment, considering how I would feel if I said no, and it turned out that I had no time to reconsider.

"Okay," I finally said, taking a deep breath and feeling a bizarre moment of truth had arrived. "Let's go."

After Noel finished paying the bill, we drove silently to Van Nuys. During the entire ride, I kept thinking, "This is insane! What are you doing? What is this about?" until it finally occurred to me that I should just say a quick prayer and hope for the best. If I did not step out in faith now, when would I?

By the time Noel pulled up in front of a small, yellow stucco house on a street filled with almost-identical homes, I felt calm. He came around to my side of the car, opened the door, and, after I got out, took my arm, murmuring, "Thank you." He rapped quietly on the front door, and Tommy opened it, putting his finger to his lips. As he put out his hand, he smiled, and I saw his mother's amazing smile. Smiling back, I took his hand.

"Thank you so much for coming," he whispered, and I nodded.

As we stepped through the door, the odor that permeates closed spaces when someone is seriously ill or dying hit me. No amount of disinfectant spray can camouflage that odor of sickness and bodily waste. It immediately brought back my mother's final illness.

The small living room was filled by the hospital bed and sofa. Tommy gestured me to a chair by the bed, and Noel brought a chair to sit down beside me. I noticed the caregiver, an older Latina, who sat on the sofa, knitting in the dim lamplight; we nodded to each other, and I was sure that she had been expecting us.

"Like you said, Papá, we haven't given her the medicine yet," whispered Tommy. "She should wake up soon."

It felt strange to realize that Noel had been sure I would come. I looked over in the corner of the room, easily visible from Consuela's bed, and saw a t.v. tray that had been set up as a shrine. The light of a Virgin of Guadalupe candle flickered next to a larger, framed image of her. A bright yellow rosary lay on the tray. Behind the candle and image stood a vase filled with fresh, yellow roses. Finally, having nowhere else to focus my attention, I looked at the woman in the bed.

Consuela was painfully thin, except for her distended belly, and her olive skin had a slight orange tint to it. Her short, dark hair had only a few threads of gray, and her heart-shaped face was still beautiful. Her long lashes fluttered occasionally as if she would awaken, a moment I both yearned for and dreaded. I studied her arm and small hand with its broad palm and surprisingly delicate fingers.

"She's always had a dedication to the Virgin of Guadalupe, and she's always loved yellow flowers so Tommy set that up." Noel's voice trailed off, and for the first time since we had entered the room, I looked at him. He was not looking at Consuela but at me. He leaned over and kissed me softly on the cheek, and then got up without a word. I heard faint noises and soon he returned with two glasses of wine and set up another t.v. tray to put them on. He smiled at me, and we touched our glasses together with the faintest clink, and I thought what an odd communion we were making, but it seemed strangely suited to the moment.

We sat for over an hour. After I finished my wine, I got up and borrowed the yellow rosary. Thinking of how Consuela had revisited her son's life earlier in the day, I chose to meditate on the Joyful Mysteries: the angel's visit to Mary, Mary's visit to her cousin Elizabeth, the birth of Jesus, His presentation in the Temple, and, finally, the worried parents' finding Jesus preaching in the temple, or, as He put it, going "about my Father's business." In some ways, these mysteries told the story of every mother's life from the moment of conception to the recognition that she must finally let her child go into the world. As I said the final prayer, the room felt deeply peaceful and I opened my eyes to find Consuela's large, dark eyes watching me. I reached out and took her hand.

"I'm Marcia," I said softly.

She nodded slightly and licked her lips.

"Are you thirsty?" Again she nodded slightly.

Tommy, who had been sitting on the sofa, went around the bed, found her cup, and expertly supported her head so she could sip from a straw, saying something softly in Spanish. She choked a little on the water, and he wiped her chin gently with a washcloth. He spoke to her again and said something that ended in "*inglés.*"

"He's reminding her that since you don't speak Spanish, she has to speak English," Noel translated.

I looked at him in surprise.

"My Spanish has come back and improved a lot in the last few weeks," he said with a sad, ironic smile.

Consuela's hand tightened around mine, and she pulled me closer. I leaned in awkwardly.

"Please sit on the bed," said Tommy, gesturing and taking the rosary. "Don't be afraid. You won't hurt her."

Tommy pulled the chairs back, Noel took away the wine glasses and t.v. tray, and I sat facing Consuela with my hip against her wasted thigh. I took her hand again in both of mine. She smiled at me with heartbreaking sweetness and then whispered something in Spanish to Tommy.

"She wants us to go," he said.

"Will you be okay?" Noel asked anxiously.

I nodded and said, "I'll call you if she needs anything."

Consuela murmured again in Spanish to Tommy, and he motioned to the caregiver who rose with her knitting and preceded Tommy and Noel down the hall to what I assumed was the kitchen.

I looked back at Consuela to find that she was studying me with her wide, dark eyes. I sensed she had so little energy that even speaking to Tommy in Spanish had required enormous effort.

"It's hard for you to talk, isn't it?" She nodded slightly. "Did you just want to see me because I'm Noel's wife?" She shook her head. "Do you want to tell me something?" Again, she nodded, the movement barely perceptible. "Is it about Tommy?" She shook her head, but I continued,

116

"We'll take care of him. I promise you that we will see to his education and make him a part of our family. I promise."

Her eyes filled with tears, and she squeezed my hand hard. I took the corner of the sheet and gently wiped away her tears, saying, "I'm so sorry. As a mother, I can only imagine how you feel."

A few moments passed, and she seemed more peaceful, but then she roused herself to speak.

"I talk to you," she said so quietly that I had to lean very close to hear her.

"What do you want to tell me?"

"Noel. Noel. Good man." The words came out slowly.

"I know that. Honestly, I do know that."

"No." She closed her eyes for a few moments, then opened them and said with visible effort, "*Mi culpa.* My fault. All my fault...I..." She stopped and seemed to be searching wildly for a word. "*Lo seduje.* I seduce him," she finally whispered.

I had no idea how to react.

"Believe me. I seduce him," she repeated, becoming more agitated.

"Thank you for telling me," I said and added, "It's okay. It was a very long time ago."

She looked at me in frustration and shook her head.

"He love you. Not me. You. Always. You." She squeezed my hand tightly.

"Thank you for saying this," I began, and her eyes widened with exasperation. She tightened her grip on my hand as if it would force me to understand.

"Not say. Not only say." She closed her eyes and murmured something in Spanish. I barely caught, "*Es verdad. Juro por la Virgen que es verdad.*"

"Thank you, Consuela," I said to her again. "*Muchas gracias.* I'm glad we met." I stroked her arm for a moment and, when she did not open her eyes, called softly for Tommy.

"I can't understand what she's saying. Something about the Virgin," I whispered when he came in.

He leaned over and spoke quietly to her. She said something, and I heard the words "*Virgen*" and "*verdad*" again.

"Okay, Mamá," he said softly, stood up, and looked at me. "Mamá said to tell you that she swears by the Virgin what she told you is true."

"'*Es verdad*' means it's true?" I asked, and he nodded.

"'*Por la Virgen*' means that she swears by the Virgin. It's a very serious oath," he explained, meeting my eyes. "She has always had a dedication to Our Lady of Guadalupe."

I leaned over and whispered to Consuela, "I believe you."

Consuela's slight smile was followed by a grimace, and Tommy said calmly, "She's in pain now and needs to sleep. We'll give her more medicine now."

I moved away from the bed as Noel came from the kitchen and handed Tommy a syringe. Consuela roused enough to swallow the liquid. Within moments, she was fast asleep with Tommy sitting by her side holding her hand. We told him and the caregiver good-night and went out to the car.

I cried all the way back to the motel where Noel held me while I cried some more. I cried for Consuela because she was too young to be dying and leaving her son. I cried for Tommy who would meet the joys and challenges of his future without his mother. I cried because whatever Noel felt, Consuela loved him. And finally, I cried because she had been more generous to me than I, given the same circumstances, might have been to her.

XIII

Barely conscious most of the time, Consuela suffered through another week. Then, just as we were trying to figure out how I could stay with Tommy while Noel went back to work, she died. Although the course of her illness had brought so much suffering, the end was peaceful. One morning Tommy could not rouse her. While he slept, she had slipped away.

We stayed to help Tommy through the funeral, and although we invited him to come home with us, he insisted on staying with his family and going back to his job.

In the following weeks, Noel talked with Tommy each night and flew out twice to help him handle the complex business that death entails. Noel was with him when the scholarship offer came from UCLA.

At the beginning of June, as we drove up to Bloomington to move the twins home, I said to Noel, "You've never asked me what Consuela said."

"I thought you'd tell me if it was any of my business," said Noel, glancing at me with a slight frown.

"She told me that you're a good man and you love me." I paused before adding, "She swore by the Virgin that she seduced you that night."

"What?" exclaimed Noel and swerved to take the upcoming exit ramp.

He pulled over to the side of the road and turned to face me.

"Honestly, Marcia, I swear to God that I remember very little about that night after the first shot of Tequila. There's a blank between that and when I realized what I had done. You shouldn't blame Consuela. I don't even believe her. It takes two people to create this kind of mess."

In that moment, when he did not take the easy way out, I loved him more than ever.

"She swore by the Virgin that she seduced you because she believed that's what she did."

Noel looked at me for a long time, narrowed his eyes, and said, "Did you think I would blame Consuela for what happened?"

I flushed and stammered, "I don't know what I thought. I've been going around and around about telling you."

Noel sat silent for a long time, staring out at the deserted road we were parked on. He finally turned to me and said, "I'm angry and hurt that you would ever think I'd blame someone else for my actions." He sighed. "I also know that I have no right to be angry or hurt after the pain I've caused you." He stared ahead for a long time and then turned to ask bleakly, "Marcia, do you honestly think we can go on?"

"I don't have anything more to say. Do you?"

Noel shook his head and murmured, "Nothing except what I've been saying from the beginning—I love you. From the first time I met you, it's always been you."

I put my arms around him and kissed him. "I love you. I know we can figure this out."

A bit later than expected, we arrived in Bloomington. After a flurry of discussion and the production of housekeeping schedules, Dana and Rita had agreed to have Will and Fernanda as their housemates. Noel and I were too distracted to produce even token resistance to this living arrangement, and when I did mention to Dana my reservations about Will and Fernanda's moving in together, she snorted and said, "Mom, they lived together in the dorm all last semester!"

They could not move into the new house until early August so we put their odds and ends of used furniture and books along with an amazing collection of random stuff as well as Fernanda's belongings into storage. The twins would begin their summer jobs the following week. Dana had found a paid internship with a software company, and Will would be waiting tables, lifeguarding, and pining for Fernanda whom he had put on the plane to Colombia at the end of May.

Late Saturday night, before beginning the drive home, we were eating at an Argentinian restaurant, the twins' new favorite, when Will suddenly asked, "Is there something wrong?"

Noel and I both jumped. We were planning to have the dreaded conversation with Dana and Will the next afternoon. We were flying Tommy out to meet them the following weekend. I met Noel's worried glance—we both knew that a restaurant is no place for this sort of conversation.

"No, why do you ask?" I replied in what I hoped was a convincingly puzzled voice.

I almost laughed out loud at how much Will looked like Noel and Dana like me as they exchanged suspicious looks.

"You both seem very tired and distracted. Like you're worried about something," said Will.

"I'm just tired from the trip to California," Noel replied calmly. "It was not much fun. Then I came back to a ton of work and ended up having to go out twice more."

"Okay," said Dana, with a shrug, and fixed her keen gray gaze on me, "But you seem tired too, Mom, and I thought that you had a vacation out there."

"I thought that's what I would be doing," I improvised, "But then Larry called me with an idea for an article so I ended up driving all over LA. You know how I hate driving out there!"

The twins seemed to accept our explanation and let the conversation move on to what they would need to do before they could move into the house in August.

We got home at midnight, and Noel did not come upstairs. I finished brushing my teeth and went down to find him sitting in the living room with the drapes open, staring out into the backyard where the full moon cast an unearthly glow. I sat down next to him and took his hand, asking, "Are you okay? Maybe I shouldn't have told you what Consuela said."

"No, it's not that. I've focused on you, Tommy, Consuela, and work. I realized at dinner that I've avoided thinking about telling Dana and Will. Now that I'm up against it, I'm terrified."

"They love you, and I think they'll come to love Tommy," I assured him.

"I've always tried so hard to set a good example, and now...." His voice broke. "I'm so ashamed."

Although I shared his concern, I put my arms around him and said, "You *have* always set a good example and been a great father. If anything, they'll admire you for taking care of Tommy and Consuela."

Everyone slept late. I made waffles and sausage for brunch with a fresh fruit salad. While Dana and Will ate with gusto, Noel barely touched his food.

"I'm going to the mall," Dana announced, pushing back her chair. "I need some new running shoes. Mine are falling apart."

"Honey, could you wait a bit? Dad and I need to talk to you and Will."

The twins exchanged an "Aha!" look as I said, "Let's go in the living room."

Noel and I sat down on the sofa, and the twins sat facing us, each hooking a long leg casually over the arm of an easy chair. The memory of many family meetings and the twins at different ages flashed through my mind as they looked at us expectantly.

Hoping Noel would begin speaking, I took his hand, but he said nothing.

"You aren't sick, are you?" asked Dana anxiously, sitting up in her chair, and looking from Noel to me. "It isn't that, is it?"

Will had also sat up and was leaning forward, his dark eyes intense.

"No, we're both fine," I assured them.

Noel cleared his throat and began, "A long time ago...."

"'In a galaxy far, far away...,'" said Will, laughing until he saw Noel's face. "I'm sorry, Dad."

"Anyway, before your mother and I ever met, when I was in college, I was in love with a young woman...." He paused and searched for words. "Later, I discovered that I had fathered a child with this woman."

Dana and Will looked puzzled for a moment and then shocked.

"Why didn't you tell us?" asked Will, but Dana just stared, her gray eyes wide. Sharing so many of Noel's intellectual gifts and interests, she had always been a "Daddy's girl." Even as a teenager, she had adored him.

"Do we have a brother or sister?" asked Will in a tone of easy acceptance.

"A brother. His name is Tomàs Noel Rodriguez," Noel replied. "Tommy lives in LA, and his mother recently died of cancer. That's why I've been out there so much and asked your mother to come out."

"That's terrible," Will said, but Dana stared at her father and remained conspicuously silent. "Who is Tommy living with now?"

"He's living with his aunt and uncle and cousins in the house his mother and aunt owned together. They're a very close family."

"We need to meet him," said Will, glancing at Dana, clearly expecting that she would agree, but she continued to stare at Noel and still said nothing.

"You will," I said. "Tommy's coming to visit next weekend."

"Why didn't you tell us about him?" demanded Dana, looking resentfully from Noel to me.

Noel put his head in his hands but finally looked up and said simply, "I was ashamed. Even your mother didn't know about Tommy until recently."

"You didn't even tell Mom?" Dana asked in surprise.

Noel and I had hoped that we could avoid or minimize the details, but in this moment, I think we both realized that no matter what we wanted, those devilish details would come out.

"Yes," said Noel in a sad voice, "I knew about Tommy. I've been supporting him by my consulting work. I was afraid to tell your mother about him."

"Why? Didn't this happen way before you met Mom?" Dana asked, glancing sharply from Noel to me.

"How old is Tommy?" asked Will.

I squeezed Noel's hand hard.

"He's four months older than you two."

It took a moment, but Dana, as always, was quick to do the math.

"So you were cheating on Mom right when you were getting married?" Dana asked in a horrified, accusatory voice, her face suddenly an angry, flushed mask. "No wonder you were afraid to tell her!"

"I wasn't...," Noel began.

"I can't believe it!" Dana continued furiously. "You've always told us we had to be honest and do the right thing, and *you* were cheating on Mom. At least, you were supporting your bastard," she ended with a sneer and began to cry.

123

Noel had turned white.

"Dana, that's not fair," I began, but she cut me off.

"Not fair? Exactly what is not fair?" Wiping away her tears, she stood up and said angrily, "What's not fair is finding out your father is a liar and a cheat!"

"Sit back down and listen," I told her sharply and glanced at Will who, upset and confused, was looking from his father to his sister.

"So when's the divorce?" demanded Dana as she slammed back in the chair, crossed her long legs, and folded her hands in her lap. With her trembling lower lip, she looked so young and vulnerable that I had a flashback to childhood hurts healed with quick kisses.

"Divorce?" said Will in a stunned voice.

"We aren't getting divorced," I said flatly. "I won't say that this hasn't been a shock to me, but I love your father, and he loves me."

"Right!" Dana snarled under her breath and stood up again. "Is that all?

"Dana, I made a mistake, and I'm sorry. I'm sorrier than I hope you will ever have to be for something you've done. I was drunk and did something stupid. Once. It was one time. I never meant to hurt anyone, especially your mother. Please believe me," Noel said, his voice soft and pleading.

He stood up, moved toward Dana, and reached out, but she jumped up and pushed his hands away as she ran past him. Grabbing her purse off the hall table, she was out the door before any of us could stop her. Noel sat down and buried his face in his hands. Will came to sit next to him and put his arm around him.

"It's okay, Dad. She'll come around," he said, patting Noel's shoulder. "You know how Dana is. She just has to have a big drama, and you know you've always been her hero."

"It probably has more to do with that jerk Chad than this," I added, hoping to sound comforting, but I also meant it.

Even given how she had always idolized Noel, the violence of her reaction seemed out of proportion. I thought how unfair she was being and how it was not like her to deny Noel a hearing when I suddenly realized that, in the past, she had shown this same harshness with friends.

The most recent example was senior year when Anne, her close friend of many years, got caught shoplifting. Although I talked with Dana about considering Anne's less affluent circumstances as a reason that she might have done this and urged her to feel compassion for the mess her friend had landed herself in, Dana remained adamant: the friendship was over. In her opinion, Anne had done something stupid that could have gotten them both in trouble. Dana could not or would not forgive this lapse. Anne pleaded with her and swore that she had never shoplifted when Dana was with her. Anne even convinced Will to talk with her, but Dana would not relent, telling him, "Fine! I forgive her, but I just don't want to be friends with someone who doesn't know right from wrong." I had hoped that with experience Dana would become less judgmental, more compassionate, but obviously that had not yet happened.

"I'm going to try to call Dana," I said, excusing myself to give Noel and Will a chance to talk.

I called and texted Dana repeatedly over the next two hours. Just as I was growing concerned, she answered, saying angrily, "Stop calling and texting me!"

"I just wanted to make sure you're okay."

"I'm with Jacey at the mall, and I'll be home later tonight."

"You can talk to me, Dana. I want you to talk to me."

"Yeah, right!" she said and hung up.

Later, Noel told me that he had told Will the truth, and, as far as Noel could tell, Will had been very understanding in a kind of male-bonding that, ironically, made Noel feel even more ashamed and humiliated.

That night I lay awake, listening for Dana. Around one, when I finally heard the front door open, I went downstairs to find her in the kitchen.

"Mom, I don't want to talk," she warned me angrily.

"Honey, I love your father, and I've found a way to forgive him. You need to work on doing the same."

"I just can't believe he did this to us," she said and started to cry. She let me put my arms around her.

"He didn't do anything to you except love you."

"That's not true! He cheated on you and then he cheated on all of us! For years! I always thought he was the most honest person I know, but he's been lying and cheating the whole time I've been alive," she sobbed.

Stunned by Dana's deep sense of betrayal, I said, "Your father's never done anything but love you and try to do what's best for you."

"Is it loving someone if you're living a lie?" she demanded, pulling away. "I don't understand how you can just be all right with years of lies! Do women always have to excuse men's bullshit?"

I made Dana sit down at the table, poured us each a glass of milk, and sat down across from her.

"No, women don't need to excuse men's bullshit, but you need to listen to me," I began. She sighed but remained quiet. "It's been horrible for me. Awful. Unimaginably hard. I spent five entire days crying on Suzanne's shoulder, but after a whole lot of soul-searching, I knew one important fact: I love your father. He's a good man who made a mistake, but he didn't walk away. He took care of Tommy even though he knew that Tommy's mother would never have pursued him for child support. You have to respect that he acted honorably and did the best he could."

"While lying to you and us," she added with a sneer. "It's hard to find anything to respect," she said, almost spitting the word, "In any of this."

"He was afraid if he told me that I would act exactly the way you're acting right now," I said, beginning to lose patience. "I have to admit he was right to be afraid."

I drank the rest of my milk and stood up.

"Dana, I want you to think about the fact that your father did not cheat on *you*. His love and support of Tommy have not robbed *you* of one moment of his love or attention. He wasn't unfaithful to *you*. I'm the one he cheated on, and I'm willing to forgive him. None of this is about *you*, and you need to stop acting like it is."

I took one last look at Dana' shocked face and went upstairs to finish my sleepless night.

The next morning, after talking with Noel, I called Lana Jenkins, an old friend who was a therapist, and got the name of a family counselor. Lana called Dr. Virginia Rubin who agreed, as a favor to her, to meet with us on short notice.

"I'm not going," Dana said flatly when, a few nights later, I explained where we were going after dinner.

"Dr. Rubin has made a special time for us as a favor to Lana. We need to show up. All of us."

"I'm not going, and no one can make me."

"Dana..., Noel began in a gentle voice.

"Don't talk to me," she snapped.

"Dana...," Will began, but I cut him off, saying, "Okay, here's the deal. You don't have to go to this family meeting or to individual counselling, and I don't have to write a tuition check to IU."

"That's not fair. That's blackmail," sputtered Dana angrily.

"Marcia, can I talk to you for a minute?" asked Noel.

We went in the living room, and he said quietly, "You didn't tell me that you were going to threaten Dana. I'm uncomfortable coercing her in this way."

"So how would you make her go with us?"

"I don't know," Noel admitted. "I had hoped she'd want to."

"Unlikely. She's so stubborn. If we don't force her into some kind of therapy, it might be years before she learns how to handle her emotions, not to mention her work. We should have done gotten her into therapy in high school. We knew then how wound up she was about her work."

Noel was silent for a few moments and finally said, "I know. Okay. You're right. I don't see another way to do this."

When we walked back into the dining room, Dana and Will stopped their whispered conversation. They both looked upset.

"Dana, you're right," Noel said. Dana did not look at him but stared down at her plate as he continued, "It isn't fair, and it *is* blackmail, but your refusal to participate with our family—the family that loves you—in trying to work things out isn't fair either."

Dana looked up at me and demanded, "What's this about 'individual counseling?'"

Before I could answer, Noel said, "Honey, you need to talk with someone about how wound up you are, about the way you obsess over your work."

"I come by it naturally," she said, tossing her long, dark hair. "You're always working, but I just didn't realize it was because you were supporting two families."

"Dana!" I exclaimed angrily, and Noel held up his hand.

127

"We need to finish dinner so we can get to Dr. Rubin's on time," he said firmly.

"Dana…," Will began again.

"Just shut up, Mr. Perfect!" Dana said furiously.

We finished dinner in silence, and when it came time to leave, without saying another word, Dana joined us on the silent drive to Dr. Rubin's office.

Dr. Rubin was a heavy set, gray-haired woman with a low voice that exuded calm. She laid out some ground rules—we were to speak one at a time, not interrupt each other or argue, and speak only for ourselves.

"This may seem corny, but…" She got up and took something off her desk. "This is a talking stick. It's a tradition in some tribes, and I find with family groups it helps to have a physical reminder of who has the floor. When you have the stick, you talk. If you don't have the stick, you listen. Okay?"

She looked around and waited until Dana reluctantly nodded. She then handed the intricately carved stick to Noel. He ran his fingers down its worn length and began with the story of how he met Consuela. When he got to the night he slept with her, he did not blame her for what had happened. He finished by telling how he had found out about Tommy and supported him. Dr. Rubin asked how he felt now.

"Ashamed, but I also feel relieved because the lying is over. Most important is that Marcia has promised not to leave me. I feel afraid that Dana will never forgive me, and I feel grateful for Will's understanding. I'm very worried about Tommy." He passed the talking stick to me.

I told about Tommy's appearance at our door, my emotional roller coaster, and finally my visit with Consuela, leaving out her claim that she had seduced Noel. I included my visit with Father Gerald.

"I know that I love Noel and have to forgive him. I'm trying. I know that what he did to support Tommy and Consuela shows the best of the man I love and married. I'm worried about each of us in different ways and know that moving forward is complicated. That's why we're here."

I passed the talking stick to Will who said, "I understand how this can happen." His brown eyes moved uncomfortably from me to Noel as he ran his fingers through his long, blond hair. "Sometimes situations just get out of hand especially when you've been drinking." He shifted in his seat, uncrossing and re-crossing his long legs before saying, "I think if Mom can forgive Dad, that's the main thing. I want our family to be together and include Tommy. I respect Dad for doing his best. Honestly," he added, looking at Dana, "I don't think this is about me. Dad's always been there for me." He then handed her the talking stick.

Dana took the stick, stood up, and handed it to Dr. Rubin, saying coldly, "They said I had to come, but they didn't say I had to talk."

Dr. Rubin smiled kindly, took the stick, and said, "I'm sorry you feel that way, Dana. I know we all want to hear what you have to say, but if you choose to keep your thoughts to yourself, we'll understand."

"I do," Dana said flatly and sat down with her arms crossed.

The image of her as an angry four-year-old flashed so clearly in my mind that I almost laughed out loud, but I also felt a deep concern for her--Dana might be hard on others, but she was even harder on herself.

"So I have a question about the future," Dr. Rubin said. "How do you see Tommy fitting into your family?"

Noel's and my answers were almost the same partly because we had been discussing this question for weeks. We wanted Tommy to be part of our family, but we also recognized that his roots were in another family, another place, and another culture.

"I can hardly wait to meet him. I've always wanted a brother," began Will enthusiastically and stopped when he saw the stricken look on Dana' face. "Dana, I love you. You're the best! You've always been and always will be my best friend, but I can love you and love Tommy too, can't I?"

Dana stared at him and said nothing.

Dr. Rubin took the talking stick and said, "Our time is up. Let's meet again next week. We'll talk about Tommy's visit. I want each of you to reflect on love. What makes you feel loved or unloved? What do you believe is the nature of love? What does it mean to be loved enough or share love? Dana and Will, I want you to reflect on your relationship to each other. Being twins is a special bond. What does it mean to have Tommy come into your relationship?"

The ride home was silent except when I heard Will say, with surprising gentleness, "Dana, it might have helped if you'd talked. We can't read your mind."

Dana did not answer. When I glanced back, she was staring bleakly out the window.

The next morning Will left early to run before work. Noel and I made Dana sit down at the breakfast table.

"Why are you always ganging up on me?" she demanded angrily.

I handed her a piece of paper and a check.

"Lana recommended this counselor for you, and you have an appointment at 6:00 on Monday."

"I might have to work late," Dana mumbled.

"You've never gotten off later than 5:30," I replied flatly.

"You know, you can make me go to the counselor, but you can't make me talk. I'm not a child."

I bit my tongue to keep from snapping, "Then stop acting like one!"

"Yes, you are. You're *our* child," said Noel. "You'll always be our child. We know you're grown, but we want to help you. This is an opportunity, Dana, not a punishment."

"So that's why you're blackmailing me?" Dana snapped sarcastically.

"I can't figure out another way to help you help yourself," I said, without disguising my irritation.

"We've been concerned about how you drive yourself for a long time…," began Noel.

"I'm surprised you had time to be concerned about anything with all that consulting work and your visits to Tommy," said Dana, jumping up from the table, grabbing her purse, and slamming the door behind her before either of us could reply.

"What can we do?" asked Noel bleakly. "What can I do?"

"I don't know, but she took the address and check with her."

Tommy arrived on Friday evening. Dana was not speaking to any of us except to announce that she refused to "play happy family" and would not meet Tommy. Instead, she chose to spend the weekend at a friend's.

Will accompanied us to the airport and greeted Tommy in Spanish. From that moment on Will acted as if Tommy were the brother for whom he had always yearned. He introduced Tommy to his friends and took him everywhere. Will tried to include Dana in their outings, but she flatly refused his overtures so, in addition to her anger at Noel and me, she felt jealous and shut out of Will's budding relationship with Tommy.

On Sunday afternoon, after she checked to be sure that Tommy was gone, she came home. I was chopping vegetables for dinner when she came into the kitchen and sat down.

"So," she said in the tone that usually preceded a sarcastic utterance, "What are you telling our friends and neighbors?"

"What do you mean?"

"What are we telling people about Tommy? We could just pretend he's our cousin. After all, in this family," she continued archly, "We're pretty good at pretending."

I felt a flash of anger until I realized that her sarcasm concealed real embarrassment.

"Your father and I have talked about this," I replied gently. "We're going to tell people the truth and simply introduce Tommy as your father's son from an earlier relationship."

"Not much earlier," she snorted. "Actually, more like simultaneous."

"Dana, stop it!" I said sharply. She fell into a sulky silence. "None of the friends Will introduced Tommy to this weekend seemed to care."

"Will's vastly clueless friends," muttered Dana.

"A lot of them are your friends too," I shot back and then added, "Most people aren't going to ask for a birth certificate or start doing math."

"So you're counting on most people not figuring out your husband was fucking another woman while you were planning your wedding?"

"Dana, he was drunk, and it was one time!" I said, going to the refrigerator for more vegetables.

"So he says," she muttered.

Just as I was turning around to answer, she burst out, "I hate feeling this way," and began to cry. "I hate it, and I hate acting like such a bitch, but I can't help it! Even Will's mad at me."

Wiping my hands on my apron, I went around the table, slid into a chair, and embraced her. She hugged me back and sobbed wetly against my shoulder, saying, "I'm just so unhappy."

When she finally stopped crying, I fixed her a glass of lemonade, sat back down at the table, and asked if she remembered the quilt called "Forgiveness." She frowned and nodded. I went into my office and came back with a print of one of the many photos I had taken of the quilt.

"This may help you think about how you feel," I said, sitting down across from her and handing her the picture. "This is why we want you to talk with a counselor." Before she could begin to protest, I said, "You've always adored your father and been very close to him, but frankly, I think your reaction is about more than just this situation. Your father and I were hoping you'd work hard in college but also make new friends and have fun. You've had a lot of things happen this year, especially with that asshole Chad, but for a while, your father and I have both thought you could use help getting some balance in your life. Honestly, honey, I wish I'd gone to counselling when I was your age."

Dana was silent for a long time and finally said quietly, "I've been horrible to Dad and also to Tommy. I've also been mean to Will."

"What about me?" I asked.

"You're the Mom!" she replied, laughing.

"I think you need to get to know Tommy next time he visits. He's a pretty special kid who's been through a lot. You'll find he's smart in many of the ways you're smart."

"I do feel sorry for him," she admitted. "If anything happened to you or Dad, I don't know what I'd do! I can't even think about it!" She shuddered and added softly, "Will says Tommy's great."

"Will you do something for me?" I asked, seizing on her momentary vulnerability.

"What?"

"I want you to talk to your father." Before she could protest, I held up my hand and continued, "Just sit down and talk with him."

"I always thought he was perfect. Now I just feel stupid," she protested, her voice breaking.

"And feeling stupid is almost as bad as being stupid, isn't it?" Dana looked at me, narrowing her eyes. "You are so much like your father. A perfectionist. When he realized that he'd not only made a big mistake but that the mistake had very complicated consequences, just think how he must have felt and feels even now. Try to have a little compassion."

"I'll see," Dana muttered.

"Can I say one more thing?"

"Sure. You will anyway."

I ignored the bait.

"No one expects you to be perfect."

"I know that," she replied with an impatient shrug.

"It's one thing to know this with your intellect, but it's another thing to know it in a way that allows you to live more fully. If you think you need to be perfect, you won't take risks. But, perhaps more importantly, if you think you need to be perfect, it makes you think other people need to be perfect as well, and the truth is no one is perfect."

"You just want me to be more like Will, Mr. Tolerance, friend of the world," she said accusingly.

"No. I just want you to be happy being Dana. I want you to be easier on yourself and also easier on other people," I said, standing up.

Instead of protesting, Dana came around the table, put her arms around me, and laid her head on my shoulder.

XIV

How to explain Tommy's presence in our lives turned out to be a non-issue. Although he visited us every few months, we soon realized (I, with mixed feelings of regret and relief) that his roots and life were in Los Angeles. He went to UCLA to study computer science. Having so much in common because of their studies and work, he and Dana eventually became good friends as he continued to prove himself the brother Will had always wanted.

Noel continued to run his consulting company because he enjoyed the work. He insisted on paying back all the money we had borrowed from our retirement fund and savings to pay for Consuela's care. I told him that he could cut back on consulting and did not have to repay the money, but he insisted that it made him feel a little less guilty. I decided that it was not up to me to deny him this expiation.

Even after he and Dana reconciled, he had a hard time because her reaction had so perfectly reflected his feelings about himself. I realized that if I felt stupid and humiliated by his infidelity and deception, I could not begin to imagine how stupid and humiliated he felt. As I watched Noel struggle, I often thought that if forgiving someone is a complex process, forgiving yourself may be an even longer, more convoluted one. As I realized how deeply shocked he, an orderly, logical, honest person, continued to feel at the consequences of that one act, I urged him to talk with someone. He would not talk with Father Gerald, our current pastor, or the counselor Dr. Rubin recommended, but he and Ben finally spent a long weekend at a friend's lake house in Michigan. When he came home, he seemed to have found some peace.

Three more times that summer, we saw Dr. Rubin as a family, and at the last meeting, Dana finally spoke, telling Noel that she loved him but needed time to work through her feelings. This stunted olive branch kept Noel's hope alive.

During the first half of fall semester, although Will brought Fernanda home, Dana did not come. Noel was upset, but I showed him our credit card bill to assure him that Dana was talking to her counselor regularly and trying to work through things.

Late one night, a week or two after mid-semester, we were sitting up in bed reading when Noel's phone rang.

"Dana?" he said in an amazed voice.

I immediately moved closer to hear their conversation.

She had called to tell him about a programming project.

"It's not just the grade, Dad. I've figured out what I want to do. I had a long talk with Dr. Kim, my prof, and I'm going to grad school. I want to do big data research in medical fields."

"Wow!"

"I've always loved science so if you and Mom are okay with it, I'll double major in biology and computer sciences. It'll probably mean an extra semester or two."

"No problem, honey, if that's what you need to do. It sounds like a perfect fit for you."

"Eventually I want to teach."

"Your first teaching job will be teaching me about medical big data," he said, chuckling.

There was a long silence.

"Dana?"

"I'm here, Dad. I just want to say I'm sorry I've been such a bitch."

"It's okay, honey. I'm sorry for what I've put our family through," Noel replied, choking up.

"No, Dad. I haven't been fair. I was just so shocked by what happened. I always thought you were perfect. And then I was jealous of Tommy when you clearly loved him and Will liked him so much."

"I understand. Really, I do. Dana, don't be too hard on yourself. You and I are both very good at punishing ourselves for not being perfect."

"I know. I love you, Dad. You were the only one I wanted to tell my news to. Only you."

"And great news it is!"

"Can I talk to Mom now?"

"Sure. She's right here," replied Noel. "I love you."

"I love you, too, Dad."

Noel smiled and handed me the phone.

"Hi, honey!"

"Mom, you won't believe it!"

"What?"

"Steve and I are going out."

"Steve?" I drew a complete blank.

"Steve! You know, the guy who told me about that asshole Chad!"

"Right! That Steve."

"He's super nice, and we have a lot in common. He got me to play intramural volleyball. It's co-ed so we're on the same team. Will and Fernanda are playing too."

"That's great!"

"Can I bring him for the weekend? We'll come with Will and Fernanda in a couple of weeks."

"Sure. Just let us know when, and I'll lay in plenty of groceries."

"Mom?"

"What, honey?"

"Thanks for making me talk to Holly."

"Your counselor?"

"Yes. She's helped me in so many ways. I'd like to keep talking with her for the next few months. I know it's expensive, but is that okay?"

"Of course. Like I told you, I wish I'd had counseling when I was your age!"

After we said good-bye, Noel and I looked at each other.

"It's a miracle, isn't it?"

He nodded and hugged me tight, murmuring, "I was so afraid I'd lost her."

Noel had always been a good father. His offense was not directly against Dana and Will, and they loved Tommy. In addition, they were young and involved in their own lives. For these reasons, Will and Dana seemed to accept what had happened and move on.

My path has not been so clear. Dr. Rubin recommended a therapist whom I continue to see. Although I mostly have good days, I still have some bad days. The bad days are full of questions: Consuela may have seduced Noel, but did he want to be seduced? Was he still in love with Consuela? Was it really only one night? Did she lie to me because she loved him enough to want his happiness? Why would he ever have chosen me over such a beautiful woman? At the bottom of these questions lies my deep sense of jealousy, betrayal, and inadequacy. Clearly, Dana is not just Noel's daughter.

Two Christmases passed before I pulled the graduation picture of Consuela out of my desk drawer for the last time. I found a nice frame, wrapped it, and gave it to Tommy. He later told me that he keeps it on his desk to inspire him.

As time passes, I find myself struggling less often in the thicket of my emotions. Suzanne talks good sense to my better self and is always quick to remind me that Consuela "swore by the Virgin." Robin reminds me that I chose to stay. On the good days, which number more as time goes by, I realize that ultimately the answers to my questions are immaterial because Noel and I have chosen each other.

Again and again, I choose to forgive Noel and, by the grace of that choice, as inexorably as our eyes move to the bright center of Bettina Lowe's quilt, my path is illuminated.

Linda Blackwell Billingsley

Old Friends

Alyssa sat at her desk correcting her second-graders' papers and sighed. She had asked them to write about their favorite place. She loved her students, and at least once during any set of their writings, she was so astonished or moved that she had to sit back for a moment. This time it was Miguel Sanchez who had written about his grandmother's house, ending "The house of my grandmother is not there now. Mi Abuela is dead in Mexico." She sat staring out the window and wondering what else Miguel had lost with his family's move to California. Suddenly there was a knock, and she looked up to find Antonio Rivera, the long-term substitute in the third grade, standing in the doorway.

"Hi, Antonio! Come in! How are you?" Since the first time she had met him a few weeks ago, Alyssa had liked his open cheerfulness.

"I'm fine. Would you mind helping me for a minute?"

"Sure. What do you need?"

"I'm trying to put up this bulletin board. When the principal visited my classroom last week, she said that it was too dull. She said that I needed to work on 'the environment.'" Antonio's dark eyes sparkled. "So I told her I was thinking of buying a hybrid."

"Did she laugh?"

"Actually, she did."

They were now in Antonio's classroom which was, indeed, drab. One bulletin board showcased flags from different parts of the world, but Alyssa knew that the teacher Antonio was temporarily replacing had put up that display.

"So will you help me put up this border? I found it in the cupboard." He gestured toward a cheerful, multi-colored pile of paper. "You hold that end, and I'll hold this, and we can tack it up."

Alyssa looked at him in astonishment before saying, "Antonio, do you have a stapler?"

He went to the desk and came back with a stapler.

"Watch this!" Alyssa said, and began unfurling the border and stapling it at six-inch intervals.

"I feel like such an idiot!" he said, flushing.

"Don't! How long have you been teaching?" she asked.

"I just got my credential, but I was kind of late getting through college."

"It's the practical stuff that no School of Education ever teaches you," said Alyssa, thinking how completely useless her own education classes had been. "Now, what are you going to put up?"

Antonio held up a map of the world.

"That's it?"

He nodded.

"Okay, get me some poster board, markers, and scissors. You need to give the kids a reason to look at the map so we'll write a geography hunt for them."

They spent the next half hour making up a range of geography questions and writing them in large, colorful letters on pieces of poster board.

"That looks great! Now what else do you have?"

"It's not my fault, you know. I'm just beginning," Antonio replied, flushing again.

"Hey, don't feel bad! Come with me, and we can look in my cupboard."

Near the geography board, they finally put up a large poster about the life cycle and migration pattern of the monarch butterfly. Alyssa also found a colorful multiplication poster.

"Look, you can put this up over there," Alyssa said, gesturing enthusiastically. "Your kids should be getting to multiplication soon. Just make sure you take it down or cover it if there's a test or math assessment!"

"I will. And I promise that you'll get everything back at the end of the year."

"Not that long," replied Alyssa.

"What do you mean?" he asked anxiously.

"Relax! I just mean that you'll want to change things in a few weeks. Also you'll start to get useful stuff in the mail—usually come-ons to use a book or product, but posters too. If you let Wendy know, she might also loan you stuff."

"Wendy?"

"Wendy Jackson-Grady, the school librarian."

"Oh, yes. She seems nice."

"She is, and she'll be glad to help you out."

They stood together awkwardly at the door to Antonio's room.

"You have grading to finish?" he asked.

141

"Yes. About half an hour to go."

"I also have work to finish, but then…you aren't married, are you?" he asked shyly.

"No," she said, laughing. "Not married, not living with anyone, and definitely not in a serious relationship, except for loving my students."

"Can I buy you dinner? As a thank-you?" he asked.

"Of course. That would be nice," said Alyssa, touched by his shy, tentative tone. "Why don't you come by my room in about half an hour? We can walk out together."

Alyssa and Antonio drove separately to a nearby Mexican restaurant and over chips, queso, and guacamole, she asked him where his family came from.

"I'm curious because you have a Latino name, but I don't hear even the whisper of a Spanish accent, and I've got a pretty good ear."

"My family has been in Los Angeles for generations," he said. "We're Spanish." Then he added, with a small grimace, "My name gets me in all kinds of trouble because people assume that I'm bi-lingual, and I'm not."

"Really?"

"Really," he said, grinning, his dark eyes twinkling. "My mother is a high-school English teacher! My parents used to speak Spanish with my grandparents, but they died when I was young. My parents have always insisted that we speak English. We live in an Anglo neighborhood, and they always made it clear to me and my sister that we were Spanish. It was sort of strange," he added. "They didn't even want us to take Spanish in school although I did in college, but I'm far from fluent. It's not my fault, but it's still embarrassing. Do you speak Spanish?"

"Yes. I've always taught in places where there were Spanish speakers. I took it in college and spent a summer in Mexico doing an immersion course. I've also taken a few additional courses at night over the years. My conversational Spanish is good enough for conferences, but I'm far from fluent."

"I may have to call you in next time I have conferences."

"That'd be pretty funny. 'I'm Mr. Rivera, but let's call Ms. Gerard to do the translating.'"

"You can see how humiliating this is!" Antonio said, laughing.

They ate for a few minutes in silence, and then he asked, "Where did your name come from?"

"What do you mean?"

"Alyssa. It's unusual. I've never heard it before."

"My mother loved flowers," said Alyssa.

At that moment, the server arrived with their order, and they spent the rest of the meal talking about school.

It was the first of many conversations throughout the rest of the semester. They sat together at faculty meetings, helped each other with projects, and shared assignments that were successful. They discussed their students and sometimes brainstormed together when teaching was not going well, a student seemed to need special help, or an assignment failed to get the expected results. After faculty meetings, they always went out to dinner, either by themselves or with other colleagues.

Alyssa had only one close friend. Throughout her difficult childhood, she had lived next door to Nan. During Alyssa's peripatetic adulthood, Nan had remained her best friend although she now lived in Boston with her husband and three children. Alyssa thought of Nan as her sister, her anchor, the one person with whom she could be completely honest and to whom she did not have to explain anything. They texted often and talked every few weeks.

"So what's up with this Antonio guy?" asked Nan in a teasing tone. "You're talking about him a lot, and now, you have Dodger tickets together. This sounds almost matrimonial."

"Stop it! We're just good friends," insisted Alyssa.

"Wouldn't you like to be more? From that picture you sent, he's good looking."

"He is. Beautiful, dark eyes. Lovely skin. Great smile." Alyssa sighed. "He's actually very good looking. He's kind of short but five or six inches taller than I am."

"Not hard, given how short you are!"

"At least, I'm not an Amazon like you," laughed Alyssa. She was just over five feet, and Nan, at five-nine, had always towered over her.

"And he isn't attached?"

"Not at all."

"Why haven't you wrestled him into bed? Or have you and didn't tell me?"

"He's twenty-seven. He'll be twenty-eight this summer."

"So what's the big deal? Men date and marry younger women all the time. So what's wrong with a little cougar action?" asked Nan, adding a playful growl.

"It isn't like that! We're just good friends."

"So what's wrong?" asked Nan, picking up on Alyssa's troubled tone.

"He assumes I'm about his age or a bit older," she said with a sigh.

"How much older?" asked Nan warily.

"I don't know. Maybe thirty."

"Thirty!" snorted Nan who, eighteen months older than Alyssa, would soon be forty-one.

"Maybe, at the outside, thirty."

"*Thirty*? Really?" Nan sounded shocked and then began to laugh. "You must be in much better shape than I am! Kids do take it out of you, but you've always looked young, Miss Skinny Bones. And you've got those freckles to cover your wrinkles. But *thirty!* Wow!"

"Even looking younger doesn't change the fact that I'm almost forty."

"You sound tragic, but maybe it will turn out that he has a thing for menopausal women."

"That's not funny, Nan."

Before they hung up, Alyssa said, "I need to ask you a favor."

"What?"

"I feel silly saying this, but please don't send any joke birthday cards mentioning my age. Antonio's sometimes in my apartment, and just in case this does go somewhere, when the time is right, I'd like to tell him myself."

"So I should cancel my order for 40 flamingos?" asked Nan, laughing. "Maybe that's the way to tell him."

"Stop it! I'm serious."

"I think you're being weird, but okay. Nothing with 4-0 emblazoned in large numbers across it. No flamingos. No forty black roses. No black balloons with the magic number," said Nan, laughing. "Okay, I promise."

After she hung up, Alyssa sat thinking about the future. Antonio would not be returning to Keating Elementary in the fall so he would no longer be her colleague. He had already begun interviewing for permanent jobs at other schools. Although they were both sad not to be at the same school, secretly Alyssa felt relieved. She had been waiting for one of her colleagues to mention when she had graduated from college, what year she had done her certification, how long she had been teaching, where else she had taught, or, worse yet, her many years of experience. She had only been at Keating three years so, at least, that fact felt safe, but a million other facts would irrevocably date her.

Her luck had held so far, but there was no guarantee for the future which might contain landmines like "Where were you on 9/11?" or "How did you feel when Obama was elected?" She felt like Kurt Cobain's suicide, Rodney King's beating, the Oklahoma City bombing, the pursuit of OJ, the Columbine shooting, and myriad other events could blow up at any conversational turn. She would miss Antonio's daily presence, but until she could tell him her real age, it would be safer to have him out of the building.

The last day of the semester, Alyssa and Antonio treated themselves to dinner at a high-end Italian restaurant. They drank wine and splurged on appetizers and dessert.

"My family wants you to come to dinner tomorrow," said Antonio. "They want to meet you."

"Okay," said Alyssa, the wine interfering with her ability to make sense of her surging anxiety. "Where do they live?"

"Pasadena."

"Can we drive together?" asked Alyssa.

"Sure, but let's take your car. I wish I could afford a new car. Not new, of course, but new to me. My Honda is on its last wheel. Lately, it's been at the garage more than it's been home."

Later, as they said good night outside her door, their hug lasted longer than usual, and soon they were kissing. Alyssa ran her hands over Antonio's muscular back, feeling secure in his embrace.

"I've wanted to do this for so long," he whispered, his lips grazing her ear.

"Do you want to come in?"

"I've wanted to be with you since the first time I saw you. I love your curls," he said, ruffling her short, red hair.

"Now don't say you like freckles," murmured Alyssa.

"But I do," he replied, kissing her pale neck as she opened the door.

The next morning, Alyssa lay watching him sleep and placed her light, freckled arm next to his, noting her arm's pale, slim, narrowness against his brown, corded muscles. She placed her small, slender hand next to his and sighed, remembering how he had gently explored her body the night before.

Suddenly she remembered her framed diploma in the second bedroom and crept out of bed. She only kept it because it reminded her of how proud her mother had been as she insisted on paying for the framing, saying, "I'm only sorry I couldn't have paid for your college."

Alyssa lifted the heavy frame off its hook and slid it behind the desk. She glanced around the room. She hid a childhood picture of her and Nan along with two other photos where the style of their clothes gave away that she was a grown woman when Antonio was probably in elementary school. She quickly shoved the photos into a drawer along with two photo albums from her teens and twenties. After a quick glance around the rest of the apartment, she went into the kitchen to make coffee.

"Alyssa? Where are you?"

"Making coffee," she called and then went back to bed.

After they had made love, Antonio suddenly asked, "What are the tattoos on your feet?"

Alyssa raised both her feet and said, "They're a pair. I got them when I was younger and had a much higher pain threshold than I have now."

"I've always been scared to get a tattoo. Besides, my parents would kill me!" Antonio laughed. "What are they?"

"If you look carefully, the one on my left foot is my initials A, C, G."

"What's the C for?"

"Clare."

"The way they're inter-twined, they look almost like a flower."

"Yes, that's what they're supposed to be."

"And the flower on your other foot?"

"Alyssum, the flower I'm named for. It's also called 'Sweet Alyssum.'"

"I like that, Sweet Alyssa," murmured Antonio, leaning over to kiss her.

Later, when Alyssa thought back to this moment, she had mixed feelings. It was the perfect opening to tell Antonio about her name-change so why had she not said anything?

She had begun to use the name "Alyssa" when she was eighteen and had, immediately after graduation, moved (actually, more like run away) to Sacramento with Troy, her high-school boyfriend. She lied and said that it was her middle name, but the "A" in her name actually stood for Ann—her birth name was Shirley Ann Donaldson.

Mark, the man she had lived with for several years after she left Troy, had accidentally seen her social security card.

"I hate my name," she sobbed when he asked about it. "I hate my father and Donaldson is his name. I hate the name Shirley."

"Why?"

"When I was in elementary school, they used to call me Curly Shirley. I just hated it."

"But your hair is beautiful."

"You don't understand! You weren't in elementary school with wild curls standing up all over your head because you couldn't help it." Seeing Mark's puzzled look, she rushed on, "There was no one at home to fix my hair or see that I got it cut. My father was long gone, and my mother was not functioning most of the time." Afraid she sounded hysterical and might say more, Alyssa went to the window and looked out.

"I didn't know," said Mark softly, coming up behind her and putting his arms around her. "You need to tell me."

As Alyssa told him about her childhood, Mark listened carefully, sympathetically, unflinchingly. When she finished, he held her quietly for a long time.

The next day, he came home from work and asked, "Do you want to change your name legally?"

"Yes, but I'm sure it's expensive," she replied.

"I found a lawyer, a friend of a friend. If you want to do it, I'll pay for it. It isn't that expensive, and I think if you want to change your name, you should."

Much later she would look back and wonder cynically if Mark had expected that changing her name would change who she was and where she came from.

She saw the lawyer the next week and began the process of becoming Alyssa Clare Gerard. "Gerard" was a variation on the name of a teacher who had nurtured and encouraged her. Alyssa was tempted to disappear into her new name but finally decided that she needed to tell her mother. She informed her of the change and was surprised and angered when her mother responded, "I'll let your father know."

"Whatever," Alyssa replied, cutting the conversation short.

By that time, she had no idea where Billy, her younger brother, was living or how to get ahold of him.

After she and Antonio ate a late breakfast, they headed to Griffith Park. The observatory spurred memories that put Alyssa on guard because she realized that the programs she and Antonio had seen as elementary-age children belonged to two different eras of space exploration. She was sure that when she had visited the observatory, the Space Station had not even been in orbit.

"I think they just showed us the night sky in different hemispheres. You know, how you see different constellations, but it's hard to remember," she said vaguely.

"It must have been a different program. We saw pictures from the Hubble. They were so beautiful," Antonio said. "That's why I took Astronomy in college. I asked for a telescope for Christmas the year we went to the observatory, but I couldn't see much in the city. It wasn't my fault. Just too much light."

They talked about his family. She already knew that his mother taught English. She found out his father was a mechanic. Belinda, his sister, was eight years older, married, and had twins. As Alyssa considered his family, her hazy anxiety from the night before crystallized. Her stomach tightened as she realized how she would have to be on guard with Belinda because of their closeness in age. She realized anew how easily she could share an opinion, memory, or fact that would reveal her age.

When they got to his family's modest home in an older neighborhood, Alyssa relaxed a bit. She had grown up in a similar neighborhood although she was sure that her family had been nothing like his in any other way.

"We're so glad to meet you," his mother said warmly. "We've heard so much about you!"

"I'm happy to meet you, Mrs. Rivera," said Alyssa, taking her outstretched hand.

"Call me Maria."

They had a pleasant dinner which Mr. Rivera ("Call me Tony.") proudly cooked on his new gas grill. After dinner, Belinda and her family stopped by for dessert--ice cream, topped with strawberries and whipped cream, with home-made cookies on the side.

"I just had to meet you," said Belinda. "Honestly, Antonio talks about you all the time. He told us that you're an amazing teacher, and also that you've been so helpful to him."

"Are you a teacher too?" asked Alyssa.

"No, I'm a nurse. I've worked only part-time since the kids were born," she said, gesturing to Madison and Mitchell who were playing a game with Antonio at the dining room table.

"They're good kids, aren't they?" said Alyssa with a smile.

"Yes, but they're on their best behavior for Antonio. They adore him. He's like a second father to them. He'll be such a great dad when he has kids of his own. He's so patient."

Alyssa smiled politely, thinking that even if, at this late date, she could have children, she did not want them.

She managed to escape questions from Antonio's mother until they were clearing the table after dinner. Loading the dishwasher, Maria said, "So where did you go to school?"

"I went to a two-year college in Sacramento and then graduated from UC San Diego, but I came back to Los Angeles to work on my credential. I'm originally from here."

"Pasadena?"

"No. The Valley. Northridge."

"Did it take you long to get a job? Antonio had to sub for almost two years."

"I subbed for a while before I got hired at Keating. I love my job—Keating's a good school and near where I live."

Alyssa had just dodged a telling fact (how long she had subbed) and collapsed twenty years of her life. Out of high school, she had not gone to college but worked full time for a florist in Sacramento. Within two years, she and Troy broke up as he began doing more drugs, working less, and acting increasingly abusive. After the second time he hit her, Alyssa had moved out with a brief stop at a women's shelter because she was broke and pregnant. Nan had loaned her money and come to be with her when she had the abortion.

Nine months later, she met Mark. He had left college after his second year and was working in tech. She changed jobs and began working at a catering company where she soon became a manager. They moved in together, and Mark encouraged her to enroll in the local two-year college. Two years later, when he got a job that required him to move to San Diego, he asked her to go with him and promised to help her get her four-year degree. After she was admitted to UC San Diego, she got a job at a local after-school program where she was soon running the homework hour. She discovered that she loved teaching and was good at it.

Because many of the students in the after-school program spoke Spanish, Alyssa tried to remember her high school Spanish and began taking courses. After homework hour, the students would delight in helping her practice. Mark kept getting promotions and was making a lot of money so when she mentioned a summer Spanish-immersion program in Mexico, Mark encouraged her to apply. She received a scholarship that covered the program cost except for travel.

The day she returned from her eight-week course, Mark told her there was someone else. Alyssa was even more devastated when she realized that Mark had been seeing this woman for over a year.

"Why didn't you tell me?" she demanded.

"I love you. I didn't want to hurt you, and…," his voice trailed off.

"What?"

"I was afraid that you might do something."

"Do something?" Alyssa was furious. "Do what?"

"Like Billy," Mark replied uncomfortably.

Shortly after they had moved to San Diego, Billy had died in a single-car accident. He was facing jail time for dealing drugs, and the accident might have been suicide.

Alyssa could think of nothing to say. She had trusted Mark who had always seemed understanding, encouraging, and loving. Alyssa could not face the idea of being either a wife or mother so they had talked about marriage and children as a pattern they would not follow. Because Mark had never asked her to change, she had assumed that he loved her enough to accept her limitations.

"She's very different from you," Mark said tentatively, and Alyssa heard, not "different," but "healthier," "saner," "less damaged," "more normal."

"You'll marry her?"

"Yes."

"Children?" She forced herself to ask.

"Probably," mumbled Mark, not meeting her eyes.

She walked into the bedroom, packed, and called Nan who was still living in Los Angeles. She stayed with Nan and her family for two weeks. Night after night, as she and Nan sat up late talking, Alyssa insisted that she had not known Mark was unhappy. She talked about how she could have made things work.

"If he had only given me a chance, I could have tried to change!"

"How could you be someone you're not?" Nan asked insistently. "Maybe you could have wrapped your head around getting married, but children? You've never wanted children."

Alyssa felt betrayed by how she had trusted Mark with details of her childhood, sharing some things she had never told anyone except Nan. She believed that because she had been honest and allowed him to know her, he had stopped loving her.

Mark insisted on not only finding her an apartment but paying her rent through the next summer when she would graduate. Alyssa wanted to throw his guilty kindness back in his face, but even with scholarships and work, she could not manage to live and pay for school. She now knew that she wanted to teach more than anything so, at Nan's urging, she reluctantly accepted his help.

She managed to graduate, but even with Mark's help, ended up with student loans. Then, just as she was about to begin working on her credential, she found out that her mother had cancer.

Since there was no one else, Alyssa moved back to Los Angeles and into her childhood home which was the same dirty dump it had always been. Her mother, the victim of depression and hypochondria, never had energy for anything except the search for a doctor who would cure her various ills. She had never cared for the children, cooked meals, or done housework. Alyssa had learned to do laundry when she was eight, and classmates began asking why "Curly Shirley" and Billy wore "dirty" clothes to school. By the time she was ten, as her mother spiraled downward, she was shopping for groceries and cooking dinner out of cans and boxes. Every day she made sure she and Billy got to school in time for the free breakfast. She hoarded and took home as much food as she could school meals.

Help came from unexpected places. When she and Billy dragged their red wagon to the market each Saturday morning, she usually tried to go to a certain checker's line. Violet was a friendly, older woman who always asked Shirley about school and usually had a treat for her and Billy. She would ask after their mother and mention if she had seen her come in to pick up a prescription during the week. One Saturday, Violet pulled a large box of powdered milk out from under the counter and said, "Somebody paid and forgot to take this. You can have it. Follow the directions, mix it up good, and put it in with your other milk—half and half. It will taste just like regular." Shirley listened carefully because they were always running out of milk.

"You kids need to be drinking milk with your meals so you'll have strong bones and teeth," added Violet.

The next week she had a bag of apples for Shirley. She called the manager over and said, "Can I take my break?"

"Sure, Vi," he replied.

"Just leave the groceries here," she said, gesturing for Shirley and Billy to follow her.

They went to the back of the store where she showed them two shopping carts full of dented cans. There was a large sign that read "50% off!"

"Now, honey, this food is just as good as what you get off the shelves regular," Violet explained to Shirley. She pointed to the sign, saying, "50% means half off. Sometimes the prices go even lower."

"They only cost half as much?" asked Shirley in wonder.

"Yeah. Now here's some beans. You can mix these into stew," she grabbed another can out of the basket, "And make it go further. Beans fill you up, and they're good for you. You can also fix 'em plain with a little tomato sauce. Add a little catsup for flavor." She pulled another can out of the basket. She looked at Shirley carefully for a long moment and then pulled out a can of corn. "You can also get vegetables. This is good with a little salt and butter."

"I like corn!" Billy said enthusiastically.

"Well, let's put these cans in with your order," said Violet, turning to lead them back to the front of the store. She glanced at her watch. "I've just got time to grab a smoke before I have to go back to work."

"I'm sorry," said Shirley hesitantly. "I don't have enough money for these things."

"Don't worry. I'll cover them. But next week, before you do the rest of your shopping, check these carts. They're always here."

"Thank you so much," said Shirley.

"How do you kids carry all this home?" asked Violet.

"We have a wagon," said Billy proudly.

When they got back to Violet's register, she rang up the cans, and then helped them carry the groceries out to their wagon. Smoking her cigarette thoughtfully, she watched them try to balance the food bags in the wagon, and finally said, "You kids wait right here."

She went into the store and returned with two sturdy, plastic milk crates. She helped them unload the wagon and put the crates in place to hold their various purchases.

"Works like a charm!" she said with a smile.

Shirley and Billy had depended so much on that red wagon that later, in high school, when her class read William Carlos Williams' "The Red Wheel Barrow," she had to pretend a coughing fit to disguise her tears and leave the room.

"Now tell me your names," said Violet.

153

"I'm Billy!" He extended his hand which Violet shook.

"I'm Shirley." She also extended her hand. Violet shook her hand and held it for an extra moment, looking into her eyes.

"You kids always make sure to come through my line, you hear? I always work Saturdays. If I'm on break, you just wait for me." They both nodded. "And, Shirley, they might hire you as a bagger when you're fourteen."

"That would be great!"

"Well, I gotta get back. See you next Saturday!" She reached into the pocket of her smock and handed them each two suckers.

"One for now and one for later," she said with a wink as they thanked her.

"What do we call you?" asked Shirley.

"Violet. Just like the flower except the flower's little, and I'm big," she said and laughed.

"Thank you, Violet," Shirley said again.

A few months later, after she had checked them out and handed them a bag of oranges someone had supposedly left behind, Violet said, "Billy, I can hardly find you under all those curls!"

"Shirley's gonna cut my hair later," he said.

"Would you like a real haircut?" Violet asked. Seeing Billy's skepticism, she added, "Just like grown men get?"

She got the manager to let her go to lunch and walked them down the small strip mall to Harvey's Barbershop. It was early, and Harvey, an older man, was just finishing a haircut. Billy, Shirley, and Violet sat watching him shave the man's neck and then brush him off.

"Be right with you, Vi," he said, accompanying the customer to the register.

"This is Billy, and this is Shirley. Kids, this is my friend Harvey." They all stood up.

"What gorgeous red hair," said Harvey appreciatively. "And there sure is a lot of it.

"Who's been cutting your hair?" he asked, looking at them both from the front and back.

"Me," Shirley admitted and added apologetically, "I'm not very good at it."

"What scissors do you use?" asked Harvey, his faded blue eyes twinkling.

"Sewing scissors. Regular scissors aren't sharp enough."

"Young lady, you've been doing an excellent job!" said Harvey. "All I need to do is clean it up a bit. Young man, do you think you can climb all the way up in this chair? Then I'll give you a ride to the moon."

Without protest, Billy clambered up into the barber chair and got several rides up and down before Harvey put the cape around him and went to work. Shirley watched carefully to see exactly how the barber cut Billy's hair, trying to memorize each snip. Suddenly, she became worried and turned to Violet, whispering, "I haven't got any money to pay."

"Don't worry, honey. Just let me and Harvey take care of it."

When Billy climbed down, smiling proudly, his wild, red curls were cut close to his head and as tame as they would ever be.

"Young lady," said Harvey, coming to stand in front of Shirley, "It would be an honor to trim your hair up a bit. I'm just a plain, old barber. Not the stylist someone with your beautiful hair deserves, but I'll do my best if you'll allow me." Shirley giggled at what she thought of as "book talk" and looked questioningly at Violet.

"If you want to, honey, go ahead," Violet encouraged her, and Shirley went to sit in the barber chair.

"Now what would you like?" asked Harvey.

"I can't see to trim the back," said Shirley, "So I know it's all messed up."

"Do you like short hair?" asked Harvey. "You have a beautiful face for a short haircut, and such gorgeous curls to go around that face."

"Thank you," said Shirley. No one had ever said anything nice about her wild, curly hair. "I think you should do what you think would look best."

"I'll try, and if it isn't perfect," he added with a wink and chuckle, "Hair grows!"

When he was finished, Shirley had a short cut that set off her pixie features and bright blue eyes.

"Vi, you need to get her some of that curl cream I told you about." He turned to Shirley. "You use the cream after you wash your hair. Just put a little bit in your palm and rub it in. It'll make your curls shiny and soft."

"I'll get it," promised Violet.

Harvey went to get the broom and Shirley said, "Mr. Harvey, I'll sweep up if you like."

Harvey handed her the broom and dust pan, saying, "Thank you." Afterwards, he told her it was the best clean-up job his shop had ever had.

A month later, Harvey hired Shirley on Saturday afternoons, his busiest time, to come in and sweep up. He paid her $20 each week. She brought Billy along, and Harvey gave him a new Matchbox car each week, and, while she worked, let him build race tracks out of empty cartons at the back of the shop. He cut her and Billy's hair until she was fifteen. When he retired, he gave her scissors, clippers, and a drape so she could continue to cut Billy's hair, but, by then, she was working at the market and making enough money to afford Billy's haircuts. Harvey set her up with a neighborhood woman who had an informal salon in her home. However, Juanita would never let her pay, only saying, "I owe Harvey a lot."

When Shirley was a senior in high school and working part-time as a checker at the market, Violet had a heart attack. When Shirley went to see her in the hospital, she told Violet that she was leaving with Troy after graduation. As she sat holding Violet's hand, she asked her why she had always been so kind to her and Billy.

"I was like you, honey, except I get tossed around among my relatives and in foster care. A lot of bad things happened to me. I wanted to help you and Billy stay with your mother." She shot Shirley a concerned look and said, "I hope I did the right thing. Especially with all this trouble Billy's been in."

"I think you did." Shirley took Violet's hand. "Thank you for all the times you helped us. It meant so much to have you looking out for us."

"You've always been such a spunky kid. You're so smart. I hope things work out for you so that you can maybe go to college, but whatever happens, remember that I've always been so proud of you."

The store manager called Shirley that night to tell her that Violet had died.

Help had also come from Ms. Girardi, her fifth-grade teacher. To celebrate their graduation to middle school, Shirley's class was going on a three-day trip to San Diego. As they studied the history of San Diego and the animals they would see at the zoo, Shirley wanted to go on this trip more than she had ever wanted anything in her entire life, but she told her teacher that she could not go.

"If it's the money, Shirley, don't worry. Your trip is paid for, and there's even some spending money for you," Ms. Girardi assured her.

"It's not the money."

"Then, what is it?" When Shirley did not respond, Ms. Girardi asked, "Is it your mother? Is she feeling sick?" Shirley did not answer but bit her lower lip to keep it from quivering. She looked at the floor so Ms. Girardi would not see the tears rising in her eyes. "Honey, you can tell me. You've worked so hard, and I know how much you want to go on this trip."

Earlier, after school, when she was helping Ms. Girardi clean out the supply cupboard, Shirley had admitted that she had never been out of Los Angeles. In fact, she was not sure that she had ever been out of the San Fernando Valley.

"Shirley, please tell me. What is it?"

"It's Billy. I can't leave Billy home alone."

"But your mother...," began Ms. Girardi and stopped at the look on Shirley's face. She thought for a moment and said, "I think I can work this out. Just give me a few days. Okay?"

Shirley nodded hopelessly and wiped her eyes.

A few days later, Billy was invited to spend the three days of the trip with Carter, a classmate and the younger brother of Simon and Philip, twins who were in Shirley's class. Their father was going along on the trip as a chaperone, but their mother would be staying home with Carter and, now, Billy. Not only did Billy have a great time, but he brought home a huge bag of clothes because Carter got double hand-me-downs from the twins. Even in high school, long after Carter and Billy had drifted apart, periodically, bags of hand-me-down clothes would appear on the Donaldsons' front porch.

The school trip was a dream for Shirley, a brief insight into how other kids lived. Adults arranged meals, transportation, and activities. All she had to do was cooperate and enjoy herself. She was partnered for the trip with Elizabeth, a tall, silent, awkward classmate who was not at all athletic and was therefore even more an outsider than Shirley. Elizabeth also loved books and animals so they were equally enthusiastic about the San Diego Zoo. When they went on the harbor cruise, although Elizabeth was shocked that Shirley had never seen the ocean, she did not make fun of her. They sat together at lunch during what was left of the school year.

Shirley was athletic so her classmates included her in games and chose her for teams, but, having realized very early that if she went to someone's house, they would expect an invitation to hers, she made no close friends at school. The only birthday party she ever attended was Nan's because she could walk over, and Nan understood that her present would never be fancy. Nan, a grade ahead of her, was her only friend, and she rarely allowed even her to come into the house. When they were adults, Nan told her that she had noticed a sticky spill on the kitchen floor that was still present a year later when she made another rare foray into the house.

"If you never see anyone clean," Alyssa told her angrily, "How are you supposed to know how to do it? Besides, when did I have time? I was shopping and cooking and being Billy's mother."

She made sure Billy took baths, brushed his teeth, and did his homework. They both loved to read and went to the nearby library often. One of the children's librarians helped them find books and made sure they were signed up for various programs, especially during the summer.

But by the time Shirley was sixteen and Billy fourteen, she could no longer control him. An excellent student, she found refuge, a source of praise, and order in school. Billy had always done well, too, until middle school when he began to run with a bad crowd. Beginning in his early teens, he stayed out late, and Shirley never knew where he was or who he was with. She had to hide money, or he would take it. When she tried to talk to him, he told her to mind her own business. One time, when she tried to stop him from going out late at night, he hit her. After that, she gave up trying to reach him.

Having dropped out of high school after doing six months in juvenile detention for theft, by the time he turned twenty, he had become addicted to drugs and spent ten months in jail for drug possession. He was facing a much longer sentence for dealing when he died in the car crash.

Over her mother's objections and in no position to afford it, Alyssa took her mother to a hotel and hired professional cleaners to come in. She then spent the next nine months working toward her credential while she lived with and cared for her dying, indigent mother. Alyssa paid bills with student loans, credit cards that were easy to get, and cash advances against those cards. She planned to pay off the credit cards when she sold the house after her mother died.

During the months of her mother's illness, Alyssa came to know her in a new way and glimpsed the person she might have been if she had gotten better treatment. She began to understand how trapped her mother felt in her intractable depression and hypochondria. She learned how increasingly abusive her father had become as he confronted her mother's inability to function. She also discovered how guilty her mother felt about her inability to parent and make a home in the way millions of other women did.

"You and Billy were the only reason I didn't just end it," her mother confessed repeatedly.

Alyssa began to feel compassion and let some of her anger go, but then her mother died and she discovered that the trickle of monthly income was from a reverse mortgage. The house was gone.

Alyssa called Nan, who was now living in Boston.

"You won't believe this," Alyssa told her tearfully.

"What?"

"The house is gone."

"You sold it already?"

"No, Mom did a reverse mortgage. There's no house to sell! I have to move out, I'm completely broke, my credit is fucked, and I can't pay my bills," Alyssa sobbed.

"What about your father?" asked Nan.

"I haven't seen that asshole in years!"

"I know, but maybe he could help. He owes you something, and he did pay for Billy's funeral."

"Yeah, but he didn't show up. Besides, I don't even know where he is. I don't want to know where he is."

"Okay. I understand." Nan was silent for a time. "I'll talk to Carl. I think we can send you some money to help you get a place, but I have a suggestion."

"What?"

"See a lawyer about filing for bankruptcy."

From childhood, Nan had been the closest thing she had to family. Nan had understood her circumstances since they were small girls playing on the swings and in the sandbox at Nan's house. Of course, Alyssa's house was never a place to play unless you hid in some overgrown bushes during a game of hide-and-seek. Nan was the person she called when she discovered that she was pregnant, Billy had died, Mark had left her, and her mother had cancer. Nan was the only person she ever told about the financial hole she had fallen into.

After declaring bankruptcy, Alyssa began her teaching career under a debt repayment program. She worked on weekends as a server and every summer in the school system. She dated occasionally, but, although lonely, was wary of getting into another relationship. When she met Antonio, she had paid her debts, quit her second job, and begun to feel that her life was finally in order. She was even saving money each month.

"So what do your parents do?" asked Maria, as she closed the dishwasher.

"My father left us when I was five, and after I was six or seven, I didn't see him anymore," Alyssa said honestly. "He supported us, but I have no idea where he is now."

"And your mother?" asked Maria, looking concerned.

"She passed away while I was working on my credential."

"What a shame! Do you have any brothers or sisters?"

"No, my only brother died in a car accident so it's just me. My parents weren't close to their families. You know how California is," Alyssa said, trying for a lighter tone. "Any family my parents had back east, where they came from, stayed back there, and we were out here."

"I understand," said Maria, sounding pleased to be on safer ground. "I've lost touch with some aunts and uncles who moved away, but we have family here. Mostly we see my younger brother and his wife, and my older sister and her husband. Their kids are almost like brothers and sisters to Antonio and Belinda."

"You're from a big family?"

"There were five of us, but my youngest sister died very young. There are three of us here, but my other brother moved with his family to Florida, and we rarely see them."

"And Tony's family?" I asked.

"Tony has two brothers. They're all mechanics, and they work together at the dealership. We see them and their families sometimes, but not as frequently as we see my family."

"It's nice there are so many of you," Alyssa said.

Maria smiled and nodded.

"So how did you decide to go into teaching?" she asked, ushering Alyssa back into the living room.

"I worked in an after-school program. I ended up running the homework hour so I was always helping students, and I began to realize how much I enjoyed teaching. We had some kids who were struggling in first grade with reading so I set up a special group to work with them. I did a book club every two or three weeks with some older kids who wanted to read more. I just loved the kids," Alyssa ended abruptly, sensing that she might be talking too much.

"You must be looking forward to having children of your own," remarked Belinda.

Alyssa had not realized that she was listening.

"Mind your own business," Antonio snapped.

"It is my business," replied Belinda indignantly. "I'm certainly not having any more babies so my kids need some cousins to play with."

"Talk to Elliot's sister and brother about that," replied Antonio, and Alyssa sensed real irritation behind his teasing tone.

"A lot of good that will do," laughed Belinda. "Let's play Scrabble."

"Anybody want to watch the Dodgers?" asked Tony, coming in from outside.

Madison, Mitchell, and Elliot followed him into the den as Antonio, Alyssa, Maria, and Belinda sat down at the dining room table to play Scrabble.

"Antonio, wouldn't you rather watch the ball game?" asked Maria.

"And leave you two to interrogate Alyssa," he replied. "I don't think so."

As they drove home, Antonio said, "I hope my family wasn't too annoying."

"Not at all. I thought they were very nice."

"They really want me to marry and have kids. The closer I get to thirty, the pushier they are," he said in a frustrated tone. "If you weren't there, they

161

would have been interrogating me about who I was dating and when I was going to settle down. It used to be about getting a job. Now it's all about getting married and starting a family."

"I guess families are just like that," Alyssa said in a neutral tone, thinking how little idea she had what other families were like.

"I think my mother and Belinda are afraid that I'll never get married and have kids."

"The two things go together?" Alyssa asked with a smile.

"Always in their minds," replied Antonio emphatically.

"So why did your parents name you Antonio? Why did they pick Belinda for your sister?" asked Alyssa to move the conversation away from marriage and children.

"What do you mean?"

"I mean, if they were so insistent on English, why did they give you both Spanish names?"

Antonio laughed before replying, "I'm named after my father and grandfather. Belinda's named for my mother's mother. I don't think they could get out of it. But Belinda changed her last name to Clark as soon as she married Elliot."

"Why?"

"She had the same problem I do. Patients would see Belinda Rivera on her name badge and begin speaking Spanish to her! She said it made her life much easier to be Belinda Clark."

"Madison and Mitchell will never have any problem," Alyssa pointed out, and Antonio laughed heartily.

Throughout the summer, Alyssa and Antonio spent a lot of time together although Antonio kept his small apartment. For the fall, he had been hired at an elementary school near Keating. That summer he worked as a playground supervisor at a community center near where he lived. Alyssa had hoped for a summer off, but always nervous about her finances, she decided to teach summer school at Keating. When their summer jobs ended, they drove to Las Vegas for the weekend.

"Did you have fun?" asked Nan, when Alyssa called her the next week.

"We had a great time! Our big splurge was Cirque du Soleil. Totally amazing show!"

"Did you gamble?"

"Only with the hotel's money. Neither of us is in a position to lose any money. I'm okay now, but you know how I worry about money, and Antonio is always broke."

"So did you tell him?"

Alyssa knew that Nan was asking if she had told Antonio her age.

"I can't. I just can't now."

"It's okay."

"We've had dinner at his parents' a few more times."

"How is it?"

"Uncomfortable. They're very nice to me, but I get this feeling that his mother suspects something isn't right."

"What makes you think that?"

"I don't know. Maybe I just feel guilty or maybe it's all the talk about marriage. I swear Belinda and Maria can't stay off the subject of babies and what a great father Antonio would make."

"How serious are you about him?"

Alyssa fell silent and finally murmured, "I'm in love with him. I wish you could meet him, Nan. He's sweet and considerate. Thoughtful. We have so much in common, and he makes me laugh. And he says he loves me."

Nan was silent for a long time before she said, "Alyssa, you need to think about telling him."

"I do. All the time, but I just can't. I don't want to mess this up like I did with Mark."

"It wasn't your fault. Mark wasn't honest with you."

"How do I know Antonio wouldn't dump me if he realized how old I am? God knows I'd never tell him the stuff I told Mark." Before Nan could answer, Alyssa rushed on, "You don't know how amazing it is to have someone care about me. It's been so long since I've had someone to depend on and do things with. I've been so lonely. I can't risk losing him, Nan. I just can't tell him now."

In late August, Nan called to tell Alyssa, "Carl has a meeting in San Diego. It's only a few days, but I'm going to come see you."

"That's great!"

They discussed travel details, and Alyssa said, "I want you to meet Antonio, but you have to promise not to give me away."

"I would never do that," Nan assured her.

Since the trip was short and Nan could only spend from noon Saturday to noon Sunday, Alyssa thought the best way for her to meet Antonio was over dinner. Nan insisted on treating them so Saturday night found the three of them headed for The Big One, an upscale seafood restaurant with a view.

After they were seated, Nan looked out the window at the sun setting over the Pacific and sighed, saying, "I love Boston, but I miss the Pacific. The Atlantic just isn't the same!"

"So how long have you lived in Boston?" asked Antonio.

"Thirteen years. Our youngest was born there so he thinks of himself as a true Bostonian," said Nan, and Alyssa found herself doing some quick, panicked arithmetic with the ages of Hannah and Michelle, Nan's older children, who were both in college.

"Alyssa's always talking about how you grew up next door to each other. Did you go to school together?"

"Not really," Alyssa said quickly, glancing at Nan who was seated across from her.

The server came with wine and took their orders. Nan raised her glass.

"To old and new friends," she said, smiling.

They touched glasses and drank.

"I was so much ahead of Alyssa that we were never in the same school, but we were always neighborhood friends," said Nan fondly. "And we've stayed friends over...," she halted, took a sip of wine, and finished, "Over the years. It's been like having a younger sister."

"You're so lucky," said Antonio. "I have all my cousins, but I haven't kept any friends from the neighborhood or school. It's no one's fault, but you just seem to drift apart."

"You have to make a real effort to stay in touch, especially when someone moves to Boston," said Alyssa, making a face at Nan who laughed.

"Especially if that friend never comes to visit," replied Nan, making a face back.

"When I get rich, I promise I'll visit," said Alyssa.

"I'd love to see Boston," said Antonio. "I've never been to the East coast."

"It's different in a lot of ways," said Nan.

They spent much of the meal discussing the differences between Boston and Los Angeles. Nan asked Antonio questions about his family and where he had gone to school. He shared funny stories about various jobs he had done as he repeatedly dropped in and out of college. The evening passed in a flurry of good food and superficial conversation.

After they dropped Antonio at his apartment, Nan asked Alyssa anxiously, "Did I do okay?"

"Great! I had a bad moment or two when you started talking about your kids."

"I did too, but I decided pretending I was much older was easier than pretending all three of the kids were younger. I didn't want to have too many lies to keep track of."

"You managed to make it sound like you're so much older than I am."

"I tried not to mess up," said Nan with a worried look. "It was a lot more of a strain than I expected."

"I know what you mean," agreed Alyssa and quickly changed the subject by asking, "Did you like him?"

"I did. He's very nice and clearly very much in love with you." Nan paused. "But seriously, aren't you ever going to tell him?"

"I'm trying to figure out how to do it," Alyssa assured her.

The next week, Alyssa and Antonio went to the beach. After a long walk, they got ice cream cones and sat watching the ocean sparkle in the afternoon sunlight.

"Alyssa, I want to ask you something."

"What?"

"Do you love me?"

"Of course. Haven't I told you every day for months?"

"Would you... I've never said this to anyone before." Antonio paused, took a deep breath, and said quietly, "Alyssa, will you marry me?" Seeing the shock on her face, he quickly added, "It doesn't have to be now, but would you just think about it?"

"Antonio, I need to tell you something," Alyssa said, looking away sadly.

"What?"

"I probably should have told you after I met your family."

"What? What is it?" he asked, taking her free hand.

"I can't have children."

"What do you mean?"

"I mean, I can't. I have endometriosis." Antonio looked completely baffled. "It's when the lining in your uterus grows where it shouldn't. It's kind of a hormonal thing. Anyway, to put it bluntly, my tubes are blocked, and I can't get pregnant."

"Is there any way to cure it?"

"No. In my case, there's no fixing it. I saw a specialist at UCLA. This is why Mark and I broke up," Alyssa added quickly. "He wanted a woman who could have children."

"I don't care. I'd like to have kids, but we can adopt," Antonio said easily.

Alyssa immediately imagined adoption applications with spaces for dates of birth, histories of employment, and other damning information, not to mention a child to raise at the end of the process.

"I couldn't do that," Alyssa said bluntly.

"Then we won't have kids. I just want to be with you for the rest of my life." Antonio met her eyes with his earnest, loving gaze, and for a brief moment, Alyssa was tempted to tell him the truth, but the moment passed.

"Marriage isn't something anyone should rush into. Because of my parents' divorce, I've never wanted to marry, but I love you." Alyssa paused as she pictured the damning documents one would have to present when obtaining a marriage license. "I'm not saying no, Antonio, but we're happy. Can't we just go on as we are?"

"Just remember that I asked and will ask again because I love you." Antonio pulled her toward him and kissed her.

Alyssa called Nan that night and said, "I've got a problem."

"No! You? A problem?"

"I'm not kidding, Nan. Antonio asked me to marry him."

"What did you tell him?" asked Nan with real concern.

"I told him I couldn't have children."

"Why?"

"Why did I tell him that, or why can't I have children?" asked Alyssa with a giggle.

"Both," said Nan, laughing.

"This isn't funny, Nan. We shouldn't be laughing. I told him I can't because, at this late date, I probably can't. You know, I love my students. Your kids are great, and you're such a good mother, and you've always wanted kids. I remember all those games of house you forced me to play with your baby dolls! But I raised Billy, and you know how that turned out. I have *never* wanted kids. Ever. So I told him that I have endometriosis blocking my tubes, and no surgery can fix it."

"That was a pretty good story to come up with on the spur of the moment."

"Don't be shitty. I've known, or, at least, been afraid, this conversation was coming."

"What about adoption?"

"He asked, and I told him that I couldn't do it. He still wants to marry me."

"What a mess."

"I know. And the worst part is that I love him. If it wouldn't reveal my age, I'd marry him, but I told him that I have issues about marriage from my parents' divorce. That part, at least, is true."

Just before they hung up, Nan said, "Don't be mad, Alyssa, but I have something to say."

"What?" she demanded in a suspicious voice.

"I hate to be blunt. I don't want to hurt you, but you need to consider how you would feel if someone did to you what you're doing to Antonio. How would you feel about being systematically lied to by someone you love?"

"But I didn't start out to make him think I was thirty," Alyssa protested.

"Yes, but you knew from the beginning that he thought you were much younger than you are, and you didn't tell him the truth."

"I know."

"So?"

"You just don't understand, Nan. You have Carl and the kids. You've always had family. I've been so lonely. Antonio's so special, and it's so good being with someone, having someone there for me."

In late November, Alyssa received a letter on heavy, cream-colored stationery from a lawyer in Phoenix. The letter informed her that her father had died the previous year, the probate of his estate was now completed, and she had inherited $150,000. First, she checked the law office online and called to make sure it existed. Then, she checked the credentials of the attorney who had signed the letter. Finally, she located her father's obituary which named as survivors only his current wife, two sons and their wives, one daughter and her husband, and several grandchildren.

Alyssa stared at the small photo on the screen thinking how this man had abandoned her and Billy to go off and make a new life. Had it turned out to be normal, orderly, and conventional? Had his abusive behavior ended when he left her mother, or had his second wife suffered the same verbal and physical abuse? The photo of her father in middle age made her realize how little she remembered him. According to the obituary, he had been a partner in a development company.

"He must have made a good living," thought Alyssa bitterly. "He paid our mortgage, alimony, and child support, but money doesn't change the fact that he deserted us. He left me and Billy with a woman he knew was incapable of caring for us."

On the one hand, $150,000 seemed like a lot of money, but on the other hand, it hardly seemed like payment enough for the instability and neglect that had defined her and Billy's childhood.

She called Nan and told her the news, asking, "What should I do with the money? I just had them deposit it in my savings account at the credit union."

"Savings account?" Nan laughed. "Pay off your credit card debt immediately. Maybe treat yourself to a trip to Hawaii or even Boston! Talk to the manager of your credit union. You should probably, at least, put the money where you'll earn better interest while you think about what to do. You need to talk to a financial planner."

"I think that I can talk to someone at the union retirement fund for free."

"Do that." Nan paused for a moment and finally said, "Alyssa, unless you win the lottery, this is the only windfall you'll ever have so you need to be careful with it."

"I know, but you know what?"

"What?" asked Nan.

"I still hate the bastard, and I hope he suffered."

"I don't blame you at all." Nan was quiet for a moment. "Don't take this the wrong way. You know I love you."

"Okay. I know. What?" asked Alyssa in a suspicious tone.

"You might spend some of that money on therapy. Get yourself some counselling. It might help you figure out things with Antonio."

It was not the first time Nan had suggested counseling. Alyssa felt a flash of anger but then realized that Nan was, as always, acting like a true sister.

"You're an amazing woman," Nan continued, "But you've had a hard life. You know I've gone to counseling, and it helped me get past how controlling my mother was. It also helped me with the kids and Carl."

"I know," Alyssa said quietly. "I've thought about it. You know I did go for a bit in college after Mark dumped me, but then my mother got sick and I couldn't afford it. I don't want to use the employee program. They say all this stuff about privacy, but it makes me nervous that I'll screw up my record."

"Just think about it."

"I will."

"Promise?"

"I promise."

Alyssa considered not telling Antonio about the inheritance, but after a month had passed, she felt bad about hesitating and thought how hurt he would be if she did not tell him and it came out later. She finally decided that she did not want another secret to keep.

"So what are you doing with the money?" he asked when she told him.

"It's in the bank. I'm meeting with a financial advisor next week. I need to think about how to invest it."

"Why don't you loan some of it to me to pay off my credit cards?" he asked and, seeing the surprise on her face, rushed on, "I could pay you back with higher interest than the bank pays. We could sign an agreement.

Seriously, my credit cards are killing me. I could almost manage my student loan payments if I didn't have so much credit card debt."

Feeling shocked and uncomfortable, Alyssa finally said, "I need to think about it."

"What is there to think about?" he demanded angrily. "I'll pay you a higher interest rate. Or don't you trust me?"

"I do, but I have student loans and some debt of my own that I need to deal with," Alyssa said hesitantly.

"What debt?"

"From when my mother was sick. I still owe some money for taking care of her," Alyssa lied.

"Surely not $150,000 worth," said Antonio, an unfamiliar sarcastic edge to his voice.

"No, but quite a bit," Alyssa murmured. "Can we just let it go for now?"

"Sure," said Antonio, kissing her. "Take your time to think it over. I didn't mean to pressure you."

But over the next few weeks, they were never together that he did not mention how worried he was about paying off his credit cards and making his student loan payments or how strapped he was for money or how much he needed a new car.

"It's not my fault," he complained. "If my parents had paid for college, I wouldn't have all this debt. They knew I wasn't going to get a full scholarship like Belinda."

Alyssa, remembering how Mark had helped her, said nothing. She finally called Nan and, after some initial chitchat, confessed, "I think I've made a mistake."

"What did you do?"

"I didn't *do* anything, but I told Antonio about the money."

"Why did you do that?" asked Nan.

"I know it was stupid of me! I can hear you rolling your eyes! Just stop. I didn't want any more lies between us. I wanted to show that I trust him."

"So?"

"He wants to borrow $50,000 to pay off his credit cards and some student loans."

"Wow! That's a lot!"

"I've never seen a stack of credit cards like he has. He carries them all rubber-banded together. I swear he's never seen a store or on-line credit card that he didn't need to have. You know how easy they are to get and what killers the interest rates are!"

"Alyssa, in general, loaning friends money is a bad idea," Nan said slowly.

"You've loaned me money! Besides, he's not just a friend!"

"I know, but I don't think you should do this. It feels risky to me. This is the only inheritance you'll ever have."

"I know, but he's pressuring me."

"That makes it feel even riskier."

Alyssa, irritated at Nan, Antonio, and, most of all, herself, fell silent.

"By the way, I have some news of my own," Nan finally said.

"What?"

"Hannah has met someone." Nan's oldest daughter was a sophomore in college. "I think it's serious. At least, that's what Michelle says." Her second daughter was in her first year at a different college.

"How long has Hannah been seeing him?"

"Mom is always the last one to hear the romance news," she said with a sigh, "But Michelle says they started 'hanging out,' as she put it, last semester."

"That's so exciting."

"So maybe there'll be wedding bells, and you and Antonio will have to make that trip to Boston!"

"Don't you think they're young to be getting married?" asked Alyssa, thinking how full of pitfalls a trip to Boston with Antonio might be.

"Hannah was born old, and, besides, Carl and I married young and haven't done so badly," replied Nan tartly.

Two weeks later, on Sunday morning, Antonio and Alyssa were eating breakfast when he asked, "Have you thought any more about giving me a loan?"

"I have." Alyssa paused and said gently, "I'm sorry, but I've decided that I can't do it."

"Why not? Don't you trust me?" Antonio looked shocked, and his eyes darkened with anger.

"It's not that. Please don't be angry. There's something I have to tell you."

"What?" He immediately looked concerned.

"A few years ago, right after my mother died, I had to declare bankruptcy. I paid her bills when she was sick. I had student loans plus some other money I borrowed while I was working on my credential. I had gotten a bunch of credit cards and done cash advances to keep the lights on. Then, when my mother died, she left me nothing. Absolutely nothing. I discovered that she reverse-mortgaged the house. She didn't even own a car. So all I had were a bunch of debts. I've spent the past few years settling my debts and re-building my credit."

"So you understand my position!" he said irritably. "I'm drowning in the monthly payments on the damn cards! It's not my fault that I can't get ahead!" He ran his hand through his thick black hair.

"Antonio, this money is the only inheritance I'll ever have, and I need to use it wisely. I need time to figure out what I should do."

"But I don't have time," Antonio said angrily. "Don't you get it? It's not my fault, but I can't manage month to month."

"What would you have done if I hadn't inherited this money?" asked Alyssa, trying to keep the anger out of her voice.

"I would have done what I always do," he said, his voice rising. "I would have asked my parents, and they would have lectured me on what a loser I am. They always want to know why I can't learn to manage money. They don't understand how much money I owe for college and how much it takes just to live!"

"I'm sorry, but I think your parents are in a much better position to loan you money than I am."

Antonio got up, went in the bedroom, grabbed his clothes off the chair, and slammed the bathroom door. In a few moments, he emerged fully dressed.

"Where are you going?" asked Alyssa, a tremor in her voice.

"Home. Just put my stuff in a box, and I'll pick it up later," he said, zipping his laptop into its case.

"You're leaving?" asked Alyssa, her blue eyes wide in disbelief.

"What do you expect?" he demanded, his dark eyes flashing. "You don't trust me. Why would I stay around?"

"It's not that I don't trust you...," Alyssa began.

"Yes, it is. I've asked you to marry me. You say that you love me, and you won't do this one, small thing for me. What does that say about us?"

"Maybe it's just about me," Alyssa said, sounding desperate. "I just need more time to wrap my head around things. Maybe we should sit down and look at your finances together. I could maybe help you get on track."

"You're not my mother," Antonio said, impatiently pulling on his lightweight jacket, picking up his laptop, and slamming the apartment door behind him.

Crying, Alyssa ran to the door, but she could hear his car starting, and then he was gone.

They did not talk again until the following Friday when Antonio called.

"I just wanted to let you know that I can't do the Dodger games this season," he said in a flat tone.

They had recently reserved their season tickets. Alyssa had generously offered to pay for an upgrade, so this year's seats would be even better than last year's.

"Are you sure?" asked Alyssa. "You love baseball, and we had a lot of fun last summer."

"I know, but I can't afford the ticket. See if you can find someone who wants it. I'll call around and try to sell it, or maybe I can just cancel it."

"Okay. How are you?"

"Not great."

"I miss you," said Alyssa, beginning to cry and trying not to sob audibly in the uncomfortable silence between them.

"I miss you, too," Antonio finally replied.

"I gathered up all your stuff. If you want, you can come by and get it," said Alyssa softly.

"Okay. Maybe next week. I'll let you know," he replied and ended the call.

Alyssa cried for a long time. When she looked at the clock, it was only six, and another lonely evening stretched before her. She did not have any friends in the sense of Antonio or Nan, but she had acquaintances from school with whom, before Antonio, she used to go out. Since Antonio, she had refused their invitations because he would have gone with her, and one of them might have dropped an age-bomb. Now there was no need to worry. Some colleagues always went out on Friday night. Before she could change her mind, she called Jennifer.

"Alyssa, we were just talking about you!"

"Saying nice things, I hope!" Alyssa could hear bar or restaurant sounds in the background.

"Of course! We were just wondering where you've been!"

"That's for me to know and you to discover," said Alyssa. "Can I join you?"

"Sure. We're at Jorge y Diego's, that new Mexican place up on Ventura."

"Have you ordered?"

"Just finishing up Margaritas so you need to hurry up. I'll order you a Margarita with salt, okay? We can hold off ordering dinner until you get here. Brian and Kim are with me, or rather, I'm with them."

"Oh, wow. They're together? I didn't know!"

"See, you just aren't up to date at all!"

"I'll be there in fifteen or twenty minutes."

After rinsing her flushed face in cold water, Alyssa studied herself in the mirror and decided that in a few minutes she would look fine. She found a green jacket in the closet to dress up her khakis and light yellow shirt, slipped on sandals, grabbed her purse, and drove to the restaurant. She suddenly felt nervous as she walked in, but Jennifer waved her over to the table, and everyone greeted her warmly.

"We wondered what had happened to you," said Kim, looking curiously at Alyssa who was taking the first sip of her Margarita. "You came out every Friday night, and suddenly, we never saw you except at school!"

"I'm sorry," murmured Alyssa. "I've been seeing someone who lives in Santa Monica."

"Someone special?" asked Jennifer, with a smile. Older than the other three and long divorced, she was so motherly that no one resented her personal questions.

"It seemed special until a few weeks ago."

"Oh, poor Alyssa," said Jennifer, putting an arm around her. "I thought you seemed a little down lately."

"Sorry," murmured Brian and Kim in unison.

"Live and learn," replied Alyssa, taking another sip of her Margarita. "So what's new?"

"We're getting married," Kim exclaimed, and Brian smiled happily as she held out her left hand for Alyssa to admire the modest engagement ring.

"The three of you," asked Alyssa, and everyone laughed. "What a pretty ring! How long have you been engaged?"

"Since last week. We've just started telling people."

"PE and Art—I can't imagine what the wedding will be like!"

"An aerobic, visual creation," said Jennifer, laughing.

"Are you walking down the aisle or swinging from beautifully painted monkey bars?" asked Alyssa, and everyone laughed.

When Alyssa got home that night, she felt better than she had all week. In spite of her aching heart, she had enjoyed her friends, and she was happy that Brian and Kim were getting married. No one had mentioned Antonio. He was just a long-term substitute who had dropped off their radar when he left for another job.

On Saturday, she spent the day cleaning, a task she had been neglecting. Unable to settle down with a book, she went to a movie. Sunday she slept late, grocery shopped, and finally, called Nan.

"How are you doing? I was about to call you. We haven't talked in ages," Nan greeted her, sounding worried.

"I'm not doing well. Terrible, in fact."

"What's wrong?"

"Antonio and I broke up. He walked out when I refused to lend him money."

"Oh, Alyssa, I'm sorry."

"It's been so hard," said Alyssa, beginning to cry. "I'm so lonely. I miss him so much."

"I'm sorry. I don't know what to say."

"It's not your fault," said Alyssa, sighing. "He was pressuring me all the time about the money." She swallowed hard, trying to stop crying. "It's just so hard after being with someone to be alone again."

"I know, but doesn't it bother you that he would leave you over this?"

"It does, but you know, I've had money trouble so I understand how desperate he is. He doesn't want to ask his parents, and he assumed that because I love him, I would help."

"But your decision isn't just about what he expects."

"I know that," snapped Alyssa and immediately regretted how angry she sounded. "I'm sorry. I just feel so bad. It's just so hard being alone after being with someone. I just don't know what to do, Nan."

"You have other friends."

"I do, but not like you or Antonio. I went out Friday night with friends from school, but the apartment is so quiet. I feel so much more alone than I did before I started going out with Antonio."

The next Friday, Alyssa called Antonio and asked him to pick up his things.

"Can I come in for a minute?" he asked at the door.

"Sure. Come on in."

He sat down on the sofa and looked uncomfortable.

"What is it? Is something wrong?" Alyssa asked with real concern.

"I want to apologize. I never should have gotten angry with you, but I was just so worried over my bills. I never should have expected you to help me."

"I'm sorry, too," said Alyssa, relief filling her voice. "I told you about the money because I trusted you. You know this money is the only inheritance I'll ever have. You have your parents, but I have no one."

"I know, and it was not fair of me to pressure you. I'm sorry."

"I was thinking about loaning you some money to help you dig out," said Alyssa disingenuously. In fact, the idea had just occurred to her. "Just not quite as much as you asked for."

"The money's not important. I miss you."

"I miss you, too."

Their eyes met, and Alyssa went to sit beside him. Antonio took her hand, twined his fingers through hers, and turned to her, saying softly, "Let's try again."

A few days later, Alyssa called Nan.

"We're back together," she announced. "I think the turning point was knowing that we would have to let the Dodger tickets go!" she joked happily.

"I'm glad you're back together," replied Nan, laughing. "If it makes you happy, I'm so glad. I have big news of my own! Hannah is engaged. She brought Justin home, and we love him. Carl and I think he's perfect. A wedding invitation will come your way next fall, and we want both you and Antonio to come. Since it's over a year away, I hope you can arrange to take some time off. Think about spending a few extra days so we can show you Boston."

A sense of dread filled Alyssa as she considered the risks of such a visit, but she said nothing to Nan who chatted on happily about wedding plans and Justin's family.

At the end of the conversation, Nan said, "So, I have to ask, when you got back together, did you tell him?"

"I just can't," said Alyssa. "Things are so good with us. Now, I'm even more frightened of losing him."

"No pressure," said Nan, "I just wondered." When Alyssa did not respond, Nan added excitedly, "It will be so great to have you here for the wedding. Don't worry about getting a hotel. You and Antonio can stay with us. We have plenty of room."

"Thanks. That sounds great," said Alyssa, thinking how much she would love being with Nan and her family but how impossible making such a visit with Antonio would be.

Although they chatted for a few more minutes and she told Nan about the mutual fund she had invested in, Alyssa did not mention the $30,000 she had lent Antonio to pay off his credit cards.

After this conversation, over the next fifteen months, Nan called, left messages, e-mailed, texted, and sent cards and letters. Alyssa did not respond. The summer before the wedding, Nan sent a save-the-date card, and the next fall, she sent a wedding invitation. No response.

As the wedding date approached and the caterer needed final numbers, Nan called and left yet another message: "Alyssa, I don't know what's wrong. I'm worried. I want to talk to you, but at least, let me know whether you and Antonio are coming to the wedding. Call me or text me. Please."

Alyssa did not respond.

After the wedding, happy and exhausted, Nan and Carl lay in bed.

"You did a wonderful job!" he said admiringly. "It was perfect."

"There was one thing missing," Nan said sadly.

"It was beautiful. What was missing?" Carl asked in surprise, sitting up to look at her.

"Alyssa."

"What do you think is going on with her?" Carl asked in a worried tone. "Do you think she's mad because you told her not to lend that guy money, and they broke up?"

"They got back together, but maybe she blames me." Nan sighed. "Actually, I don't think that's it." Nan met her husband's concerned gaze. "I think she's made a choice."

"About what?"

"She's decided that she'll never tell Antonio how old she is."

"What does that have to do with you?" Carl asked, puzzled.

"It was him or her old—and I am stressing *old*--friend."

"I don't follow."

"Alyssa knows that I'd never purposely give her away, but after that very awkward dinner I had with her and Antonio, I'm sure she realized that I might accidentally reveal her age. A visit for the wedding would be a huge risk. Anyone in our family could give her away."

"Honestly?" asked Carl. "You think that's it?"

Nan nodded and said, "Just by being in her life, I would always be a threat."

"I just can't believe it!" Carl said angrily. "You're her oldest friend. Since you were kids, you've always been there for her. You've helped her so many times."

"I know, and I also know that it's nothing I said or did. In the end, Alyssa felt that to protect herself, she had to make a choice. She chose Antonio," said Nan in a sad but matter-of-fact tone.

"She could at least have told you!"

"Given me the courtesy of an explanation?" asked Nan, with a smile. She shook her head, saying, "No, I don't think so. Alyssa could find no way to conceal or explain this choice by lying." Nan fell silent and then added, "We're sisters. She knew that I would figure it out."

Becoming My Mother

I did not intend any of this to happen. Writing these words, I feel like a child who, having acted impulsively, is now faced with unimagined consequences. However, I am not a child but a woman in her forties. Did I act impulsively? I like to believe that I did, but I'm a writer so the question remains: why did I, of all people, not imagine that my action would have consequences? The answer is simple: I was sure no one would ever know.

In the spring of my second year of college, my father died of a heart attack. Although Dad was only thirty-eight, he and Mom had been married for twenty years. They had eloped after their Senior Prom, and I was born six months later. Dad—affectionate, playful, full of jokes, fascinated by how everything from can openers to cars worked--may have wanted more children, but Mom did not, so I am an only child.

Dad's death was not a total shock: his own father had died of a heart attack when Dad was only nine. Working hard at low-paying jobs, his mother, who died when I was three, managed to bring up her four boys. They all began working as soon as they could and later scattered across the country. As a result, I knew none of my uncles or their families. When Dad died, Mom called them all, and we receive condolences, but, as we expected, no one came.

Mom's sister, Aunt Sylvia, twelve years older than Mom, was the only relative I knew. She lived in New Jersey, managed a large office for a manufacturing company, and did not marry until she was forty. She and Uncle David had no children so he joined her in loving and spoiling me. Aunt Sylvia and Mom were so close that I sometimes felt excluded, especially when they talked about the past, before their parents had moved with Mom to California. Aunt Sylvia, almost through college, had stayed in New Jersey. I was jealous and wanted their attention, but I also realized at some point that sisterhood, with its closed, charmed circle of shared memories, was something I would never have.

Mom and I had expected, at most, thirty people to attend the simple service at the funeral home. We were amazed when ninety people showed up. Dad, medium height, muscular, with a quick smile and clear blue eyes, had made friends everywhere. As the receiving line moved past us, we heard story after story of his kindness, honesty, and helpfulness. It was the first time I had a clear vision of my parents having an existence entirely separate from mine.

The morning after the service, Mom, Aunt Sylvia, Uncle David, and I scattered some of Dad's ashes around his favorite rose bush in the backyard.

"We really ought to scatter some at the station," Mom said, "But it's all concrete!"

The four of us laughed and then cried.

We made plans to scatter the rest of his ashes at the beach in the summer. Uncle David returned to New Jersey, but Aunt Sylvia stayed for another week. Both she and Mom insisted that I return to school for the final few weeks of spring quarter.

I knew how important my getting an education was to my parents, both of whom had only a high school diploma. Dad was a gifted mechanic. He had taken a car repair course in high school and co-oped at a local gas station. The owner hired him part-time, and after high school, full-time. When Mom's parents died within a few years of each other, she inherited the money that had allowed Dad to become a partner in the station.

Mom stayed home with me and kept the station's books. She had taken a single bookkeeping course in high school and learned what she needed to know by borrowing books from the local library, ordering U.S. Government tax pamphlets, and, eventually, searching the internet. When I was five, she learned what she needed to know to computerize the business. I later realized that she was a financial wizard who had helped Dad make very lucrative business decisions.

She had urged Dad and his partner to sell to a larger chain that brought in a manager for the gas station. Dad and his partner, both good mechanics with reputations for honesty, retained ownership of and ran the garage. They worked hard and took home excellent money. Although Dad sometimes grumbled, Mom insisted that he invest in a retirement fund, buy life insurance, and, above all, save for my college.

I finished that spring quarter with good grades, and when I came home for the summer, I told Mom that I would transfer to UCLA, closer to home.

"No, you're happy at Santa Cruz and doing well."

"But I want to be here with you," I said, gesturing at the house. "You must be lonely and need help with gardening and stuff," I added vaguely.

We still lived in the small, post-war tract home my parents had bought when I was four.

After a long pause, Mom said, "Honey, I hope you won't be upset, but I'm going to sell the house. I'm going back to school. I'm planning to rent a place near Cal State Northridge."

"What?" I was astonished.

"I've already applied and been admitted for the fall."

"I never knew you wanted to go to college," I said in amazement.

"Sylvia went to college. I was a very good student, and everyone expected that I would go too. That's where I was headed when I got pregnant with you," she replied with a smile.

"But you never took classes or mentioned anything about wanting to go to college!"

"I was busy with you and the business, but now Dad's gone...." She stopped and swallowed hard.

I rushed to put my arms around her, and we cried for a few minutes, blew our noses, and then laughed at each other.

"I thought you might like to travel," I said.

"Why would I do that 'when I'm living in paradise?'" quoted Mom, making us both laugh and cry again.

Dad had rarely taken time off, complaining jokingly, "I *am* the business!" But when the subject of travel came up, he always said, "Why would I travel when I'm living in paradise?"

We rarely vacationed, except for occasional weekends away, sometimes in the mountains but more often at the beach. From late April to October, every Saturday or Sunday, we packed a picnic and headed for the beach.

"I'm glad you have a plan for moving forward," I finally said. "I was afraid you might just give up or something." In truth, I had also been worried about what she might expect from me.

"Kristin, I'm only 38! It may seem old to you, but it's way too young to give up," she laughed, her brown eyes sparkling. I studied her trim figure, smooth olive skin, and abundant dark hair and realized that she was, indeed, still young.

"So what will you study?"

"English. I've always wanted to study literature."

"Just like me?"

"Not at all! You want to be a writer. I just want to read books. I'll probably minor in Business."

"Piece of cake for you," I teased. "Maybe you can become a financial analyst or investment broker and make us rich!"

"I don't think I'm headed for Wall Street, but I can probably finish my bachelor's degree in three years with some credit for work experience. Then I'll get a job. I don't need to work while I'm in school. Dad's life insurance and the sale of the business will see us both through college and a bit beyond if we need it. I'm trying not to touch his retirement savings because it's my retirement too."

"You're such a planner," I said, resenting a bit how clear her path seemed.

"Because his father died so young, I always knew this could happen," she said quietly.

"But the money—that's all thanks to you."

"No, it's thanks to how hard your father worked."

"No, Mom. Dad always said you were the brains of the business and he was the brawn."

She smiled sadly.

"I want to ask you something," she said later over lunch.

"What?"

"Will you help me with school? When I have to write papers, can I call you and discuss the assignment? Can I email you stuff to look at? I haven't been in school for twenty years, and I'm pretty scared."

"Mom, you're the smartest person I know. You'll do great! But if you need a sounding board, you can call or email me, just the way I've been calling and emailing you!"

That summer Mom insisted that I not work. She quickly sold our house for an astonishing amount. In a haze of shared grief, I helped her clear out the house. She was less sentimental and more clear-headed than I as she chose what to keep, what to let go, and what to store. I helped her move into a tiny apartment in Northridge within walking distance of campus. At her apartment, I shared her queen-sized bed. Like room-mates, we often laughed, watched movies, and shared books. I wrote several stories and discovered later that they were mostly about grief and loss.

In September, before I went back to school, we went to the beach in Venice. We slipped bags of Dad's ashes under our bathing suits and swam out beyond the waves. As we let his ashes blend with the ocean he had so loved, we said good-bye and our tears mingled with the salty water.

That fall, we talked two or three times a week. We both missed Dad, and Mom also missed the house, garden, and neighborhood more than she had expected. Although she soon discovered that she was not the only older student on campus and loved every class with a passion that made me envious, she worried constantly about her work. By mid-semester, realizing that her brain had not gone dormant, she had shown herself to be the excellent student that she had always been.

After that first semester, she felt more confident, I saw fewer of her papers, and we slowly drifted back to our weekly conversation.

I came home to visit in the middle of the fall quarter. The morning after I arrived, Mom announced that I should pack up because she was taking me to a "secret destination." She drove over the mountain, down through Santa Monica to the end of Venice Beach, turned down a side street that ran toward the ocean, turned again, and pulled up behind a modest, older, turquoise, stucco apartment building.

"Hop out!" she said.

She opened the back door of the building, we climbed two flights of stairs, and she let us into a bright, airy, third-floor apartment. We had come in next to the kitchen, but in the adjacent living room, I discovered a large bay window with an ocean view.

"Oh, my God, Mom! This is great! Are we spending the weekend? Can we rent it next summer?"

"No, I own it." She laughed at my surprise, adding, "After I finish school, I'm going to move down here permanently."

"Are you sure it's safe?" I asked.

Mom looked at me with raised eyebrows.

"I mean it's always been kind of sketchy down here...." My voice trailed off.

I had gone to the beach in Venice since I was a small child. Dad loved it because the wide, sandy beach was beautiful, and, always thrifty, he hated to pay for parking the way you had to in Santa Monica. Dad had also loved the mix of people doing crazy things on the boardwalk. We had watched jugglers, musicians, dancers, and magicians, all working for the coins tossed into a hat. I suddenly remembered how much Mom had loved it too, especially the ocean, where she would swim deep into the surf and float over the waves, letting the sea rock her in its giant cradle. I had taken swimming lessons, but swimming, riding waves, and playing in the ocean with Mom and Dad had truly taught me how to swim.

"Venice has always been a kind of border town," she admitted, with a grin, "And it is a place with a past, but I asked around, and, as one of my neighbors put it, Venice is now 'eccentric but respectable.'"

"But the appeal has always been the craziness."

"I don't mean middle-class, suburban respectable, but livable and interesting. I've always wanted to live by the ocean. I hadn't meant to buy until I graduated, but this condo came open. It was a stretch, but I can afford it. Harriet is a widow and lives on the first floor. She bought the building with her husband and turned it into condos. Rachel, who lives on the second floor, is single. They're both older than I am, but we all like each other."

She grabbed my hand, saying, "Let me give you the grand tour. Kitchen, where we came in." she said, gesturing to the small galley kitchen. "The living room—isn't it big? Don't you love that view?" She led me through the living room to a short hallway. "There are two bedrooms. I'll always have a place for you to visit or even live with me when you finish school."

"Mom," I hesitated, and then plunged ahead, "I don't think I'll be coming back here. I want to do an MFA in creative writing, probably at San Francisco State. I'm going to try to find something up north. I love the Bay Area," I finished lamely.

She quickly concealed her disappointment and said firmly, "You have to choose what's best for you, Kristin. I didn't realize you wanted to go on for a master's, but if you do, I can afford your tuition."

"I'll work. I thought about taking a break and working. Maybe I'll get a fellowship or assistantship."

"That would be great, but you'll always have my support in whatever you do," she said and smiled at me.

Relieved this dreaded discussion was over, I smiled back, saying, "I love this place! It's perfect. And your bedroom has another great view!"

"Dad loved this area so much that I almost feel he's here with me."

I hugged Mom tight against me, our sadness an almost tangible bond, as we stood looking at the Pacific, sparkling in the sun.

"Do you stay here?" I finally asked.

"I do. I've worked out my schedule for next term so I can be here Friday through Monday. I don't mind the apartment in Northridge, but I love it here."

"I'll love thinking of you here when I'm away. What a great place to visit!" I added, making Mom laugh.

I visited whenever I could and began to consider Venice home. One weekend, almost a year after Dad died, I came home a day early to surprise Mom for her birthday. I sat looking out the living room window and saw her walking across the beach, toward the condo, with a man. They were holding hands, and she was laughing. She looked young and carefree. She held her dark hair back in the sea breeze as they kissed, and then, with a wave, he walked away.

When she came in, she was happy to see me and did not seem worried that I might have seen something. I didn't say anything and agonized over whether it was any of my business. The next day, I asked her casually if she ever went out with anyone.

"You mean like dates?" she asked, coming out of the kitchen and sitting down at the other end of the sofa.

"I wouldn't object," I began awkwardly. "I'm just asking."

"I've had a few dates, but nothing serious. Kristin, I don't want to marry again. I loved your father, and we made a good life together, but now I want my own life."

"Yes, but you could fall in love with someone. You aren't that old, and you're still very attractive."

"Thanks," she said, smiling. "I'm enjoying making friends these days with all kinds of people. Did I tell you that I joined the neighborhood association?"

"No."

"It's been fun. I've met many neighbors and some local business owners. I've also made new friends at school."

As always, I was struck by how different we were: Mom with her quiet yet easy sociability and me with my shy awkwardness. I never joined anything. It took me days to work up courage to ask a classmate to have lunch or coffee. Each year brought a new roommate and close friendship which seemed to evaporate over the summer. I often had dates, but no relationship lasted beyond a few months. I forced myself to pay attention to what Mom was saying.

"You know, your father worked so hard that we never had much social life. We just held on to our friends from high school."

I thought how I sent Christmas cards to but now rarely saw Melissa and Angie, my best friends from high school.

"You still see Helen and Jack, don't you? And Mark and Naomi?"

"Of course. We all have dinner once a month, just like we've been doing for years. I usually go to the valley, but sometimes they come over the hill, and we eat by the beach. Mark and Jack made a visit after I moved in. They helped me hang pictures, move furniture, set up the television, and put together those shelves from Ikea. They also changed out the light fixtures and installed fans. They were very funny and sweet about all of it. I'm lucky that I still have our old friends. Some women get left out when they're widowed, but *our* good friends are still *my* good friends. In fact," she added, laughing, "Naomi is always trying to set me up. She just can't believe that I'm not interested."

Over the years, I suspected that Mom had lovers. Occasionally, an odd razor, toothbrush, t-shirt, or jacket would turn up in the apartment. I found it impossible to say anything since she never talked about or introduced me to anyone special. However, I did meet her other friends, mostly women, at a few holiday parties and on lunch or dinner dates. The variety of people she knew seemed endless. Her closest friends were still Naomi and Helen, but, she rapidly became good friends with Rachel and Harriet, her neighbors.

The year I graduated, I won the Senior Short Story Prize. The prize and a recommendation from my writing professor opened the door at a small publishing house in San Francisco. I began working part time as I pursued my MFA in writing fiction. By the time I finished my degree, Mom had graduated and found a job at UCLA, reasonably close to Venice.

She worked in the Bursar's office where she soon became the office manager. Her bookkeeping background and degree had gotten her the job, but her intelligence, people skills, and good sense earned her rapid promotion. The first time I stopped in to pick her up for lunch, it was clear that her co-workers already adored her. She loved her job, especially the contact with students.

"They're keeping me young!" she would often tell me.

While Mom was thriving, I stagnated. I had Dad's clear blue eyes with Mom's olive skin and dark hair. I was slim like Mom but taller, like Aunt Sylvia. Dad had never met a stranger, and Mom, quieter, still managed to make good friends, but I possessed none of their social ease. My life-long pattern continued: I made few friends, and, although I attracted men effortlessly, the relationships never lasted.

I slogged through failed relationships, writer's block, the completion of various short stories, the start of many novels, myriad rejections, the fruitless attempts to find an agent, different jobs in publishing, and unpromising dates.

I cycled through various editing jobs and, at one point, the particular hell of producing a company newsletter which involved interviewing people. Not my forté. Just as every new boyfriend seemed to turn out to be a recycle of a previous boyfriend, every job seemed a recycle of previous jobs from the boss to the techie.

The only consistent bright spot was Sarah Sloane, my best friend. We had met at the MFA orientation when Sarah chose to come over and talk to me. A gifted poet and generous soul from a large family, Sarah always urged me to reach out and give people and circumstances a chance.

She constantly urged me to enter contests, and finally I won the Delia Forsyth Short Story Prize. Like most of my writing, this new story was partly autobiographical. I had always been slightly embarrassed that Dad worked with his hands. My story was about a teen-age girl whose father is a mechanic. She manages to get into the "in" crowd at her high school and after attending several parties, finally gets the attention of a boy she has been loving from afar. When asked, she has always said that her father is in the "gas and oil business," adding coyly, "I don't really know what he does."

Dream boy asks her out, picks her up from the house, and drives straight to her father's gas station to fill up the car. Not only is her father at the station, but he is helping out the driveway attendant, so it is her father who walks up and asks if they need any help. The girl has no choice but to introduce him to her date. When her father won't shake because his hands are dirty, her humiliation is complete.

As the girl and her date drive away from the gas station, dream boy says, "Didn't you say your dad was in the 'oil business?'"

"Actually, gas and oil. It was kind of a joke," she replies in embarrassment.

"I think it's great your dad knows how to fix cars. He worked on my mother's car when no one else could figure out what was wrong. Do you think he might let me hang out some time?"

At the award ceremony, the presenter, an author of some note, talked about the perfect balance of comedy and pathos in my depiction of the young woman's desperation to fit in.

The award included publication in a prestigious magazine, and that mythical person, a literary agent, contacted me on the heels of a publisher calling to ask if I had a novel they could "take a look at."

Did I have a novel? Is the sky blue? Did every fiction MFA who has ever lived have a novel? Or two? Or three? Actually, I had only one novel that was anywhere near finished. It was a *bildungsroman,* the mis/adventures of a woman who defines success as marriage by the time she is thirty. The main character, who wants to be a writer (Of course!), has a kind of Moll Flanders verve and always finds the funny side of even the worst date or relationship. For this novel, I recycled all my bad boyfriends and a few of my roommates' and acquaintances' even worse boyfriends. In the final chapter, our heroine turns thirty, gives up men, and, since she cannot retire to a nunnery, decides to go to law school.

My agent, Melodie Summers (Not a made-up name!), a bossy, fashionably thin, bleached blonde, always dressed in the latest fashion, called or e-mailed me daily as I re-wrote my novel. I had everyone whose opinion I remotely trusted read the novel and give me feedback. Finally, Summers read my manuscript and (frustrated English teacher?) wrote her suggestions/corrections in red, returning a manuscript that looked like a mass murder had been committed on it. I assumed that she knew what she was doing and made most of the changes she wanted. She then submitted it to the publisher and, after some additional changes, miracle of miracles, my novel was published.

Mom proved that she was no prude, but when she read a late draft of my novel, she remarked, "If this weren't so funny, it would be sad."

I asked what she meant and after some urging, she said, "Your main character, this young woman, has no friends. I understand the men she dates are impossible, but where are *her* friends?"

As I had my entire life, I read the concern in her soft, brown eyes, but then she quickly added, "But it *is* very funny and well written. I'm so proud of you!"

Insisting on paying list price to boost my sales, she bought my novel for all her friends and had me autograph every copy. She got friends to post reviews and rate my book online. She came to any bookstore in her area where I spoke and listened as I read from my novel and answered people's questions. She took me out to dinner after I signed books and bought me more than one drink when the crowd was thin.

I was now working as an editor at a company that published technical writing online and sometimes in print. I had taught part time one semester and discovered my personal circle in Hell. I did not want to help people fix their writing, find their "voice," or work out their problems. I hated everything about teaching from class discussion to the way it followed me home and filled my mind. Editing prose on technical subjects was a much easier process because when I walked away from my cubicle at the end of the day or week, I was done. My time was my own, and I had energy to write.

For six months, I promoted my book. I got several positive reviews from people other than Mom's friends, and the book sold well enough that the publisher signed me for a second novel. The completion date was eighteen months away. I got a moderate advance, paid Melodie Summers her percentage, and began figuring out what to write next.

All my life, voices had been telling me stories, the objects around me had been speaking volumes about how they got where they were and who had used them, and the most random circumstance had morphed almost automatically into a full-blown narrative. *All my life...*but suddenly, as if I had crossed from technicolor into black and white, I had no idea what to write.

"You could write a sequel to your first novel? I mean, law school, that's an adventure, isn't it?" Melodie Summers suggested.

"I haven't been to law school and don't intend to go. It's a joke," I replied sharply.

"How about a prequel? High school must have been pretty funny for her?"

"Is high school funny for anyone?" I asked, making no effort to keep the irritation out of my voice.

"Well, give yourself some time, Kristin. Maybe get away for a bit and something will come to you. You're a good writer! Don't give up!"

"Yeah," I said cynically, "If I give up, I have to give back."

I went to Cancun with Chris, the guy I had been with for almost two years, my longest relationship to date. While there, I realized that I could not just keep drifting on a wave of good sex. I spent our get-away drinking myself stupid, letting him fuck my brains out, and in my brief moments of sobriety, planning my good-bye speech: "You're a great guy! I know you'll find someone who shares your passion for mountain-biking, snorkeling, and snowboarding, but I don't think that person is me."

Why had I stayed with this clear mismatch for so long? If I were honest, it was not just good sex. I liked Chris' friends who had become my friends. I enjoyed being part of a group and knew from experience that once "TheChKrises," as they had dubbed us, were over, these friends would disappear too. In truth, Sarah was my only friend. Other friendships I might claim were transient work relationships.

"How can Mom have so damn many friends?" I grumbled to Aunt Sylvia. "She's not out-going like Dad was, but people just seem to gravitate toward her."

Aunt Sylvia pondered my question for a few moments before saying, "I think it's because she's interested in people, and she listens to them."

"Most people make me want to read a good book," I said, only half joking.

To cope with my writer's block, I took a long weekend. I meditated, took walks, performed every writing warm-up exercise I had ever heard of and then invented new ones, for example, The Hate Soliloquy wherein the writer describes for ten minutes how much s/he/they hate/s writing and then describes for ten minutes what bliss would ensue if s/he/they never wrote anything ever again.

I read and reread Yeats' "The Circus Animals Desertion," and then mocked myself: Yeats had a long career to look back on when he hit the wall (and, note, wrote a great poem about it!) whereas I had a single novel, a few stories, and random praise from teachers, friends, and co-strugglers as the backstory for my crisis. Yeats also believed in the power of sex. I was nearing forty and had had a fair amount of experience, but, especially after Cancun, I no longer believed in the power of sex to kick start anything creative except pregnancy.

I avoided going to the library and bookstores. I tried not to open the Amazon app on my phone. I stopped reading books because any written word of fiction was a fresh reminder of my sterility. Trying not to think about the writing behind the programs, I entered a television coma and binged on sit-coms and detective shows.

I had experienced blocks where for a day or week I didn't know what direction to take with a piece of fiction, but I had never before entered this desperate, blank, wordless, endless Sahara-of-the-White-Page. I had stopped dreaming--even my sub-conscious refused to offer me its creative lunacy.

I was happiest at work because I had to focus on the text in front of me and, like a good mechanic, tune it up to run more smoothly. I found myself wondering if this pleasure in fixing something was how Dad had felt when he did his work. Perhaps I was a fixer, not an inventor.

I would like to say that I was in this state for a few days or weeks, but actually it had gone on for six miserable months when Mom called one Wednesday.

"Can you come down this weekend?" she asked. "You haven't been home in a while."

"I'd love to. I'm still having terrible writer's block, and a weekend at the beach might inspire me."

192

Friday night Mom picked me up from the airport, and we ate a late Chinese dinner. She asked me about Chris (long gone but still texting me), my work, and the writer's block. As always, I felt better after talking to her and slept more soundly than I had in months. I even dreamed. I was scuba diving in clear blue water, floating above huge clams, watching and waiting for them to open. I awoke and immediately understood that the dream was a metaphor for my life: the floating, the sense of waiting and expectancy, was my writer's block, and the clams were my imagination that I felt had closed me out. No clams opened in the dream, but just remembering it gave me hope.

Feeling invigorated for the first time in months, I got up, threw on my cotton robe, and followed the smell of bacon.

"How do you want your eggs?" Mom asked as I kissed her on the cheek.

"Scrambled. Want me to make the toast?"

"Sure."

I poured myself a cup of coffee, and we worked in companionable silence. As we had hundreds of times before, we sat down to breakfast side by side so we could both look out across the white sand to the sunny, gleaming ocean.

"I never get tired of it," I remarked, and Mom nodded.

"I've never regretted moving here. Even when it's gray and dreary or stormy, I still love being near the ocean."

When we had finished eating, I cleared the dishes and poured us a second cup of coffee. As I sat down, I realized that Mom was watching me intently.

"Mom, what's wrong?"

She took a deep breath and said, "Kristin, I have cancer."

"What?"

"I got the diagnosis on Wednesday, and I didn't want to tell you over the phone."

"Are you sick? You seem fine. How did you find out?"

"I haven't been sick, but I've been having these periods of nausea for a while now so I went to the doctor. I had a bunch of blood tests that all looked okay so she ordered a colonoscopy, and that was fine. Then she ordered an upper GI test, and when that came back fine and I was still having nausea, she ordered abdominal imaging."

"So how long has this been going on? You didn't say anything." I sounded accusatory, but Mom seemed to realize that I was just scared.

"The nausea? Several months off and on. The tests and everything have been over the last month or so."

"Why didn't you tell me?" I demanded.

"I didn't have anything to tell except I was having tests, and I didn't want you to worry."

"So what kind of cancer is it?"

"Pancreatic."

"Oh, no!"

I began to cry, and we moved to the sofa.

"What's the treatment?" I finally asked, pulling away from Mom so I could see her face.

"I had a biopsy about two weeks ago and saw the oncologist yesterday. Chemotherapy may slow it down, but," she swallowed hard, "There isn't a cure, honey. It's in my liver as well."

We huddled together, hugging each other tightly and crying.

"When do you start chemo?" I finally asked, beginning to consider the practical implications.

"On Monday."

"Okay, I can stay. I'll call my boss and let him know that I won't be back until later this week, depending on how you feel."

"You know, Rachel and Harriet have already offered to take me to chemo and stay with me to make sure I'm okay. I also have Helen and Naomi and other friends I can call on."

"Mom, I love you. I need to be with you. Please let me do this."

"Thank you," she said quietly and hugged me.

"Have you told Aunt Sylvia?"

"Yes, I called her when I found out, but David has his second knee replacement next week so she can't come for a while."

I did not go back to work the following week. Mom had an allergic reaction to the anti-nausea drug and ended up spending the night in the hospital. I stayed with her, and we were both so terrified that she did not object to my spending the rest of the week. She felt okay for a day or so, slept the next day, and then slowly began to eat again. By the second week, she was insisting that she could go to work half days.

Although her boss and co-workers were accommodating and Mom had accrued much sick/vacation time, she had already told me that she did not want to be a burden on her co-workers: when she could not do her job effectively, she would quit. I wanted her to quit immediately, but she just laughed and said, "I like working."

Mom insisted that we have a detailed conversation about finances. I broke down when we got to her retirement account, money she had carefully saved and would not live to enjoy.

I called Melodie Summers, explained my situation, and offered to return the advance, but she negotiated with the publisher and got an extension on my contract. One year. I had no idea what that additional year would bring. The only writing I was doing were short, frightened, heart-broken journal entries.

Two months of chemo brought a reduction in the size of Mom's tumors and a small respite from treatment. She came to San Francisco for a long weekend. Even short walks exhausted her so we drove up and down the coast to enjoy the sunshine and vivid blue water. I found as many seaside restaurants as I could, and we spent hours lingering over drinks or meals, talking, and enjoying the view.

"Are you sorry you didn't have more children?" I asked her idly over coffee one afternoon.

"I'm sorry that you don't have a brother or sister to be with you now," she said slowly. "I was so young when I had you. Imagine! In less than a year, I graduated from high school, got pregnant, married, and became a mother. I was only eighteen. It was so overwhelming and scary. When I got pregnant, my parents were furious—I don't think Mother ever forgave me." She stopped, gazing away from me and out to sea for a long time. "No one seemed to worry about how I felt or what it meant to have my life completely derailed. I loved your father, but he was so young and scared to death that he couldn't make enough money to support us. His reaction was to work all the time. Honestly, Kristin, I have never felt so alone." She sat looking down at the table and shaking her head. "It never occurred to anyone that I might have had...and your father might have had...different

195

plans for our lives. Everyone just cared that we had gotten married—'done the right thing,'" she said, putting air quotes around the phrase. "It was awful."

I reached over and put my hand over hers.

"You've been a great mother," I assured her. "I never had any idea that I wasn't exactly what you and Dad wanted."

She smiled at me, murmuring, "That's the nicest thing you've ever said to me." We fell silent for a moment, and then she asked, "Did you want brothers and sisters?"

"Sometimes. I got lonely, but most of the time I knew that I was lucky to have you and Dad. As I got older, I realized how much you have to share if you have siblings."

The second round of chemo weakened Mom so much that she decided to quit her job. I went to her going-away party and was touched by how much her co-workers cared. That week I made a brief trip to San Francisco to negotiate a way to work part-time from home. My landlady let me out of my lease when I told her about Mom and offered to forfeit my deposit. Sarah helped me pack and put my books, furniture, and household goods in storage. Although Mom protested when I moved home, I could feel her relief at having me with her.

The weekend I moved in, I went into Mom's room to get a blanket. As long as I could remember, she had had a small, low book-case by her bedside. Her father had made it for her when she was a girl, and she had always kept her journals and library books on its shelves. It now held only a few library books. The orderly row of her journals was gone.

"Where did you put your journals?" I asked at dinner that night.

"I got rid of them."

"Why?" I was incredulous.

"I thought it over—actually I've been thinking about it off and on for years—and I finally decided that they had served their purpose and didn't need to be shared."

"But you didn't ask me!" I wailed and quickly added, "I've always looked forward to reading them and finding out how your life was—what you felt about things."

A stubborn, closed expression came over her face as she said, "I'm sorry, Kristin, but I didn't feel right about leaving you with all those loose ends."

"Loose ends?"

"Journals are nothing but loose ends. One day you're upset or angry or hurt so you write about it and either feel better or come to a resolution or stay upset—which you may or may not write about--but tomorrow or next week or five years later, you've moved on or forgotten about what happened. Even if you haven't forgotten, your feelings may have changed, but you probably only wrote about the issue once when you were upset. Journals have no structure. No resolution. Just loose ends."

"That doesn't mean they're useless," I protested.

"No, of course not! They're very useful to the person writing them, but I didn't want my musings on my life and my muddled emotions to cast shadows on your life."

"It would be a way to have you with me. To hear your voice. Couldn't you trust me to understand?" I demanded in a hurt tone.

"I'm sorry, dear. I would trust you to understand, of course, but, for example, when I first started keeping a journal, I was pregnant with you. I didn't want you to read how angry I was sometimes. I didn't want you to read the terrible things Mother said to me. And those are just two examples. I decided that I didn't want to force you to deal with things that aren't yours." Her voice was firm. She paused and then added, "Especially if I weren't here to explain."

"Mom, don't say that!"

She smiled at me and, taking my hand, said sadly, "Kristin, I hope for a miracle but plan for adversity."

We developed a routine. I worked early in the morning or late at night so I could spend as much time as possible with Mom. We watched all our favorite movies. We re-read our favorite books, and I read aloud when Mom complained that she was having trouble focusing on the printed page. We took short walks on the beach. When she could no longer walk on the sand, we used the newly-installed chair lift to get her downstairs and sat under an umbrella close to the building. When she became too weak to go out, we placed her hospital bed in the living room facing the sea. On warm days, we opened the windows wide to let in the fresh, salt air.

Between Mom's first and second rounds of chemo, Aunt Sylvia came for a week-long visit that was like a slumber party with alcohol. Mom could not drink, but Aunt Sylvia and I made up for it. We looked at family pictures, and they reminisced about their girlhood. Aunt Sylvia told stories about people scorning her or saying awful things because they assumed the toddler in the stroller or little girl holding her hand was not her sister but her child.

We played cards and soon realized that Mom could not focus on strategy so we switched to Dominoes, Uno, and an endless game of Monopoly. Sometimes Mom would not play but lie on the sofa watching us with amusement as Aunt Sylvia and I tried to beat each other at Scrabble or different versions of Gin Rummy.

When the next scan showed that the tumors were continuing to grow, the doctor tried a new, experimental chemotherapy. After the first treatment, Mom was barely conscious for three days and remained nauseous for the rest of the week. The second week she rallied a bit, but the next treatment proved even worse than the first, leaving her unable to eat and complaining that her mind was completely foggy. The day before the third treatment, she made me sit down beside her on the sofa.

"Honey," she said, taking my hand, "I'm sorry, but I can't do this anymore."

"But maybe it's so bad because it's killing the cancer," I protested.

"I don't think so. I think this chemo is not stopping the cancer but killing me faster."

"Let's talk to the oncologist tomorrow. She may have some suggestions."

The oncologist reluctantly suggested lengthening the time between treatments. Mom thought that having more recovery time might help, and it did, for a couple of treatments. She forced herself to have the final treatment in the series. By then she was so thin and weak that she could no longer walk.

A month after her final treatment, she had a scan. The tumors on her pancreas were larger, and those on her liver had multiplied.

Mom listened to the results of the scan and said, "Let's call Hospice."

"I'm so sorry," the oncologist said, hugging my mother as we all cried.

We had three more months together. Mom was not well, but for two of those months, she could still enjoy brief drives in the car, listen to me read her favorite books, listen to music, and watch movies. Her hair began to grow back, without gray, very dark, and surprisingly curly. As they had throughout her illness, her friends stopped in regularly to visit and give me time to go to the grocery and walk on the beach.

I finally got in touch with Melissa and Angie, my friends from high school. Melissa was divorced and Angie, still single. We discovered that we all still loved books and enjoyed being together so we went out to lunch or coffee occasionally. I was grateful for any respite from Mom's illness.

Sarah came down several times to spend the night or weekend. Mom had always liked Sarah and perked up when she visited. I was grateful for these visits because I could be frank with Sarah in ways I could not be frank with anyone else. In addition, we could talk about writing and not writing. She sympathized, recognizing how, beneath my fear of losing Mom, ran the fear of never writing again. She constantly urged me to be patient with myself. I had been a writer since I knew what a story was and could write words, but I feared that words and images, like a flock of seagulls, had now flown away to parts unknown.

The last month of Mom's illness was a blend of grueling physical care, broken sleep, sweet moments of memory and affection, and the horror of watching her body slowly fail.

"I'm taking a lot of killing," she whispered to me one morning as I was snuggled next to her in the hospital bed.

"You've always been tough."

"I've been seeing Dad lately," she said in a matter-of-fact tone. "He's waiting for me, but I think he'll just have to be patient. I want to see Sylvia again."

"You really saw Dad?" I asked in wonderment.

"Yes. This morning he was standing at the foot of the bed. He just stands there and watches me like he used to when he was waiting for me to get ready to go somewhere. He's been visiting a lot lately."

"I love you, Mom," I said, snuggling closer. "I don't want you to go."

"And I love you, honey, with my whole heart. I'm so sorry to leave you. I want to see you settled with your writing career and maybe a husband. Maybe kids. I want to see you settled and happy in the life *you* want."

"I want to write more than anything," I said, "But I just feel so blank, so empty."

"You have the gift. You've always been a writer so don't be too hard on yourself. As you live, you'll meet people and gain experience, and the stories will come. I just wish I could stay to read all the wonderful books you'll write."

Aunt Sylvia arrived that afternoon and had time to visit with Mom who seemed remarkably alert.

The next morning, we could barely rouse her. We sat by her bed for three more days, but she never fully regained consciousness. We administered her pain medication. When she became restless, we would wet her lips and wipe her forehead. We held her hands and talked to her, reminiscing, telling her we loved her, and, hardest of all, giving her permission to leave us.

I don't know what went through Aunt Sylvia's mind, but I prayed as I had not since childhood: "Oh God, please take her peacefully. Oh, God, please don't let her suffer any more. Oh, God, please let this be over."

And then it was. With a breath like a deep sigh and a groan, Mom was gone.

She had arranged to be cremated and have her ashes scattered at sea. I invited everyone, her co-workers, her many friends, my few friends, to the scattering. On a sunny, clear, perfect day, we sailed out from the harbor at San Pedro to where seals were swimming and sunning themselves on buoys. We then sailed beyond to the open waters. The captain read the 23rd Psalm. As Aunt Sylvia, Uncle David, and I leaned over the back of the boat to scatter Mom's ashes, I saw her. The lithe, young mother I knew as a child dove gracefully into the sea she had always loved and swam off. I never asked Aunt Sylvia if she had seen the same thing perhaps because I wanted this final, miraculous, oddly comforting vision of my mother to be mine alone.

Aunt Sylvia and Uncle David stayed for another week. I was exhausted and would have slept away the days, but Aunt Sylvia insisted on helping me go through Mom's clothes and take them to a women's shelter. We went through her jewelry, and, knowing they would one day return to me, I let her choose whatever she wanted. They fed me good dinners and helped me begin to settle the estate.

Always a planner, after Dad's death, Mom had put me on everything from her bank account to her credit card and utility accounts. She owned the condo and had made me a co-owner. She'd given me her car when she stopped driving. In the case of a miraculous remission, we had agreed that she, always having purchased used vehicles, would deserve a new car. We had laughed, imagining her zooming up Route 1 in a red Porsche with the top down. She had left a will. I was her sole beneficiary so the business was as simple as possible, but it still seemed overwhelming. The only real surprise was how much money Mom had left me.

It was good I had these details to occupy me, blunting my focus on the ineluctable fact that Mom, my life-long source of advice, support, encouragement, and love, was gone.

Aunt Sylvia talked to me about going home with them for a visit and maybe thinking about moving to New Jersey.

"We're your only family," she said. "We want you close to us."

"I know, but I still have a job in San Francisco. But, actually, I think I'll stay here." Until I spoke the words, I had not realized that I had decided. "I want to keep this condo and live here, on the beach. How about I visit you at Christmas?"

"I'd rather have you living near us," Aunt Sylvia grumbled, and then smiled. "A Christmas visit would be wonderful!"

"I need to find a full-time job here, but I may wait until the first of the year to start looking."

"What about your friends in San Francisco?"

"I have two good friends from high school here, and Sarah likes to come down. Maybe I can convince her to move and share the condo. Most of my friends from school have scattered to the four winds. I could only manage to hang on in San Francisco because Mom helped with my rent," I confessed, feeling embarrassed.

"I can see you've thought it all out. You're so much like your mother."

"I wish!"

"No, you are. Did you know she wanted to be a writer?"

"What? She never told me."

"When she was a girl, she was always making up stories. After she moved out here with Mother and Father, even though Mother fussed about the

201

postage, she would send her stories to me. She always had a lot of imagination."

"I never knew! Why didn't she tell me?" The hurt at once again being excluded from Mom and Aunt Sylvia's relationship must have shown on my face.

"I don't know why she didn't tell you."

"We were so close, especially this past year. I can't imagine why she didn't tell me." I could feel tears welling in my eyes.

"Honestly, Kristin, I don't know why except I don't think she told many people." Aunt Sylvia hugged me and added, "I'm sure she never intended to hurt you. Since the day you were born, you always came first with your mother."

The next morning the phone rang. It was the editor of the UCLA alumni magazine. She wanted to do a story on Mom for a local newspaper.

"What about?" I asked.

"I posted a small item online about your mother's passing in our current issue."

"Why? She took courses, but she wasn't an alum," I said, suspecting a scam.

"I know, but when I was an undergraduate, my father died. I'm from Alaska, and the loan I could get from the Bursar wasn't enough to buy a plane ticket home. The financial aid counselor sent me to your mother who told me not to bother with the loan. She took me to a travel agent she knew in Westwood. The agent not only waived her fee but got me a bereavement fare, and your mother wrote a check for the ticket. She even drove me to the airport. I paid her back when I got my first job. She didn't even know me and was so kind that I wondered if there were other students out there who had had similar experiences."

"Were there?"

"Yes. I've gotten fifteen e-mails with stories very similar to mine. Apparently when students came to borrow money, if they couldn't qualify for a loan or the loan wasn't enough for what they needed, they would get sent to your mother. She often found them other resources at the university or in the community or helped them out of her own pocket."

"She was always generous to me, but honestly, I had no idea."

"Can I send you the e-mails?"

I gave her my email address and later that morning received a file containing the fifteen stories. One student, like the editor, needed airfare home to Trinidad when her grandmother died. Another had exhausted his loan eligibility and needed money for food until his next paycheck. Mom helped him, found him an on-campus job, and met with him several times to teach him how to budget his money. Ironically, he became a financial planner. Another student needed to pay tuition for a study-abroad course in advance of receiving her travel scholarship. Several students came from poor families they themselves were helping and needed clothes for job interviews. The most compelling story was from a woman who got pregnant her first year. The amount she could borrow did not come near covering the cost of an abortion so Mom had not only given her the money but taken her to the appointment and had her stay with her afterward.

"I had no idea. She never told me any of this," I said, gesturing toward my laptop as Aunt Sylvia finished reading the stories.

"She didn't tell me either, Kristin, but why would she?" she asked gently.

I thought about this question for a long time. Each of these students had a problem that Mom had the means to solve. Why would the situation need discussion? It was not as if her generosity had required my permission or harmed me. Yet I knew that had I encountered these people and their problems, I would have shared my experience with Mom. Of course, I had to admit that I would never have been in such a situation. Maybe it was grief, but I felt excluded and hurt. I did, however, give my permission for the story. After it ran in one of the local papers, the author sent me several additional e-mails from other students Mom had helped.

When Aunt Sylvia and Uncle David returned to New Jersey, I rattled around for a few days, and then convinced Sarah to come for the weekend. I told her that I had decided to stay in Los Angeles.

"But your job!" she protested.

"I have enough money to support myself until the beginning of the year. I can write my novel and then look for a full-time job here."

"Lucky you!" she said enviously and then, seeing my sad expression, added, "I'm sorry, Kristin. You know how much I loved your mother."

"I know. Lucky me, money, but unlucky me, writing," I said grimly.

"If you just relax, something will come. Have you considered writing about your mother?"

"I don't write nonfiction," I replied flatly.

"No, silly. I mean a novel about a young woman who gets pregnant. Or how about a novel about the daughter finding out?"

I remembered "finding out." I was twelve. It had been like doing a word problem in math: Mom and Dad got married on this date, and I was born on this date. Gestation in humans takes nine months. How long before they were married did Kristin's father get her mother pregnant?

I was so embarrassed that I was a senior in high school before I said something to Mom who just laughed and said, "Well, you've always been advanced!"

"No, I've never considered writing about that, but now I wish I'd asked her if she ever thought about having an abortion or giving me up for adoption. I always felt awkward or shy about asking her, but now that I know about that young woman she helped, I wonder. I wonder if she wished that she hadn't had me."

"Of course not! Your mother adored you! I've always wished my mother and I were half as close as you and your mother."

"I know, but still, I wonder. It's one of the worst parts of losing someone. Suddenly there are all these questions you didn't ask and conversations you should have had."

"I know," Sarah said quietly. "Why not ask your aunt? See what she says."

"I will. Next time I talk to her."

Aunt Sylvia admitted that she had not discussed it with Mom because "By the time I knew she was pregnant, she and your father were married. Then I was not with her until you were born." She proceeded to assure me that Mom and Dad had loved each other and welcomed me at my birth.

"So what kind of job do you think you'll look for?" asked Sarah.

"I am *not* going to get a job where I edit or write."

"Really?"

"Yes, I think maybe that's why I feel so blank. I need to do something different from writing to earn a living."

"Maybe your next novel will be a best-seller that gets made into a movie or original series or tv show," teased Sarah, and I rolled my eyes.

"Would you consider moving here?"

Sarah looked surprised and asked, "Are you serious?"

"Yes. You're always saying you want to get away from your family. You could share the condo with me."

"I hate my job! I never meant to stay at the bank for more than a few months. It doesn't pay anything, and the last thing I ever want to be is a bank manager. Of course, I may not have to worry because, although that's the next step, the stupid bank mostly promotes men."

Sarah was a rare bird: a woman of words who was also a whiz at numbers.

"You could probably get a bank job here."

"Maybe. Or do something else. Danny and I are finished," she continued thoughtfully. "I finally told him last week that our relationship was going nowhere, and I'd like to be friends, but nothing more."

"You didn't tell me."

"I knew that I was coming this weekend, and you've been so busy!"

"If you were here, we'd talk every day!"

"We already talk almost every day," Sarah laughed.

"We'd talk every night too!" I said, and we both laughed. "Are you upset about Danny?"

"I've known for a long time that we were just drifting along, but then, last month, he asked me to marry him."

"You didn't tell me!"

"Your mother was dying. You didn't need my drama, and actually the decision was so mundane. I knew immediately that much as I like and even love Danny, I don't want to be married to him. I don't want to have children with him, and as far as I can tell, that's the only reason to get married. I'm just glad we never moved in together."

"How's Danny taking it?" I had always liked him but had never sensed a real spark of passion between him and Sarah.

"He was pretty upset at first, but I have this feeling that he's relieved. I think he felt obligated to propose because we'd been together for so long, and all our friends have gotten married and are starting families. He argued with me when I said no, but he never said that I was the only woman he'd ever love or that he'd die without me," she said dramatically, making me laugh. "We're taking six months apart, and then we're going to see if we want to stay friends."

"You're so sensible. You do a much better job of breaking up than I do. I know I need to do it for a long time before I finally do it, and then my break-ups always involve a lot of yelling and crying."

"Chris?"

"I thought four drunken days in Cancun was not serious, but he apparently thought it was the equivalent of a marriage ceremony. He's still texting me every few days and asking how I am which generally leads to his asking when I'm coming back to San Francisco and 'can't we just see' although I have explained repeatedly that we have nothing, absolutely nothing, except sexual attraction, in common. He's an outdoor guy, and I'm an indoor woman. I'm trapped in words and books. He never reads a book unless it's instructions for sports equipment and even then he generally goes on YouTube."

"Opposites attract?"

"And we do. Great chemistry, but we have nothing for the long haul." I paused and then added, "Frankly, I miss our friends, really Chris' friends, more than I miss him."

"Any chance you'll stay friends with them?"

"Alice and Jeff contacted me when Chris told them about Mom, but it was awkward. Jeff is Chris's best friend. They only called that once. Not a word from anyone else."

"I hear what you're saying. The few friends of Danny's I've met, I can easily live without," said Sarah with a laugh, making me think how she could afford to lose a few friends because she had her family and a circle of friends so much larger than my own. "Speaking of the long haul," she said, interrupting my thoughts, "When are you moving your stuff down here?"

"Next weekend. James, Melissa's older brother, is going to fly up with me. He'll help me load everything and drive the truck back."

"Great. What's he like?"

"He's two years older than Melissa so we were in high school together, but I only knew him in passing. He's a nice guy. Quiet."

"What's he do?"

"He's a carpenter. He works in The Business building sets."

"Did he go to college?"

"Some, but he liked his part-time job more than school so he quit. He makes good money and enjoys his work, according to Melissa."

"Married?"

"Divorced, but I don't know anything about it."

"Good-looking?"

I thought for a moment. James was tall and solid. He looked like he did physical labor. He had curly, light brown hair and clear blue eyes. His best feature was his slow, engaging smile.

"Yes, he's okay. But, Sarah, this is not a date or hook-up!"

"Well, I wish you a moving experience," she replied with a smirk.

After Sarah left, I spent the next week going through Mom's books. We owned many of the same books because if either of us liked a book, we usually bought a copy for the other person. Sadness overwhelmed me as I remembered how, when I first went to college, Dad had jokingly dubbed this new habit our "PBC"—Private Book Club. I was moved to tears by finding cards I had written Mom in books I had sent and remembering how we had talked about certain books. I remembered our argument over Elizabeth Jane Howard's *The Long View*. Mom had insisted it was one of the most brilliant novels she had ever read, and I had had trouble getting through it. I set it aside to try again. Finally, I made a list and decided to sell my copies of books we had in common.

Going through the bookcases that lined two walls of her bedroom, I found my childhood books, a mix of Mom's old books: *Heidi, Heidi Grows Up* and *Heidi's Children;* Nancy Drew; *Little Women* and the rest of Alcott including *Jack and Jill*, the one I loved best; *The Wizard of Oz* and books bought specially for me: all of *Harry Potter;* all of Judy Blume, Beverly Cleary, Madeleine L'Engle, and Laura Ingalls Wilder; and various picture books. I sat looking through my battered copy of *Where the Wild Things Are* and wept, not just for Mom, but for myself and the children I might never have to share these books and memories.

On Friday evening, Melissa dropped us at the airport. James and I ate a quick dinner while waiting. Once we boarded the plane, he muttered, "Sorry. I'm really tired" and slept throughout the flight. I had gotten us rooms at an airport motel. At eight the next morning, Sarah, showing herself to be a true friend (and also wanting a look at James), drove us to the storage facility which also rented trucks. As she drove off, she gave me a lecherous grin and laughing thumbs up.

As James patiently helped me unpack, go through the list, and repack the duplicate books, I discovered that he too was an avid reader and ended up giving him several books. Soon we were chatting easily as we repacked the books and loaded the boxes into a taxi that we took to a second-hand bookstore. Business done, we ate lunch, took a taxi back, claimed our rental truck, and loaded up.

On the way out of town, we stopped to drop some furniture, dishes, pots, and pans at a co-worker's new apartment. We then dropped linens, towels, curtains, and anything else that was left at a refugee organization.

After the last stop, James remarked admiringly, "You sure had this all planned out!"

"Yeah," I said, thought of Mom, and turned away so he would not see the tears in my eyes.

As we finally drove out of San Francisco, James asked, "Which route?"

"I assumed you'd want to take the 5 and get home as quickly as possible."

"No. I'm off Monday so if you want to drive down the coast, I'm for it. This truck is easy to handle."

"If you don't mind, that'd be great. Let's take our time. I don't think we need to push on after dark. I can cover another night in a motel. Where do you think we'll stop?"

"How about Santa Cruz? It's probably two to three hours from here."

"I went to school there, and if it's still open, I know a hotel where Mom used to stay. It isn't fancy, but I think it'd do." I quickly called and got a reservation for two rooms.

"Now, sit back, relax, enjoy the trip," said James with a smile, "And look at that ocean!"

As always, the wide expanse of blue water, glittering in the sun, made me feel relaxed and at home.

"Do you like the ocean?" I asked.

"Love it! I used to surf."

"Did you ever surf around here?"

"Never. Mostly I surfed Ventura and south."

"I wish I'd learned to surf. I never had a chance, but I love to body surf."

"In my teens, before I could drive, I used to hitchhike to the beach. Then I got to know some guys who were older, and they'd take me along. It was awesome! I used to cut school on Friday afternoons to go surf."

"I'm surprised. You always seemed so well-behaved and quiet."

"Quiet, yes. I think Jessica talked for both me and Melissa," he said, naming his youngest sister.

"I can imagine that happening with you, but not with Melissa!" I replied, and we both laughed.

"Probably right, but I was a quiet kid. I read a lot of books and until Melissa caught up with me on reading, I didn't have anyone to talk to. My parents aren't book-ish people, but obviously your mother was!"

"Yes, she was. When I think back to when I was a little girl, I can remember waking up at night, and she was always in the living room or in bed reading a book. It was hard for her when she got so sick she couldn't read."

"Did you read to her?"

"Yes, until she couldn't follow the plots or keep the characters straight. I could tell that frustrated her so we switched to music. Even movies were hard at the end because she fell asleep so often, and even with the movies she knew, she stopped being able to follow the plots."

"I'm so sorry. It's a rotten thing to have to go through."

"It was hard for me, but I saw how hard it was for Mom, and that keeps me from feeling too sorry for myself."

We stopped on Saturday night at the small hotel which was much as I remembered. We found an Asian restaurant where we had a delicious dinner followed by a walk on the cliffs overlooking the vivid blue ocean. I watched James stride along on his long legs and thought how much I liked him. He seemed to like me too, but neither of us made a move so we said a friendly good night and went to our separate rooms.

The next morning, after a leisurely breakfast, as we drove down the coast, James suddenly said, "You know I was married?"

"Melissa told me."

"It's been over for ten years now—over three times as long as it lasted."

"So what was she like?"

"Beautiful. Talented. She had just gotten a small role in a television show. Her dad's a carpenter so on the set one day, we got to talking. We had only known each other six months when we got married, but all my friends were getting married, and I was in love."

"What's her name?"

"Lisa Caruso."

"You mean, *the* Lisa Caruso of *Night Wings* and *Remembrance?* She's a very good actor."

"I won't disagree. She's also a good person, but our relationship was a disaster. She wanted and needed to be out and about, constantly in the spotlight. Her career was just beginning to take off. I wanted to come home and settle in for the evening."

"Her career versus your career?"

"Not exactly. More a matter of personality. I'm an introvert, and she is an extreme extrovert. We run into each other occasionally now, and we always end up laughing at how we could have ever imagined a life together."

"Hormones."

"Definitely. I have no bad feelings about her. It was an amicable parting."

"And since?"

"A few short-term relationships, but nothing that felt like it could go the distance so I settle for dating people I like and seeing what works out. I'd like to get married and maybe have kids, but I wouldn't mind just settling in with someone I love."

"That's pretty much where I'm at, too," I said with a sigh. "I think it shows I'm slouching toward forty."

"I've rolled right over forty now, and it's still what I want. I'm just not sure how to find it or even how to go about looking. I guess it just has to happen."

We were driving along in easy silence when James said, "Melissa told me your dad died really young. Did your mother marry again?"

"No. When Dad died, she was only thirty-eight, but she seemed pretty clear that she did not want to remarry. I'm sure she had some affairs, but she never talked about them. At least, not to me."

"But she didn't want to remarry?"

"No. She loved my dad, but I don't think she was carrying a torch for him. She was only eighteen when she got married and had me. I think she didn't want to be confined again. Now I wish that I had asked her more about why."

I sighed and looked out the window to hide the tears welling in my eyes. James touched my arm lightly and handed me a clean handkerchief.

"Thanks." I blew my nose and leaned back with a sigh. "It just catches me at the oddest moments."

"I know. My best friend drowned when we were in our twenties."

"I'm so sorry. What happened?"

"No one knows. He was in Hawaii and went out to surf early one morning before anyone else was up. Going out alone was a dumb thing to do. When he didn't come back, they began searching and found his board had washed up. They searched, but the ocean had swallowed him. I still miss him. When I look out at that water, I always think of the conversation we would have had about the day and the waves."

"I'm so sorry."

"I stopped surfing when Sam died. I tried to go out, but it was just too hard to do something we had both loved so much and done together for so many years. I felt guilty for a long time that I wasn't with him in Hawaii." James cleared his throat. "You probably knew him in high school."

"Sam who?"

"Sam Rhodes."

"I did my theatre elective with him."

"I bet that was excruciating."

"He was the only person in the class more uncomfortable and less talented than I was."

James laughed, saying, "How he hated that class!"

"Hate is too mild a word for what I felt. It was just endlessly humiliating."

"Sam was furious. He was the only senior in that class and got stuck with it because he needed an arts elective to graduate, and it was the only class that fit his schedule. He just hated everything about it. He did hilarious impressions of the teacher."

"Mr. Campion."

"He used to do a routine about camping out with the camp Mr. Campion."

"Ouch."

"Yes, ouch, but remember we were young and ignorant and cruel."

When we got home, James helped me carry everything up to the condo. I followed him to return the truck, drove him home, and tried to give him $300.

"I know it isn't enough, but I'm so grateful for your help."

"No way. I had a great time, and now Melissa owes me forever," he laughed.

"I insist that you take it."

"How about this? You can take me out to dinner. Pick your favorite ocean-side restaurant."

"When?"

"How about next Saturday night? 7:00?"

"No, let's go earlier. 6:00 so we can sit outside and enjoy the sunset."

"It's a date! I'll pick you up at 5:30 unless we need to go earlier."

"No, 5:30 should work."

We shook hands and then quickly hugged. As soon as I got home, I called Geoffrey's in Malibu to get a reservation.

On Monday, my boss called. I thought for a moment that I might be fired, but it turned out he wanted to tell me about a large project that he was moving me to and that would guarantee my twenty hours per week (and insurance!) for the foreseeable future. I still planned to get a new job, but for now, I thought working might help me get organized to make my writing time more productive. What I might write remained a painfully open question.

For the next week, I spent the mornings working and the afternoons unpacking. On Friday afternoon, in search of hangers, I steeled myself, went into Mom's bedroom, and opened the closet doors. I inhaled the slight scent of her perfume and looked down at an old steamer trunk. It was made of black metal, measured about three-feet long, and had worn leather handles at each end. There was no lock through the center hasp so I popped the side locks and raised the heavy lid.

On top lay my baby book. I opened it and found, documented in Mom's precise, even handwriting, everything from my height and weight until age 5 to my first words, my first steps, and the first book I read by myself at age four. Below was that first book—*My Book of Animals*. The next layer was carefully folded baby clothes I recognized from pictures. Below were a few of my favorite outfits which I remembered.

Beneath the clothes were large boxes of file folders and other office supplies. Puzzled at this uncharacteristic evidence of hoarding, I opened the first box and took out a printed manuscript, entitled *Through the Door*. I opened the next box and found another manuscript called *The Next Time: Stories of Choices Made and Unmade*. I was stunned. Each of the twelve boxes contained a manuscript of 200 to 500 pages with a title and no author's name, but I felt sure that Mom had written them.

Beneath the boxes were loose papers and shorter manuscripts, many hand-written. I recognized my mother's handwriting even in its juvenile form.

I was shocked. When we were clearing out the condo, Aunt Sylvia had brought out Mom's clothes. She must have opened the trunk and assumed it held only mementos from my childhood.

Why hadn't Mom told me that she was a writer? I tried to think back to my childhood and later stays at home. Had I ever seen Mom writing anything other than a letter, card, or grocery list? Aunt Sylvia had said Mom wrote stories when she was young, but I felt sure that if she had known Mom were still writing, she would have told me.

Hoping to find a letter that might explain, I spent the next two hours searching. I opened Mom's laptop and realized that she had reset it to the factory settings. I went through her files, discovered an empty drawer in her desk, and realized that she had not only disposed of her journals but also her letters. I had already been to her safety deposit box so I knew there was nothing there. I searched everywhere in the condo and finally concluded that she had, without explanation, left me these boxes full of her words.

I gathered up the loose papers, got a cup of coffee, sat down on the sofa, and looked out at the sea.

"Okay, Mom," I said, "Now I'm going to start reading."

Some of the loose papers were school essays on set topics that had all received high praise. Her early forays into fiction were surprisingly like mine. She had written a few stories about a group of girls who solve neighborhood mysteries à la Nancy Drew. She had written several high school romances. I could tell that she had found *Roget's Thesaurus* by this time because the stories were filled with the sort of unlikely word choices I recognized from my own discovery of *Roget's* in eighth grade—not red, not even scarlet or crimson, but *vermillion*.

Although nothing, except the school essays, had names or dates, the handwriting on the most disturbing story looked like my mother's adult handwriting. The story was about a high-school girl who gets pregnant. Her boyfriend wants to marry her, but she knows that she does not "love him a life-time worth." The story ends with her planning to "glide into the ocean and swim away, my life and the life inside me merging with all the life in that deep water." I wondered if Mom had written this story when she knew that she was pregnant. Had it been a way either to figure out what to do or to accept what she had decided to do? Had she seriously considered suicide?

I put the loose papers back and picked up the box that contained the manuscript called *Through the Door*. The opening chapters were about a wife and mother who, her life a constant juggling or balancing act, never goes through a door without having her hands full. Groceries through the side door. Laundry through the kitchen door. Folded clothes through the bedroom doors. Books and bags through the front door. Water for the dog and snacks for the kids out the back door.

I sat back after reading the first ten pages and thought how perfectly Mom had captured the constant, monotonous, insistent intrusion of *everyone*'s daily life into this mother's mental and physical space. The woman begins to dream of going through a door alone, unimpeded, without having to carry anything, flying "like an angel on the wings of her own thoughts."

One day she empties her purse onto the kitchen counter. It is full of pencils, pens, markers, everyone's candy wrappers, enough tissues for an army, band aids, several different chap sticks, lipstick, a set of chopsticks, several drawings by the kids, her wallet, her keys, an extra key to her husband's car, keys to her parents' house, acetaminophen, a comb, a book, a comic book, hair barrettes, ponytail holders, small notebooks, and a small coloring book with crayons. She divides everything into two piles. Her pile has six objects in it: comb, lipstick, packet of tissues, pen, notebook, and her keys. She decides to add a band aid and bottle of acetaminophen to her pile. She stands looking at the other objects for a long time, retrieves the keys, and then puts this graphic evidence that her life is full of things *she* does not need in a box at the back of the cupboard.

I wanted this woman to find her way to a new life, but in the end, she gets cancer and suddenly everything she had thought burdensome becomes precious.

I turned the last page over—no mistaking my mother's handwriting here. As if reading my thoughts about her story, she had written:

"Is this ending convincing? Would someone this miserable in her marriage and life stay? Lots of women do, but would *this* woman? Or would she find the courage to fly out the door to a new life? What about the kids? How do they fit into this new life? What if in her new life she just recreated the life she's left? What if the real problem is *how she's made*, not who she's with or how she lives?! Cancer seems too convenient here. Maybe she gets cancer *and* flies out that door!"

I wondered when she had reread this manuscript and written this note which was much like one I might have written to a fellow writer. It seemed ridiculous to think that she had written the note to me, but she must have known that I would find the manuscripts.

I gazed out at the ocean and thought about the story. What if the woman left, met someone, married again, and realized her new life was becoming her old life? What would she do? Would she stay, try to go back, attempt a second escape? I thought about who this woman might be and what circumstances might have shaped her. Then I stopped myself, put the manuscript pages back in the box, and put the box back in the steamer trunk.

Bereft, I stood gazing out at the ocean. In the story's turn of phrase, I had heard Mom's voice and, in some of its characters and situations, seen her wry sense of irony and humor, perceptions which pierced me with inextricable joy and sorrow. I finally noticed the sun was starting to set so I grabbed my keys, went down to the beach, and did not come home until it was dark.

After dinner, I went to the trunk and picked another box—*Nothing Being What It Seems*-- a murder mystery set in Venice and fueled by a gentrification scheme. Long past midnight, I finished it. The subject matter, complexity of the plot, and development of the characters made me think it a more recent book. I thought that with very little work, it might be publishable.

Saturday morning, when I got up, I picked another manuscript and started reading over breakfast. I suspected this one was earlier, but I had no way of dating it. It made me laugh on almost every page because, in spite of its contemporary (1990s?) setting, it was a parody of every pseudo-Gothic romance mystery I had read as a young teen-ager. I remembered my irritation when Mom had once pointed out, "You know the heroine survives because the story is told in the first person."

The plot was ludicrous. The heroine, a blonde, beautiful, sixteen-year-old girl, her eyes like "melted pools of chocolate," had an innocence that verged on stupidity. Of course, her young, handsome, leering tennis coach (depicted with a sly irony uncomfortably reminiscent of *Lolita)* marries her mother, but he is clearly after the heroine. The narrative was filled with "hard manhood," flushes, blushes, and "heaving bosoms." The heroine's description of her first physical contact with the "tall, dark, and unbearably good-looking" tennis coach put paid to any doubts I had about the tone of the story: "As he demonstrated how to swing my arm all the way through, he held my thin wrist in his strong grasp. He was so close that I could smell his cologne (*Animal*, I later found out.), and my stomach moved in a way it had not since the last time I had the flu." After the mother's conveniently fatal car wreck, the stepfather/guardian marries the heroine on her seventeenth birthday.

The final chapter entitled "Five Years Later," finds the heroine, twenty-two, pregnant for the fourth time, and almost penniless, resolutely standing by her walking sperm bank who is charged with raping two fourteen-year-old girls. His only defense, in his final address to the judge, is "I thought they were sixteen. How was I to know that they lied to me? They came onto me. Besides, a little romance and sex is what all young women want."

The woman judge replies, "No, rape isn't what women want, and it certainly is not what children want. Castration not being an option, enjoy your stay in prison."

There were no notes, and I wondered what had made Mom write this. I vaguely remembered her talking about a study of romance-fiction readers she had read for a women's literature course in college. She had sent me the article. I don't think I read all of it, but I remembered how shocked she had been at what some of the readers' said about rape.

I finished this manuscript with barely enough time to get ready for dinner.

James arrived on time and was delighted with my restaurant choice. Once we were seated in full view of the ocean and had ordered wine, he turned to me and said, "I've thought a lot about you this week. I enjoyed the time we spent together more than I've enjoyed being with anyone in a long time."

"I enjoyed it too. And I have to admit that I've thought about you this week." Only a white lie. I had thought about him until I got engrossed in the manuscripts.

"So maybe this could be a first date?" he said, smiling.

"Meaning there would be other dates?" He nodded, and I said, "I just have to ask one question."

"What?"

"Do you like heavy metal?"

He frowned and looked puzzled before saying, "No, I actually don't."

"Okay, then, we can go out. The only music I absolutely abhor is heavy metal. Just thinking about it gives me a headache."

"Not an issue," said James when he stopped laughing. "I just have to warn you that I work a lot so I can only see you on the weekends. Don't ever think there's someone else. It's just I work late most nights and have to get up early so I don't do anything during the week."

"That's fine," I said, relieved to be able to limit my commitment so clearly and easily. "Let's enjoy the weekends and see what happens. But you can't tell Melissa."

"Oops."

"You told her?"

"She called, and I told her how much I liked you."

"I was just kind of non-committal when she called," I said, with a wink, "Because I suspected she thought that she was setting us up."

"I know. She must have called me after she called you because when I said that I liked you, she kept saying, 'You owe me!' I told her that she was being juvenile."

"What'd she say?"

"She just laughed and said I needed an injection of young blood since I'm over forty."

We had a delicious dinner, watched a beautiful sunset, and went back to my place where, after a walk on the beach, we went to bed. James proved to be a gentle, thoughtful lover.

After lunch the next day, as soon as James left, I continued reading through the "Mystery Manuscripts," as I had begun calling them. In the fifth manuscript, I found a first-person narrative about a young woman who is a talented writer, winner of a prestigious, national prize in English, and shoe-in for a college scholarship until her birth control fails. In the successful meeting of sperm and egg, her life is changed forever. She waits four months before she tells anyone and then marries the young father of her baby.

The birth, overseen by a condescending, older, male physician, is horrific—a kind of knock 'em out, drag 'em out that I believed, in my ignorance, the women's movement had ended. The woman loves her young husband, but they are different in every possible way. Their only common ground is their mutual attraction and love for their baby. As the young mother struggles along in everyday life, books become her only consolation.

The writing had a desperate immediacy, and I found the novel a gut-wrenching version of my mother's story. In the end, the young woman embraces her child and accepts her life because she finally realizes that she *is* young. Her secret mantra becomes, "I am young. I have time." I wondered when Mom had allowed herself to revisit those life-changing moments, and I no longer wondered why I was an only child.

Each day, I worked four hours in the morning and then, in the afternoons and evenings, read the Mystery Manuscripts.

One manuscript told the story of a forty-year-old widow. Two years after her husband dies, she meets a widower. They begin dating, and she enjoys his company, but when he asks her to marry him, she equivocates until he insists that she give him an answer. She loves him and realizes this may be her last chance at marriage. Each of her friends is in a marriage that has issues so not one of them is completely happy. Although they understand and sympathize with her reservations about marrying again, each friend tells her, "You don't want to grow old alone."

After much soul-searching, she tells her lover that she loves him and wants their relationship to continue, but she cannot marry him. She cannot accept the responsibility, constant demands, and day-to-day compromises that marriage entails. She explains, "If I want to eat crackers in bed and read a book until 3 a.m., I want that freedom. If I want to leave dishes in the sink and my clothes on the floor, if I want to talk or be silent, if I want to spread out like a starfish in bed, I want that freedom. I spent years shackled to the daily demands of others where my every action required negotiation, compromise, or explanation. I love you, but I can't face being in that situation again."

He loves her, but, given that he wants a full-time companion, he is unwilling to compromise and walks away. Although heart-broken, the woman realizes that she will heal and, most importantly, still be free. I wondered who the man was based on. I wondered if the "crackers in bed" and other details were code for time and space to write.

I still had many manuscripts to go when Sarah arrived for the weekend. We spent the afternoon at the beach, although it was too cold to swim, and had dinner with James. Sarah and he got on well.

"I don't think I'll be moving down here," she said as we got ready for bed late Saturday night.

"Why not?"

"I think you may be getting another room mate before long."

"I don't think so," I said. "It's early days yet, and his place is closer to his job. We both agree that commuting is a big waste of time."

"Maybe so, but I think, even though I miss you like crazy, I'm going to stay up north."

Late Sunday afternoon, after dropping Sarah at the airport, I met Melissa and Angie for dinner. When I got home, I called Aunt Sylvia for our weekly chat.

As I fell asleep that night, I realized that I had not told anyone about the Mystery Manuscripts. Neither my best friend, nor my new guy, nor my old friends, nor Aunt Sylvia. Not pausing to reflect on this fact, I thought how much I was looking forward to the next manuscript: *The Klatsch*.

The Klatsch was set in the 1950s. A group of women, all feeling lonely in their new, post-war subdivision, form a coffee klatsch that meets several mornings a week. They trade books and magazines, get to know each other, often share stories about their pasts, and tiptoe around the three taboo subjects: religion, politics, and money. Each one of them feels trapped in a different way. Gloria got pregnant and had to get married. Jeanie, a WAC officer during World War II, is now stuck at home with an infant and toddler. Nancy loved teaching third grade, but when her pregnancy showed, she lost her job and is now home with twins. Martha married to escape an abusive father, but her friends gradually realize that her husband is an abusive alcoholic.

The murder in the book is not planned but opportunistic. Jeanie has to make cookies for a bake sale and late one night goes to Martha's house to borrow vanilla. As she passes the attached garage, she hears the faint sound of the car motor running. After answering the back door, Martha goes to quiet one of her children, leaving Jeanie alone in the kitchen. She finds the vanilla, listens at the door to the attached garage, and then pushes a rag rug snugly up against the bottom of the door. Without waiting for Martha, she goes home to bake cookies.

Martha thinks nothing of her husband's absence. He often comes home late to pass out on the sofa, but when she wakes up the next morning, he is not home. She opens the kitchen door to see if the car is in the garage. It is, but the gas has run out. Her husband, sprawled across the front seat, is dead from carbon monoxide poisoning.

Once they open the car door, smell liquor, find the open bottle of scotch on the seat, and hear Martha's confirmation that her husband "had a problem," the police don't give the situation a second thought. The mandatory inquest quickly declares it an "accidental death."

Mom framed the tale with a reunion story. Having kept in touch over the years, when they are in their sixties, the women meet for a weekend at the beach. The last night Jeanie asks each one to share the worst thing she has ever done. Freed by alcohol and age, they each tell a story. Nancy had an affair with her husband's best friend. When Gloria could not face a fourth pregnancy in five years, she had an abortion without telling her Catholic husband. Martha got gonorrhea not once, but twice, from the same man! Worse yet, he had gotten it from his ex-wife with whom he claimed to have no contact. Then Jeanie introduces her story by saying, "Martha, all us gals knew that Al was hitting you."

"I thought I was doing a pretty good job of hiding it," Martha replies, and her friends all shake their heads.

"I stuffed the rag rug at the bottom of the kitchen door even though I heard the car running."

"Don't feel bad. The night Al died, I heard the car and saw the rug. I knew that he had worked to get that garage sealed up tight because, from the war, he had a thing about rats getting in. That night, I could have opened the door, but I just went to bed. After he broke my arm, I was sure that next time he would kill me or go after one of the kids. My father beat my mother and us kids for years, and he was always sorry, but nothing ever changed. I knew Al wouldn't change. Don't waste a minute feeling sorry. The cops said it was an accident, but he killed himself. It was his own damn fault."

As I read the manuscript, I knew that it could be strengthened by changing the murderer. Jeanie was a take-charge person, but if I incorporated the earlier manuscript about the pregnant teenager to give Gloria a back story and then made her the one who takes charge of her friend's problem in a way she has not been able to take charge of her own, it would be much more interesting. Perhaps I would add a fifth woman with another story to tell.

I found the "pregnant teenager" manuscript and sat down, skimming it to see how the narratives could fit together, strengthen each other, and build toward my novel. Before I knew it, the sun was setting.

The next morning, I did my four hours of editing. My conscious mind was on my job, but underneath I could feel the electricity of creation humming. I felt like a kid who knows a sucker is coming at the end of a mundane meal.

In the afternoon, I sat down at the computer and began writing. Drawing on an album of photos Mom had inherited from her parents, I created a fuller picture of the post-war suburb with its new houses built close together with bushes, trees, and lawns just beginning to grow. I drew on memories of hearing my parents talk about their older neighbors who would have belonged to that post-war generation. I found a list of the best movies of the fifties and a list of noir films, but I wanted the ordinary stuff. I needed a librarian for my research.

I called Los Angeles Public Library to see if my card could be updated. I chatted with a clerk who told me what documents to bring and then put me through to a helpful reference librarian who suggested that I look at newspapers and magazines from the period as well as movies and television shows. She found several histories of the period that contained photos and also a list of novels from the fifties: *The Best of Everything, The Group, The Man in the Gray Flannel Suit*. I wrote down her name (Diane Carmody) and promised to see her within the week.

I searched Mom's bookshelves and found *The Feminine Mystique*. Betty Friedan had done her research on this generation of women. I re-read several chapters, including the one on "The Happy Housewife Heroine" about how housework can expand to fill vacant hours.

I set the first chapter of my book about a month after everyone has moved into the neighborhood and met casually. The husbands agree to help each other build fences and pour concrete patios. This work creates a weekend ritual so when the men are done working for the day, everyone gathers at another house for a potluck supper. Everyone brings the makings for "high balls." They are all just starting out on strict budgets, but Al has three to everyone else's one drink. The men talk about sports. Jeanie, saying the men's work group is like a club, suggests that the wives form a "coffee klatsch."

When I looked up, the sun was setting again. I went for a quick walk on the beach, trying to remember everything Mom had told me about Mrs. Owen. When I was small, the elderly Mrs. Owen was the only remaining original owner in our neighborhood. I wondered now if Mom had been using those neighborly visits to interview Mrs. Owen for her book. I remembered her telling Mom that back in the fifties, everyone knew each other and everyone had kids who played outdoors and freely roamed the neighborhood. She had talked about how the men all helped each other with home improvement projects. I remembered her pointing out the window to the gray concrete-block wall around her yard and saying, "My husband and the guys built that and the one around your yard too. They also poured my patio. Yours, too."

I had one other clear memory from one of these visits. On the way home, I asked Mom what "kidnap" meant. She explained the word, but then added, "Mrs. Owen was talking about a 'kidnap party,' Kristin. No one does it anymore, but when she was young, some women would arrange a breakfast and then go to their friends' houses and, as a surprise, 'kidnap' them. No matter what they were wearing or if their hair wasn't combed, they had to go to the party."

"What if you were naked?" I remembered asking.

When Mom stopped laughing, she said, "I think they'd let you put on a robe, at least."

I thought about using a kidnap party to reveal Martha's bruises, and the controlling, anxious personality of Patricia, the new character I was creating, who would both hate and fear the surprise of such an event.

I felt ecstatic that I was finally writing again, but when James called to talk about the weekend, I felt tired and distracted by the voices in my head.

"Are you okay?" he finally asked.

"I'm fine, but I've been working—actually writing. That's why I sound so out of it."

"I bought your novel," he said. "I've only read about twenty pages, but it's really funny. I like it, but I sure don't want to end up in your gallery of assholes."

"Thanks. Don't worry! I don't have enough years left to gather material for a sequel. I love that you like it, but this book is different. It has some funny stuff in it, but it's more serious."

"What is it about? Will you read me some of it?" he asked eagerly.

"I'm sorry, but I need to finish a draft and see where I'm going before I share it." Irrationally, I felt impatient—maybe this probing was what the widow in that manuscript did not want. But it was my fault. I had forgotten my cardinal rule: *Never talk about writing.*

When I was in the MFA program, I had seen students talk about an idea and have it stolen or, worse yet, bettered in the work of others. I had seen students talk about an idea eloquently and endlessly until there was no excitement or sense of discovery left to propel the act of writing. I had seen students talk about an idea with enthusiasm and have others judge the idea so harshly that creation was never even attempted.

I had always been a private person and had to be at ease before I could share anything, especially something as personal as my writing. At the beginning of the program, I had quickly decided that to survive, I would share only work as finished as I could make it. Out of fear, I wrote and re-wrote constantly, almost maniacally, so that I would have polished stories to present. When I had nothing to work from to fulfill an assignment, I often turned work in late, but most professors, impressed by the quality of my work, were understanding and indulgent.

Impromptu writing was a special hell for me, and I avoided classes where this would be required.

I knew the other students found me aloof and ungenerous. I made no friends in my program. I dated one of the young professors for a short time, but, my exact opposite, he wanted to talk endlessly about *his* writing. I was not lonely because early on, I had met Sarah who, although she concealed it better than I did, also felt distrustful of and impatient with her fellow students in the poetry program.

The next day I called Melodie Summers to tell her my idea for the novel. I was succinct and surrendered as few details as possible. She was not just relieved but enthusiastic.

"The seamy side of the Greatest Generation," she chortled. "That should sell!"

I rolled my eyes but did not argue with her.

"When can I have it?" she asked.

"I've been dealing with my mother's death so I'm just getting down to writing. I also need to do research."

"Okay. How about six months?"

I calculated quickly and said, "I think I need nine months."

"You're not having a baby--you're writing a novel!"

"I need time. I know I'm way behind schedule, but I never expected my mother to get sick."

"I'm sorry, Kristin. I know it's been hard. Let me talk to the publisher."

Melodie called me back in an hour and said that the novel had to go to the publisher in its final form in August of the following year. I agreed to the deadline.

For the next few weeks, in the afternoons, I wrote and did research. Aided by Diane Carmody, I looked at miles of microfilm and hauled stacks of books home. Diane was almost seventy and had grown up in exactly the sort of post-war neighborhood I was writing about. When I asked her about unwed mothers and abortion, she suggested that I watch two films she remembered watching as a teenager: *Three Secrets* (where the unwed mother is forced into giving her baby up) and *Beyond the Forest* (where Bette Davis dies of a botched, illegal abortion). She also suggested that I watch *The Best Years of Our Lives* to understand the post-war period. She often admitted to enjoying "the walk down memory lane," adding, "The fifties were a lot more complicated than people think."

We had lunch or dinner together several times, and her memories helped me grasp the insularity of families, pressure to conform ("What will the neighbors think?") and intense code of privacy within families that informed everyone's life and led to many secrets although families lived so close to each other.

At Diane's suggestion, I watched episodes of *Father Knows Best, Dragnet, The Stu Erwin Show,* and *I Love Lucy.* I watched great films, but I also watched potboilers to get a sense of clothes, décor, slang, and behavior. I was surprised by the high level of writing and acting in these "B films." I was also astonished to discover that there were far more Westerns and costume dramas produced than contemporary dramas. *Rebel Without a Cause* and *The Man in the Gray Flannel Suit* were the exceptions, not the rule. It seemed as if, in the fifties, few people wanted to examine contemporary society.

I inhabited that place where creative people go when their work takes over. I was in that state where you pour a cup of coffee, take a sip, and realize, an hour later, that you forgot to drink it. Each time I closed my laptop, I was tired but excited to find out where my story would take me the next day.

When I went to visit Aunt Sylvia and Uncle David for Christmas, they both remarked on how well I looked. I told them that I was working on my novel. One afternoon I asked Aunt Sylvia if we could look through some old photo albums together. I told her that I had already looked through Mom's albums and "I've found people that I don't know." This was true, but since Aunt Sylvia was born in 1950, my real interest was in the images from her childhood, her memories, and her sense of the era.

She enjoyed telling me about the people in the pictures and identified many relatives who were gone by the time Mom was born. As we moved on to pictures from her childhood, I observed, "These pictures were all taken on Christmas, Easter, or some other special occasion, like a birthday or graduation. It seems odd because now we take pictures all the time."

"Pictures were expensive to develop back then," Aunt Sylvia explained. "One time when I was around ten, Father let me use the camera to take a picture of the bear at the zoo. There was a big grizzly bear that I just loved! Father was furious when he found out that I'd shot the whole roll of film. He gave me a lecture on the price of film and developing. Taking photos was expensive enough that we only did it on special occasions when everyone was dressed up and looking their best."

"It's hard to tell what ordinary life looked like," I said, musing as I turned the page to several group photos of Aunt Sylvia's elementary school classes. "These pictures, for example. Are those the regular clothes kids wore to school?"

"Yes and no. We didn't exactly dress up, but on picture day, we always wore nice clothes and felt bad for the kids who forgot it was picture day or had no good clothes to wear." She pointed to a small, thin girl in a plain, dark cotton dress with a white Peter Pan collar. "Izzy Jenkins' family was very poor. She had three dresses her mother made her, all black or navy blue, all just alike. She was so sweet that none of the kids made fun of her, but we all knew how poor she was. Sometimes she brought catsup sandwiches in her lunch, so I used to share my lunch with her."

The night before I left, as Aunt Sylvia and I sat up late, drinking a last glass of wine, she said, "Maybe we can come out for a visit."

"How about in the spring? March? By then, I'll probably be happy to have company and a break from writing. You can escape the end of winter and meet James. I know that's why you're coming!"

Aunt Sylvia laughed and then looked at me seriously, saying "Kristin, you'll be forty next week."

"I know," I sighed. "Incredibly old, isn't it?"

"No, that's not what I mean. I know it's your business, but I'd like to see you married. I never understood why your mother didn't re-marry."

"Maybe no one wanted to marry her," I replied.

"Not true. There were several men over the years," said Aunt Sylvia, shaking her head. "One of them was wonderful. It was in the year or two right after your father died, and Joseph was just perfect. They came to visit us for a few days. He was crazy about your mother, and she seemed just as crazy about him."

"So what happened?"

"He asked her to marry him, and she said no."

"Why?"

"She said that she didn't want to be married. It was hard for me to understand because I wanted to be married my whole life and thought it would never happen. Then I met David. I always wanted children, but it was too late when we met."

"But you've got me," I said, patting her hand. She covered my hand with both of hers and we sat quietly until I said tentatively, "You know, Mom was very young when she married Dad, and they had me right away. When he died, even though he was so young, they had been married almost twenty years."

"I know, dear. Your mother tried to help me understand. We were best friends always, but we were very different, and there was always the age gap. I just don't want you to miss your chance," she said with a sweet smile.

"I know." I hugged her and wondered what Mom would have said about this conversation.

"It's so good having you here," Aunt Sylvia said. "I appreciate our Sunday talks more than I can say. I miss your mother so much. Sometimes I re-read her letters so I can almost hear her voice." She stopped and sipped her wine, her eyes bright with unshed tears.

"I know," I said, drawing her close and thinking about the Mystery Manuscripts. If I shared them, Aunt Sylvia could experience those moments when the narrator's voice or a character spoke in a manner or with a humor so familiar that for a heartbeat, it was almost like hearing Mom again. I let the impulse pass.

227

One chilly evening in February, Diane Carmody and I were having dinner at a Mexican restaurant in Santa Monica.

"I've put in my retirement notice," she said. "So margaritas are in order. My treat."

When the salted rims of our cold glasses touched, I said, "To the next stage." We drank. "What will you do?"

"I'm moving to San Diego. Years ago, when my husband passed away, I bought a house down the street from my daughter. I've been renting it out, but now it's time for me to move. It will be especially nice to be closer to my grandchildren."

I had no idea that she was a widow or had a daughter or grandchildren who lived in San Diego.

"I'll miss you," I said and tried to lighten the moment by adding, "Who will help me find things?"

"Merisa Nolan," laughed Diane. "She's three times as smart as I am! I've already told her about you."

"It's been so great working with you."

"I've enjoyed your project, but I've been meaning to ask you something," said Diane, eying me curiously. "Where did this book come from?"

I must have looked puzzled because she added, "How did you get interested in the fifties?"

Although for an instant, I was tempted to tell her the truth, I said instead, "I'm close to my aunt who is twelve years older than my mother. Aunt Sylvia was born in 1950. She has always seemed so different from Mom that I began to wonder how the times they grew up in influenced them."

"Interesting. Over the years I've helped lots of writers find information, and I'm always curious about where their ideas come from. Speaking of writers, have you read the latest Kate Atkinson?"

"Tunnel vision here. I love her writing and didn't even know she had a new book out!"

At Diane's retirement party, a punch-and-cake gathering in a library meeting room, I found a large group composed not just of co-workers but of writers, filmmakers, and artists. I suddenly realized that I was not special. In fact, I overheard one of the librarians complaining to a co-worker, "We always give the creative types to Di. What are we going to do now?"

By spring, I was ready for Sarah to read *The Klatsch*. She loved it, was generous with her praise, and made smart suggestions. After I had worked through another revision, my confidence in the novel grew so I asked my college writing teacher if she would be willing to read it. She replied that after the quarter ended, she would be glad to.

After watching several films from the fifties with me, James was curious about my book and would have read it, but I was reluctant to bring my writing into our relationship. Although I had shared many books with Melissa and Angie and respected their opinions, I was also reluctant to ask them to read my book. I always feared that people close to me would either not be honest with me or be too honest. I could not risk losing the few friends I had.

I asked one of my work colleagues to read my book. Layla always seemed friendly, read a lot, and liked many of the same books I did. I thought that she would give me an honest reading, and I offered to pay for her sharp, editorial skills. She set her hourly rate low, saying she was happy to read "something besides crap technical writing badly translated from foreign languages."

I used Aunt Sylvia and Uncle David's visit to put my novel out of my mind. James and I took them to the old Getty in Malibu where we had lunch on the patio while enjoying the spectacular ocean view. Spring had not yet come to New Jersey so they delighted in the sunshine and gardens. We took them to lunch at Geoffrey's and told them the story of our trip to fetch my belongings. I could tell that Aunt Sylvia noticed when James reached over and took my hand as we described our first date.

Amid the pleasure of their visit, I realized that Aunt Sylvia and Uncle David were beginning to age. I was terrified to think of losing them, the only remaining link to my past. If anything happened to them, I would be an orphan, truly adrift on my own.

My readers all loved the novel, especially the ending and made many helpful suggestions. They found the characters convincing, especially Patricia, the anxious woman I had added to the original cast. They were moved by Gloria's story of getting pregnant in high school. I was happy because I had put so much into writing this novel. It had challenged me and taken me out of myself in a way my earlier writing never had.

229

I now focused on revision. Finally, as I read the draft aloud (yet again) and made only a few small changes, the book felt more and more finished. In July, bribing her with the promise of a spectacular dinner on her next visit, I asked Sarah to read it one more time. A week later, she announced that she, too, felt it was finished.

Feeling how short Mom's time had been, I typed her birth and death dates beneath her name in the dedication: "To Mom--You are with me always."

Since I had sent her the first two chapters in June, Melodie Summers had been e-mailing me every few days to ask about the novel. I now sent her the completed manuscript and settled in to await her response.

I worked in the mornings at my job and spent the afternoons at the beach swimming, walking, or just sitting and reading. I watched movies and occasionally had dinner or lunch out with Melissa or Angie. I spent more time visiting with Rachel and Harriet who were delighted that I had decided to keep the condo. I spent my weekends with James who announced, "It's good to have you back."

"What do you mean?" I asked, irritated as I thought of how I had forced myself to make time for him while I was writing.

"These past few months, you've been very distracted."

In a flash, I knew why my mother had not remarried: she never wanted anyone ever again to feel they had a right to her undivided attention. She never again wanted to explain or apologize for who she was or what she was doing.

"I'm sorry," I said angrily, "But when I'm writing, I'm either distracted or tired."

"Hey, Kris, don't be mad," he replied gently. "It's okay. You just have to help me understand."

I was disarmed but still annoyed and daunted at the prospect of helping someone "understand" where I could go mentally for months at a time. Exciting places. Far away. Alone. Not lonely. James had no idea how much conscious effort, at a real cost to myself, I had made to be with him over the past months.

I soon heard from Melodie who liked the book but, of course, wanted changes. They seemed minor so I did not bother to argue. I was finished with *The Klatsch*.

I have never understood how to explain this feeling, but it just comes and you know you are done. The work is the best you can make it. The act of creation is over. For a while, you drift, and then it is time to tell the next story. Something grabs you and, adrenaline pumping, you are down Creation Road before you know it. Although I still had a lingering fear of writer's block, I also had a trunk full of inspiration.

The Klatsch came out in mid-September and garnered several positive reviews. I did book-signings at a few local bookstores. A small mention in the *LA Times* resulted in a few radio and podcast interviews. Melodie Summers reported that sales in the local market were quite brisk and hinted that the publisher might send me on a wider publicity tour.

When I received my author copies, I sent one to Aunt Sylvia and Uncle David whom I had promised to visit later in the fall.

The next week, when Aunt Sylvia did not answer her landline for our Sunday call, I became concerned. After leaving messages, I sent her an e-mail but received no answer. I tried both her and Uncle David's cell phones, but no one answered. I sent texts to both phones. Still no word. I was frightened when I realized that I had no other way to contact them.

Mid-week, Aunt Sylvia finally called.

Heart pounding with fear, I answered, "Aunt Sylvia, are you and Uncle David all right?"

"We got your book," she said flatly.

"Do you like it?"

"Kristin, how could you do this?"

Shock zipped through me and I stammered, "Do what?"

"How could you take your mother's work and pass it off as your own."

"It is my own work! I wrote every word of *The Klatsch*."

"That's not true! You took her story and characters. You even took her title."

"You made me think Mom only wrote stories when she was a kid," I said accusingly.

"She made me promise not to tell anyone about her writing."

231

"And you didn't trust me enough to tell me even after she died?"

"She didn't want you to know, Kristin. She had always loved writing, but she wanted it to be *your* special thing. She thought you were so gifted. She made me promise I wouldn't tell," Aunt Sylvia insisted. "She called me her 'secret reader.' When she found out she was sick, she told me that she was going to get rid of all her papers."

"So how many 'secret readers' did she have?" I asked, making an effort to keep my voice steady.

"Just me," Aunt Sylvia said, adding quickly, "Don't worry! You won't be getting a bunch of calls from her friends."

Her sarcastic tone and accurate reading of my fear stung.

"You didn't even put a note in the book to say her writing inspired you," Aunt Sylvia continued in an accusing tone. "You should have said your book was based on her novel."

"I dedicated my book to her," I replied defensively.

"Not good enough. You just took her work and used it. How could you?"

"I'm sorry, Aunt Sylvia. It's just…. I was struggling. I couldn't write at all and suddenly I found this manuscript and felt so engaged. It inspired me and made me feel I could finally write again."

"But what you wrote wasn't *your* writing," she insisted. "Didn't you think about this?"

I was silent. What could I say?

Finally, Aunt Sylvia asked angrily, "Where did you find it?"

"In the steamer trunk in Mom's closet."

"I looked in that trunk. I thought it was just your baby book and clothes."

"The manuscript was at the bottom, under the clothes."

"Not just *a* manuscript," snapped Aunt Sylvia. "You used at least two of her stories for your novel."

"Yeah," I said vaguely. "There were a few manuscripts."

"Why didn't you tell me you had found your mother's writing? Did you find her emails too?"

"No. Mom deleted her account when she got so sick that she didn't want to deal with it anymore."

"What about letters? Did you find any letters? If you did, I'd like to have mine back. Immediately," she added angrily.

"No, there were no letters at all."

"Good. What about her journals? She always kept a journal."

"I know, but she disposed of them when she first got sick."

"Are you sure?"

"Of course, we talked about it when I noticed they were gone."

Although Aunt Sylvia's distrust hurt, it also made me feel defensive. I hoped that she would not ask how many manuscripts there were or what I was going to do with them because I was already imagining how to revise the murder mystery set in Venice and how to use the bodice-ripper as a story-within-a-story about a writer who brings her teenage daughter into a second marriage to a younger man.

"Aunt Sylvia, I only did what many writers are doing now," I said defensively. "They take a character from another writer's book. They recreate or re-imagine the story from that character's point of view."

"But *you* didn't write *The Wide Sargasso Sea*." Her angry voice rose. "You used *her* plot, *her* characters, and even, in many places, *her* words!"

I was silent for a few moments and finally, to change the subject, asked, in a tentative tone, "So what did you think of the book?" I barely stopped myself from saying "my book."

"It's well written. You've always been a good writer," she said coldly.

"I'm sorry, Aunt Sylvia." I did not say what I was sorry for because mostly I was sorry that Aunt Sylvia was so upset with me.

"Kristin, I think your mother would be as shocked as I am."

Invoking my mother was a low blow, and I resented how it made me feel like a small child caught deliberately doing Something Very, Very Bad.

A few minutes later, we said good-bye. Neither of us said, as usual, "I love you. Talk to you next Sunday." Avoiding words like "borrow" and "plagiarize," I had apologized several times and assured her that I had never meant to do this, a "this" I deliberately left unreferenced. Aunt Sylvia, still angry, made it clear that she was "disappointed" in me and made no suggestion about how to repair our relationship. I did not mention visiting her and Uncle David in the fall.

I sat staring out the window at the sea, gleaming in the sunlight, rolling rhythmically up on the shore as the tide pushed in.

Mom's name appeared nowhere on the manuscripts. Her few hand-written notes were like instructions for revision. Who had she expected to read and use those notes? Had she intended me to use them? Had she not destroyed the manuscripts because she knew how I was struggling? Had she left her stories to me as a gift I could make my own? Mom had always taken care of me. What if she had not forgotten her writings in the trunk but had intentionally left them to help me?

Finally, did it matter whose stories they were as long as they were told?

Made in the USA
Monee, IL
20 December 2022